Praise for the Book

"Kept me guessing till the end. Andi Grace is an excellent amateur sleuth . . . and *Caught and Collared* is an engrossing and enjoyable cozy mystery."
— *The Book Decoder*, Best Books of 2022

"Andi Grace is adorable, resilient, and has a doggedly curious need to solve a murder. A pleasure to read."
—C. Hope Clark, award-winning author of *Edisto Tidings*

"Completely charming—and exactly what a cozy mystery should be. Amateur sleuth (and dog whisperer) Andi Grace Scott is wonderfully endearing, and her devotion to her pooches—and to justice—will have you rooting for her from the absolutely irresistible page one. Bow *wow*—What a terrific debut!"
—Hank Phillippi Ryan, nationally best-selling and award-winning author of *The Murder List*

"I promptly fell head over heels for this cast of characters, and the dogs burrowed quickly into my heart. The plot of *Bite the Dust* was intriguing and complex, with plenty of surprising twists and turns. What impressed me the most, though, was the warm tone of the author's writing voice . . . you just want to snuggle in and keep reading."
—MeezCarrie

Books by Jackie Layton

Low Country Dog Walker Mysteries

Bite the Dust
Dog-Gone Dead
Bag of Bones
Caught and Collared
A Killer Unleashed

A Killer Unleashed

A Low Country Dog Walker Mystery

Jackie Layton

BEYOND THE PAGE
PUBLISHING

A Killer Unleashed
Jackie Layton
Copyright © 2023 by Jackie Layton
Cover design and illustration by Dar Albert, Wicked Smart Designs

Beyond the Page Books
are published by
Beyond the Page Publishing
www.beyondthepagepub.com

ISBN: 978-1-958384-99-2

I dedicate this book to my husband, Tim. He encourages me on a daily basis, and I appreciate him so much.

I also want to thank my family for their support. They buy and read my books and cheer me on.

I don't remember a time when there wasn't a dog in my life. I'd like to dedicate this to Andy, Barney, Cindy, Blackie, Tinker, Maddie, and especially Heinz. Heinz has been my constant companion while writing A Low Country Dog Walker Mystery Series. Sometimes he lay by my feet, and other times he nudged me to move around. He's also been a good sport posing with my books.

Chapter One

"THIS IS THE ONE I'M MOST EXCITED ABOUT." I cut a white chocolate raspberry cupcake in half for my fiancé, Marc Williams. His hair had lightened to blonde over the summer and his tan had deepened to a bronze, highlighted by the yellow polo he wore. After putting Marc's portion on a small plate, I slid it across our table at Daily Java and grinned. "Tell me what you think."

It was the Friday of Labor Day Weekend, and we'd agreed to enjoy time together and make decisions on our upcoming wedding.

Marc stared at the cupcake, then one side of his mouth tipped up. "Yeah, I know you're excited. But raspberry? It seems too girly."

"Try it first." I forked a bite into my mouth and sighed. Sweet and tart deliciousness filled me, and I leaned back into my wooden chair at the table for two.

Marc bit into a forkful. He chewed, and his eyebrows rose. "Better than I expected."

I wiped my mouth with a napkin. "But?"

"What's wrong with a traditional wedding cake?"

Marc had agreed to most of my wedding wishes. Small wedding. Outside. October. How could I not agree? "You're right." I waved to Erin, the owner of Daily Java. She nodded and finished waiting on a customer at the counter.

Marc cleared his throat. "Say what?"

"We should go with a traditional wedding cake, but for my next birthday, I want this."

"You've got a deal." Marc's wide smile was sweeter than the cake.

Erin joined us. "Have you decided?"

"We're going with the traditional wedding cake," I said.

"You can never go wrong with the tried-and-tested option." She quizzed me on the date and size. "Juliet and Nate are scheduled for a cake tasting this afternoon. Do you want them to know ahead of time what you chose?"

My brother and my best friend were also getting married. In fact, we would be having a double wedding with them. "No. I don't want to sway their decision. We've already decided on food stations so we can incorporate different foods into our big day. They should pick the cake they want, even if it's the same as ours."

"That makes sense to me. Y'all don't need to make every food choice to make guests happy. Plus, you'll want to freeze the top layer and eat it on your

1

first anniversary." Erin smiled and the skin around her eyes crinkled.

My phone buzzed, and Ivey Gilbert's name appeared. "Oh, sorry. I should take this."

Erin reached for the samples. "I'll box up the leftovers, and you can enjoy them later."

"Thanks." I swiped my phone. "Hello."

Marc carried a tray of cupcakes and followed Erin to the counter.

"Andi Grace, this is Ivey. I need you to check on Lady. Do you still have a key to my house?" Ivey was a cancer survivor, real estate agent, wife of the ill-reputed attorney Norris Gilbert, and a bigwig around Heyward Beach. She'd somehow remained sweet despite her spouse's shenanigans.

"Yes, ma'am." I had a system for my dog-walking clients. House keys and notes on pets were secure in a fireproof lockbox.

"Norris was supposed to meet me near Savannah. He's not answering his phone, but the laws in Georgia are strict about using cell phones while driving. Still, he should be able to use the car's hands-free capability. Anyway, it's possible Norris forgot to bring Lady. My security system alerted me to movement in the house, but I don't see anybody."

"Okay. How can I help?"

"I'm probably overreacting, but would you verify Lady's not home alone? The family is meeting us here for a big vacation. We've rented a home on Tybee Island. If Norris accidently left the dog at home, do you mind watching her? I'll compensate you for the last-minute request. I know it's a holiday weekend, and I will definitely make it worth your while."

"It won't be a problem." There was no way I'd turn away from a dog in need, and Ivey seemed unglued. We discussed the details. "I'll call you as soon as I know more."

"Thanks, Andi Grace. I appreciate your help."

"Don't worry. It's not a problem." After telling her bye, I joined Marc by the counter of baked goods and updated him on the situation. "So, I'm heading to check on Ivey's dog."

"I'll go with you."

"Nice." I'd been happy when Marc told me he planned to take off Friday and Monday, making it a true long weekend. We'd have four glorious days together. This would be the only interruption I'd allow. "You know I wouldn't have agreed to check on Lady if it wasn't a possible emergency."

He wrapped his strong arm around my shoulders and kissed my cheek. "I get it. Let's roll."

After digging through the lockbox in the back of my Highlander, we took off. It was a short distance from the coffee shop to our destination. The Gilberts lived in the gated section of Heyward Beach, and the security guard sitting in the little building stood and opened his door.

I stopped and lowered my window. "Good morning."

The scrappy man looked at me. "Morning. What's your name?"

"Andi Grace Scott. I'm here to check on Ivey Gilbert's dog."

"Let's see if you're on my list." He checked his clipboard then he looked at a computer screen. "I don't see your name here. You'll need to turn around."

"Sir, it's an emergency. I'll call Mrs. Gilbert and let you talk to her."

"Nope. Not a chance, lady. You could be calling anyone. I'll give her a call myself." He shut the door to his little building and studied the computer screen before picking up the phone.

Marc sighed. "You gotta give him credit for doing a thorough job."

"You're right. I only hope Lady is okay." I looked at Marc and drummed my fingers on the steering wheel. "Do you think it's possible Norris left the house and forgot his dog?"

"Yeah. People have forgotten their kids before and left them in a hot car. It's tragic, but it does happen."

"Ma'am."

I turned back to the guard. "Yes, did you get her?"

"She says you're legit. Mrs. Gilbert also said if you find the dog, you may need to come and go more than this one time. You've got a pass for the next ten days." He held out a piece of paper. "Put this on your mirror, and we'll wave you through next time."

"Great. Thanks." I took the temporary permit allowing me into the neighborhood. "Have a good day."

"You too, miss."

Marc laughed as I drove to the Gilberts' house. "I wasn't sure we'd get approved. At least you won't have to stop if Ivey needs you to make multiple trips." He tapped the official permit.

"No kidding." I'd been to Ivey's place before and parked in front of the luxurious beachfront home. The manicured landscape included timber, rocks, palm trees, and coastal shrubbery. The yard enhanced the impressive air of the Gilberts' home.

The pale yellow two-story home invited visitors to come inside and relax. The exterior blended in with the beach yet stood out enough not to be boring. Tasteful and modern. I would've expected no less from Ivey Gilbert.

Marc whistled. "This must've cost them a pretty penny."

"No doubt." I hopped out of my SUV, and we walked to the steps leading up to the front door of the raised house. Most homes on the island stood on stilts to protect them from flooding. It was part of the current building codes, and only the oldest homes weren't elevated.

"It doesn't surprise me that Norris owns the largest house, but I would've predicted all the houses to be big." He met my gaze. "You know. Because it's gated."

I unlocked the door. "Yeah, but the small one next door was here before the rich people wanted to close off this end. I admire the family for sticking with their traditional beach house."

"There's something unique about the older beach homes. Oh, by the way, Lincoln bought Dirk Cutter's house earlier this week."

The radio personality and podcaster Dirk Cutter had been murdered earlier in the year. Lincoln Zane was a friend of Marc's and a country music star. "Really? What about his family?"

"His wife decided she needed an extended break from Lincoln." Marc frowned. "Linc's going to hunker down here and focus on writing new music."

"Good for him." I entered Ivey's bright and airy house. It was streamlined with a comfortable vibe. "Hello. Norris, are you home?"

Silence greeted us.

"Norris, Ivey asked me to come over and check on Lady." I stood in the empty room and examined the space. With a dog-walking career, it wasn't unusual for me to enter a vacant house. "It doesn't look like he's home."

Marc stood with his hands on his hips. "Wonder where the dog is?"

"I'm not sure. She's a schnoodle."

"Bless you." Marc chuckled.

"Very funny. A schnoodle is a mix of schnauzer and poodle. They're not too big, but I'm surprised she hasn't greeted us. Maybe Lady is on the way to Tybee Island with Norris." I walked into the kitchen area of the open-concept space. "It's odd, though, Ivey said the motion sensors picked up movement earlier."

"Wasps have triggered my security system before. It's possible the same thing happened here." Marc paced around the furniture in the living area. There was a long white slip-covered couch on one edge of the cream and blue floral rug. Two armchairs faced the couch and a dark leather recliner completed the living area. "There's no sign of Norris or the dog, at least not in this room."

I peeked in the well-stocked pantry. "Some owners keep their pets crated in the pantry, the laundry room, the bathroom, or honestly, you might find a pet in any room. Then other families don't crate their dogs. So, I'm going to search until we're certain there's no dog in the house."

"Never doubted it." He moved in the opposite direction and paused at the window overlooking the beach. "The water's flat today. Maybe we can go paddleboarding later."

"That'd be fun." I checked the laundry room. "Here's her crate, but no Lady. There is a basket of dog supplies, but I don't think that means anything. Norris could have Lady's stuff in the car. Well, if it wasn't Lady who triggered the motion sensors, we'll chalk it up to your wasp theory."

"Empty crate? Does that mean she's allowed to roam when nobody's home?"

"Haha, nice rhyme. No wonder Lincoln collaborates with you." I moved to the kitchen island and picked up a blister pack of pink tablets. "Diphenhydramine?"

Marc looked over my shoulder at the medicine. "It's an antihistamine. Once I used it for a bad case of poison oak, and it knocked me out."

"I hope Norris didn't take one and fall asleep driving to meet his family. If he had a car accident, it'd explain why he hasn't answered Ivey's calls." I laid the medicine packet down and walked through the living room to the home office. "Lady, are you here?"

Marc met me at the closed office door and knocked. "Mr. Gilbert?"

I met my fiancé's gaze. "Don't you feel like he would've heard us by now?"

"Not if he took that allergy medicine." He winked.

"Touché." I turned the doorknob. "Norris?"

As soon as the door swung open, we saw Norris Gilbert. He was slumped in the upholstered desk chair. His head listed to the side, and a neon pink dog leash was tied around his neck.

Chapter Two

"NORRIS!" I ran to his body and pressed my fingertips against his wrist. Where was his pulse? I pressed harder. Nothing. I shifted closer to the thumb, then closer to the forearm. Right then left. Why couldn't I feel a beat? I blinked against the tears pooling in my eyes.

Marc leapt into action across the chair from me and loosened the pink leash. He paused and felt the man's face. "I'll call for help."

"There's no pulse." I couldn't deny the truth, and my words warbled.

"Not surprised." Marc tapped on his phone. "His skin is cool to the touch."

My legs shook, and I collapsed onto the carpeted floor with my back to gray bookcase. Norris wore black shorts and a spotless white polo shirt. I closed my eyes to avoid looking at his dead body.

The cupcakes Marc and I tested earlier tried to come back up. I wrapped my arms around my upset stomach.

Marc spoke to the emergency operator in a quiet voice.

Memories of encounters with Norris flooded my memory. He hadn't been a nice man, but he'd wielded power. How had Ivey put up with his mischief throughout the years? Despite his bad behavior, he didn't deserve to be murdered.

Marc reached for my hand. "Let's sit on the front porch. The fresh air will do us good."

I wrapped my fingers around his and squeezed. "Is there something we should do?"

"The operator doesn't believe CPR will help at this point. Maybe a few hours ago, but not now. Help is on the way."

"Okay." I inched my body up the bookcase. "You'd think by now the sight of a dead body wouldn't affect me so badly."

"I can't imagine it not affecting you." He slipped his arm around my shoulders and led me to the porch. We sat on a bed-type swing and waited for law enforcement to arrive.

How had a day of making fun wedding plans turned to death so quickly? I shivered despite the late-August heat. Poor Norris. Poor Ivey. His life was gone, and hers would never be the same.

A wind gust shook the house, drawing a groan from the structure.

Chills crept up my arms. "Did you hear that? It's as if Ivey's home is mourning the loss of Norris."

"Shh. If you listen carefully, you'll hear the sirens."

"Good, because this is more than I want to handle." Breaking the news to Ivey was not on my wish list. The authorities could handle the announcement. Before long, the town would learn Heyward Beach had suffered another blow.

The timing stunk. Ivey and Norris hadn't even gotten to enjoy one last family vacation.

I closed my eyes and leaned against Marc's shoulder until a vehicle screeched into the driveway and came to a sudden stop.

I sat up straight and opened my eyes to see who'd arrived.

Sheriff Wade Stone was the first to arrive at the Gilberts' house. He climbed the steps and stopped when he spotted Marc and me on the front porch. "Should've known it was you who found the body."

I gasped.

Marc stood and glared at the sheriff. "Take it easy on her, Wade. We didn't start our day planning to discover a dead body."

The sheriff grimaced. "Sorry, Andi Grace. That was uncalled for. What are you two doing here?"

"Ivey asked me to stop by and check on her dog." I took a deep breath, trying to compose myself.

"You have a house key?"

"She's a client, so yes. I have a house key just like I have one for your place and everybody else who is on my client list." I took care of Wade's dog on occasion. Duke was a fun mutt and well-behaved. He loved to chase sticks more than any dog I'd ever met.

"Okay. Where's the dog now?"

"I never found Lady, and according to Ivey, Norris was supposed to bring the schnoodle to meet her near Savannah for vacation."

"Stay right there. My deputies are on the way. If the dog is here, we'll find it." Wade entered the house, then returned. "What kind of mutt are we looking for? I don't want any of my people to get attacked."

"A schnoodle. Lady's a small black, white, and grayish dog. I can't imagine her attacking anyone under normal circumstances. But who knows what she's been through this morning? Please, be gentle with Lady. If you find her, just holler. She's used to me." I stood and gazed up and down the street in hopes of spotting the little creature. There was no traffic, which wasn't a surprise given it was a gated community.

"You got it." Wade reentered the house.

My brother-in-law, Deputy David Wayne, was the second official to appear. "Andi Grace, are you okay?" He gave me a brotherly hug.

"Not exactly, but I'll be fine in a bit." I stepped back. "Are you going to question us?"

David straightened and crossed his arms. "Afraid not. Because we're related, another deputy will do the official questioning."

"I get it." Still, I was disappointed. Some of the other deputies thought I was a pain who hindered their investigations just because I'd helped solve past murders.

David shot me a quick smile. "Well, if you two are okay, I'll see what the sheriff wants me to do."

Marc said, "We're fine. Don't worry about us."

After David entered the house, we sat on the porch's swing bed. Once again, I leaned my head on Marc's shoulder. "He's a good guy, isn't he?"

"Yep, and he loves your sister. Lacey Jane's got a winner." Marc had a soft spot for my younger sister.

Two more deputies rolled up to the house with sirens wailing. They exited their vehicles and jogged up the stairs. Both glanced at us before going inside.

I snuggled closer to Marc and placed my hand on his chest. While my fiancé appeared calm, his heart raced. Finding Norris had affected him more than I'd suspected. "I love you."

He kissed my temple. "Love you, too."

Again, footsteps clumped up the front stairs. Lovely. It was Deputy Hanks, and he was not a fan of mine. "Morning, folks. I'm going to take a quick look-see at the crime scene, then I'll question you."

I gulped. "Yes, sir." The fifty-something balding deputy gave us a curt nod, and like all the others, stepped into the beachfront home.

Marc held me closer. "It'll be good to get the questioning behind us. Do you want Deputy Hanks to talk to you first?"

"It probably makes sense. I took Ivey's call and relayed the message to you. I've also been in the house before to walk Lady and knew where to look even though we haven't found her yet. I wonder where she could be?"

Marc swiped a hand over his face. "You said Lady has greeted you at the door in the past. Maybe the killer entered, and the dog ran away."

"That makes sense, unless the killer was waiting for Norris. Why do you suppose Ivey and Norris didn't travel together? It'd only take them two to three hours to drive to Tybee."

"It's possible he had a meeting he couldn't reschedule."

"I guess. Marc, do you think Ivey could have killed her husband then staged it for me to find his body?"

"Yeah, it'd be smart to have you find Norris. It'd possibly lessen suspicion of her being the guilty person."

"Could she really be so devious? I always felt sorry for her being married to Norris, but if she's a scheming bitter wife, I don't know what to think." The humid breeze increased my rate of perspiration, and I would've loved a cool towel to dab my forehead and neck.

Deputy Hanks returned. "We'll talk at the dining room table. Who wants to go first?"

"Me." I squeezed Marc's hand before standing and walking into the house with the deputy.

He took the bench on one side of the long oak table, and I sat across from him in a chair. He opened a small notebook and met my gaze. "Let's start with how you came to find another dead body."

I rubbed my trembling hands together. Would he believe my story? It was unbelievable to think I'd found another dead body in Heyward Beach, South Carolina. Had I been set up, or was it an accident? There was no point in stalling any longer. "Ivey Gilbert called and asked me to come check on her dog. Lady is a schnoodle, and I still haven't found her."

"How'd you get inside? Was the door open? Unlocked?"

"The door was closed and locked, and I used my key. You should know that I keep keys for all of my clients in case of emergencies. And again, Ivey asked me to enter the house."

"Right. So you came in here. Then what?"

I explained the events leading up to finding Norris's dead body.

Deputy Hanks studied his notes. "No sign of the dog but you found Norris strangled with a dog leash."

"Right." I folded my hands. "Wait, you know how sometimes you get ready to leave your house only to realize you forgot your sunglasses or purse or phone? Then you have to run back inside and find what you left behind?"

"Yeah. What's the point you're trying to make?"

"I didn't look in the car. What if Lady is in Norris's Lexus?"

His eyebrows rose, and he called Deputy Denise Harris over. She was a relative newcomer to Heyward Beach but seemed to fit in with the sheriff's department. Deputy Hanks spoke to her in such low tones, I couldn't make out the words. The Black female deputy hurried out of the house, and I hoped she was on the way to check the car.

I met his gaze. "Thanks."

"No problem. Now, have you shared the news with the victim's wife?"

I shook my head. "No. I thought you or the sheriff would want to call Ivey and gauge her response in case she's guilty."

"Smart move. Is there anything else you need to share?"

Nothing came to mind. "No, sir."

"Fine. Why don't you send in Mr. Williams?" He scribbled something on the small sheet of paper.

I left him sitting there and rejoined Marc on the front porch. "Your turn."

He stood and gave me a hug. "Are you okay?"

"I've been better, but you should go in there before Deputy Hanks comes looking for you."

Marc chuckled. "Yep. There's no need to get sideways with the man."

Deputy Harris approached me. "No luck on finding the dog. I'll let the others know."

"I appreciate you checking." After the deputy went inside, I sat on the swing, but restlessness drove me to my feet. I walked down the wooden stairs and paced in the sandy driveway, keeping alert for a sign of Ivey's schnoodle.

Sunlight glinted off something in the grass. I walked over to inspect the item. Without touching anything, it was easy enough to identify an oyster knife. Shiny and probably new. I snapped a quick picture with my phone. Norris didn't seem like the kind of guy to get his hands dirty shucking oysters, so why was it here?

"Hey, what's going on?" The voice sounded familiar.

My heart skipped a beat. Had the killer come back? No. The place was crawling with law enforcement. I turned, and relief flooded through me as I recognized the man dressed in shorts and running shoes. He held a rolled-up T-shirt in one hand. "Oh, hi, Ethan. You scared me." Ethan Seitz was a local pharmacist and one of my dog-walking clients. I was also giving obedience lessons to his black Lab, Yoyo.

"What's happening? Did someone get hurt?" He pulled the shirt on over his sweaty body.

"I'm not sure if I can say anything yet, but I can't find Ivey Gilbert's dog. Have you seen Lady? She's a little black-and-white schnoodle."

"Not this morning, but I know this many deputies didn't show up to look for a lost dog." He pointed toward the official vehicles.

"Funny, but true. Have you seen any strangers wandering around this area today?"

He lifted the bottom of his shirt and wiped the sweat on his face. "I saw an unfamiliar Mini Cooper when I was playing in my front yard with Yoyo. I think a man was driving, but I wouldn't swear to it."

"What color was the car?"

"Blue, which surprised me. It was a fun blue, like turquoise. It seems as if most of the people around here drive white Minis."

"Good point. You know I'd tell you more about what's going on here if I could, but the sheriff wouldn't be happy. I sure don't want to obstruct his investigation and get tossed into jail." I didn't think Wade would resort to such drastic measures, but I didn't want to interfere and push my luck with the sheriff.

Ethan laughed. "Isn't solving murders what you do when you're not working with dogs?"

"Shh. Don't say that when there are so many deputies around." I smiled. "Thanks for the tip about the car though. If a deputy questions you, please tell them."

"Right. Let me know if there's anything I can do to help. Right now, I better finish my run. See you around, Andi Grace."

"Bye." I watched him take off in the direction of the entry gate.

I returned to pacing. Lady needed to be found, and it'd be great to locate the driver of the blue Mini Cooper. The person probably had nothing to do with the murder, but it was a starting place. I also needed to point out the oyster knife in case it was a clue.

During Heyward Beach's last murder investigation, I had told myself to focus on planning my wedding. This time I was completely focused on preparing for my nuptials. No stinking murder was going to hinder my progress.

Chapter Three

"DO YOU KNOW ANYONE who drives a blue Mini Cooper?" I pulled out of the Gilberts' driveway with my fiancé riding shotgun.

"Not that I can think of." Marc drummed his fingers on his thigh. "Where are you going?"

I drove deeper into the gated community. "While you were being questioned, Ethan Seitz ran by. Like literally he was running, and we talked for a minute. The only odd thing he noticed today was a man driving a blue Mini Cooper. Probably a man."

"I take it we're looking for the mysterious car." He pointed out the window.

"Yes, please." I drove until the road ended then turned and retraced our path. "Get comfortable, I don't plan to give up until we've covered every possible inch of this island."

He laughed. "It would've surprised me if you didn't look for the car after Ethan's clue."

My phone rumbled in the cupholder.

Marc picked it up. "It's Ivey."

"Don't answer it. I think Wade needs to break the news to her about Norris's murder."

"You're right. I'm kinda surprised he hasn't called her yet. Unless she ignored his call and wants you to tell her what's going on." He replaced my phone. "I agree not answering her call is the best move."

"I'll drive past the pier. We'll watch for the car and Lady." I remained well under the speed limit as we searched. "Thanks for helping me."

"No problem. Black-and-white schnoodle and a little blue car. On it." Marc whistled an unfamiliar tune as we headed up Ocean Drive. When we neared the pier parking lot, he said, "How about I hop out and scan the area on foot while you continue driving down the street? Divide and conquer."

"I like your plan." I slowed the SUV and stopped in front of Cutter's Landing, the house Lincoln had bought.

Marc jumped out. "Call me if you need help."

"Sure. See you in a bit."

I cruised down the street and adjusted my sunglasses. The sun blazed bright on the last unofficial Friday of summer.

Tourists unloaded vehicles at rental homes. Suitcases, coolers, groceries, totes of towels, and beach paraphernalia. Excitement filled the air. I stopped at a crosswalk to allow two young women to walk to the beach side of the street. They smiled and carried collapsible chairs and water bottles.

My phone vibrated in the cupholder, but I continued my search. At the end of the street, I pulled over and checked my messages.

Ivey had texted. *The sheriff broke the news to me about Norris. I'm heading home. Do you have Lady?*

I gulped. *No, but Marc and I are looking for her right now.*

Ivey's quick reply appeared. *There will be a bonus for finding her.*

Ivey was quick to throw her money around in most situations. I would do my best to locate the schnoodle with or without a bonus. How could she think offering more money would make me work harder? I counted to ten in French before calming myself enough to turn my SUV around and head for Crab Street.

If we didn't find Lady soon, I'd make posters and place the signs around the island. Social media would also be a good way to alert people to Lady's predicament. The little dog was so sweet, and I hated the idea of her being alone and scared. I'd do everything possible to find her.

Thirty minutes later, I parked on a side street and walked to the pier to meet Marc. I waved when I spotted my tall fiancé and darted through the crowd to join him. "Any luck?"

"I'm sorry to report no luck yet. I talked to the ladies in the diner. They'll call us if they hear anything. I also ran into Jeremiah Prichard. He's on the beach with his metal detector and will be watching for the dog. What's next?"

"Let's go to my place and make flyers. We can even mention a reward." I told him how upset I'd been with Ivey's offer of a bonus.

"Aw, honey. She's distraught. Her husband has been murdered, and her dog is missing. I'm sure she knows how much you care about all animals." He reached for my hand.

"You're right. It was silly to feel hurt over Ivey's offer. Let's go." It was a quiet walk to my Highlander. A piece of paper secured under my windshield wiper caught my attention. "Surely I didn't get a ticket."

"Heyward Beach tickets are yellow. That paper is white."

"I guess it could be an advertisement from one of the merchants." I lifted the wiper blade and removed the generic white paper. There was a message written on it with a fat black marker.

"Well?"

Unable to process the words, I read the note twice before meeting Marc's gaze. "Lady has been dognapped."

"You're kidding."

I read the note out loud to Marc. "I have the dog. It'll cost you to get her back. I'll be in touch."

"Somebody dognapped Lady. This is crazy, especially on top of Norris being murdered." He ran a hand through his blonde hair.

"Oh, Marc. This is terrible. What are we going to do?" My heart raced. Who'd take an innocent dog? "How did they know to leave the message on my SUV?"

"I don't know, but we'll figure it out later." He shook his head. "We need to notify Ivey immediately."

"You're right." I dreaded the conversation, but there was no other option. First, I'd break the news to Ivey, then I'd post pictures of Lady on social media. It was a good thing I kept pictures of my animal clients in the lockbox. It made at least one of my tasks easier.

Chapter Four

DEPUTY DAVID WAYNE MET US AT MY HIGHLANDER, and I turned over the ransom note. I'd taken a picture of it with my phone earlier, even though I had no intention of investigating Norris's murder.

"I'm glad you called us, Andi Grace." With gloved hands, David dropped the paper into an evidence bag. "Can you tell me anything else?"

"I posted a picture of Lady on social media, but I just said she's missing. Did you see the oyster knife in the Gilberts' front yard? I forgot to mention it earlier."

"Nope. I'll check with the others. Do you believe it's important?" He wrote in his little notebook.

"Possibly." I watched a car pull into the driveway across the street. People spilled out and the trunk popped open. "It's hard to believe Norris would use one himself. Hey, do you think any of these houses have a doorbell camera? Maybe the dognapper was caught on camera."

"It's doubtful any of the homeowners are around with it being the last big week of rentals for the summer, but I'll check." He rubbed his chin. "Is there anything else you want to add?"

I glanced at Marc, who was leaning against my SUV.

He said, "Have you heard about the blue Mini Cooper?"

"It sounds like another thing I missed out on. Sheriff Stone is about to have a meeting for us to compare notes. For now, the Gilbert house is a crime scene. Have either of you spoken to Mrs. Gilbert?"

I shook my head. "She called me earlier, but I didn't answer in case the sheriff hadn't told her about Norris. Then she texted and told me she knew about Norris. She's on the way home and even offered me a bonus to find her lost dog."

"That's good to know." He stuffed the notebook into the pocket of his uniform shorts. "Be careful. It doesn't make me feel good that the dognapper involved you."

"Do you think the murder and dognapping are connected?"

"Yeah. It stands to reason they're related."

Marc stood straight. "I don't believe in coincidences. They're connected."

I said, "If we discover the link, we'll probably find the killer."

David pointed at me. "Not you. The sheriff's department will catch the killer."

The firmness of his voice surprised me, but I wouldn't make any promises. "When I woke up this morning, I only wanted to spend time with Marc and taste cake."

"That's what you two should do. Plan your wedding." He glanced at his watch. "I need to shove off, but I'll check the houses later today. You two be careful."

"You be careful too, David."

After he left, Marc faced me. "Would you rather go paddleboarding or hunt for clues?"

"Um, let's do something fun."

"Fun, as in ask if any of the neighbors saw the person who left the note on your windshield?"

I hugged him. "You really do get me."

"Your desire to find the truth is one of the reasons I fell for you."

I stepped back and looked up and down the street of beach homes. "Shall we begin at the closest one?"

"Yep, but we're sticking together this time. In case the dognapper is also the killer, I don't plan to let you out of my sight."

"Sounds good to me." I squeezed his hand. "You know, we should also ask if they saw the dog. The dognapper may have had Lady with them when they left the note."

"Brilliant. So we'll ask about the dog and the person leaving the ransom note."

We began with a narrow white beach house.

Two hours later, we hadn't come across anyone who'd seen the person who'd left a note or Lady.

"What next?" Marc pushed his sunglasses up.

"Let's go to my place and get something to drink. I also want to check out the oyster knife. Maybe we can learn who sells them."

"I can fix lunch while you research."

"Sounds like a plan." I pushed the fob button to unlock my SUV and drove the short distance to my house.

Sunny and Chubb greeted us at the front door. Sunny was my loyal German shepherd, and Chubb was Marc's golden retriever.

I loved on both of them and laughed. "Hey there. Did you miss us?"

Woof. Woof. Sunny nuzzled me.

Chubb turned his attention to Marc.

After a few minutes of loving on our dogs, we let them out into the fenced-in backyard. Marc laughed. "You'd think we'd been gone for days instead of a few hours. How will they manage when we go on our honeymoon?"

I filled two glasses with ice and water. "I'm not worried a bit. They'll be well cared for at Stay and Play." My dog-walking business had expanded into a place in the country where we cared for animals when their families left town. We also gave obedience lessons, doggie day care, and grooming services. Next up was a dog shelter.

Marc drained his glass. "It's too hot for tomato soup, but how about a grilled cheese sandwich?"

"Aw, my comfort food. Yes, please." If there was ever a day I needed comfort, this was it. "Can I help?"

"Naw, you go do your research."

Once I settled in my office, I looked at the pictures of the oyster shucking knife. I Googled the brand name from the picture on my phone.

It turned out the knife was the newest version of the tool. There was a link to contact the company, and I emailed and asked where I could buy their products near Heyward Beach.

"Lunch is ready."

I let the dogs inside, and they headed for their water bowls.

"Wow, what a spread." Besides sandwiches, there were apple slices, grapes, and carrot sticks on our plates. My stomach growled at the sight. "Let's eat inside at the table where it's nice and cool."

"It's a scorcher today for sure."

Ignoring my water, I pulled two Cokes out of the refrigerator and met him at the table, where my kitchen blended into an eating area and family room.

Marc waited for me to sit first. "I should've known to get your favorite drink."

"After our morning, I need all the comfort food and drinks I can get."

We ate lunch with the dogs resting nearby. Sunny snoozed, and Chubb gnawed on a safe dog bone. I updated Marc on what I'd learned. "Here's what we know. Norris was murdered. Lady was stolen, maybe by the murderer or another random bad guy. The oyster knife is the newest model the manufacturer makes. A strange Mini Cooper was driving in the Gilberts' neighborhood this morning."

"I wonder how the driver made it past the security guard?"

"Good question."

Marc pushed his chair back and stretched his long legs. "Who do you suspect of killing Norris?"

"The spouse is always the first person of interest. Right?" I poured more Coke into my empty glass and waited for the fizz to settle.

"Usually, but Ivey was in Georgia. Norris wasn't a nice man. There could be a long list of people who wanted to kill him. The dog is different. Why take Lady?"

"Especially if you killed Norris. Adding a dognapping to your crime would add to your danger of getting caught." It didn't make sense to me.

Marc nodded. "Why risk it? It strikes me as a stupid move."

"Yet, deep down I believe the two events are connected." I took a drink.

"I agree. If we determine how, we'll be one big step closer to finding the killer."

"Whoa, look at you. Are you thinking we'll try to help solve the case?"

"It's what you usually do, and you're good at it."

"Yeah, but the wedding is only a few weeks away. I want to focus on our future and not Heyward Beach's latest murder."

Marc lifted one side of his mouth, and his eyes twinkled. "I'll be supportive either way."

How had I been so blessed to be engaged to Marc Williams? He was smart, nice, caring, and so much more. He was a man of integrity, and I loved him with my whole heart.

My thoughts drifted to Ivey. Norris hadn't been faithful or nice during their marriage. Yet she'd dealt with his bad behavior for years. Had something happened recently that would've caused her to resort to murdering her husband? If so, it must've been bad. Really bad.

Chapter Five

IT WAS EARLY EVENING by the time I met with Ivey. She'd already been questioned by the sheriff, and when she arrived at my house, the poor thing looked done in.

"Andi Grace, thanks for seeing me. I'm so upset over Lady's disappearance." The woman wore black linen slacks and a white linen sleeveless tunic.

"Come inside." Was she more upset over her dog than her husband? I waved her in. "Can I get you a glass of water?"

"No, I'm fine."

I led her to the family room. "Please, have a seat."

Ivey sat in a chair, and I chose the couch. She placed her large leather purse on the floor before speaking. "We need to discuss Lady's situation."

"Yes. The person left the ransom note on my windshield. I'm so sorry." I swallowed. "I'm also sorry about Norris's death."

"Thank you. Can you believe the sheriff questioned me as if I'm a suspect?" Her nostrils flared.

"They just need to rule you out. It's probably standard procedure to suspect a spouse first in murder cases. Do you mind telling me what happened?"

Sunny wandered into the family room from my home office and sat next to Ivey.

The widow reached out and stroked my dog's head. "There's not much to tell. I went to Savannah early this morning to pick up food from our favorite deli. We were to meet our family for a vacation on Tybee Island, but I already told you that. I can't think clearly. The drive home was a complete blur." She shook her head.

"I'm sure it's the stress. Go ahead and tell me more."

She took a deep breath. "I wanted to get our rental home prepared before everyone arrived. There were groceries and flowers to order. I also like to organize the bathrooms with soaps, shampoos, and my personal towels."

"I'm curious about why you chose to go to Tybee. Your home is so beautiful. Why didn't your family come to Heyward Beach?"

"It's impossible to vacation here for Norris and me. We've tried, but people stop us and ask business questions. In order to relax and focus on our family, we've learned physically leaving home was the only way to go."

"I understand." Although my last vacation had been when I was a child, so what did I really know? "When did you begin to worry about Norris?"

She sniffed, then pulled a tissue from her pocket. "No doubt you're aware we've had our problems, but through counseling we'd learned not to neglect each other. He'd gotten much better about taking my calls. When he didn't answer this morning, I thought he'd call back soon. For the next couple hours, I called him about every fifteen minutes. I didn't know if there'd been a wreck, or if he forgot Lady, or what. By the time I reached out to you, I'd gone from annoyed to concerned."

"I would've been frantic in your situation."

"Can we talk about Lady? I'm waiting for the ransom demands. Did you see anyone suspicious around your vehicle?" She dabbed at a teardrop rolling down her cheek. It was still hard to determine if she was more upset about her husband or her dog.

"No. Sorry. I was focused on looking for your dog and had no idea she'd been snatched at first. After we discovered and reported the ransom note, I asked around to see if anyone saw who put the paper on my windshield. No luck with that, but one of your neighbors saw an unfamiliar blue Mini Cooper in your community this morning. Does the car sound familiar to you?"

She met my gaze. "Not really. Do you believe it's important?"

I shrugged. "Possibly."

Ivey stared at Sunny and went back to rubbing my dog's head. The woman's lips pressed together. Everyone handled grief differently, and her marriage hadn't been hunky-dory.

The silence became uncomfortable. "Is there anything you need me to do?"

The older woman stood and crossed her arms. "I can't stay at home tonight. The police haven't finished processing it. Would you see if there's a room available at Kennady Bed and Breakfast?"

I pulled the phone from my pocket and stood. "I'll text Juliet right now."

"Thank you." She stood and knocked over her purse but didn't give it a second glance. Instead, she walked toward the kitchen. "If you don't mind, I've changed my mind about a drink."

I shot a quick text off to Juliet, then joined Ivey in the kitchen. "I have Coke or water."

"A Coke sounds good."

I fixed her a glass of ice and reached for two cans of the soft drink. "How about some crackers and pimento cheese? You probably haven't had much to eat today." In very little time, I organized a snack for Ivey.

"Thank you." She stood ramrod straight by the island and reached for a thin wheat cracker.

My phone rang. "This is Juliet. I'll take her call on the back porch. Make yourself at home." I hurried outside and answered. "Hi, Juliet. I guess you got my message."

"Yeah. I heard Norris was murdered."

"It's true. Can you fit Ivey in tonight?" A balmy ocean breeze blew back my hair.

"You don't need space for her family?" Juliet sounded surprised.

"She only asked for herself. The family may be waiting in Georgia until the house is released to Ivey. I really don't know much else."

"You know it's Labor Day Weekend," Juliet said, "and we were booked solid."

"Do I detect a but?"

"I just had a cancellation for a corner room with an en suite." She described the room to me.

"It sounds perfect. Save it for Ivey. I'll let you know when she leaves here."

"Okay, thanks."

I returned to Ivey. She sat at my long table between the living area and my kitchen, petting Sunny. A quick glance at the counter revealed she'd finished her drink and had eaten a bit. "Juliet has one room available, and I told her to hold it for you."

"Very good."

"What about your family? What are they doing?"

She sighed. "I suggested they stay in Tybee until I had more details. The place is paid for, so they may as well use it for now."

I sat beside her, and Sunny lumbered to the kitchen. "Did Norris have any enemies?"

My dog lapped water from her bowl.

"Plenty. You sound like the sheriff." He eyes widened. "Oh, yes, you like to track down killers in your spare time."

Like wasn't how I'd describe it. Each time I'd jumped in to help solve a murder, there'd been a good reason. "Sorry. I didn't mean to butt in, but Norris is gone. Besides that, Lady is missing, and you could be in danger. Please, be careful."

She stood and glanced toward the kitchen. "If you don't mind, could I get a refill?"

"Absolutely." I hurried and poured more Coke into her glass.

Sunny wandered to the family room area and stretched out near the coffee table.

Ivey joined me in the kitchen and took another cracker. "I don't know how to deal with the dognappers. Norris was one of Lady's favorite people. When he was in the house, she stayed right with him. I was always second choice even though I'd been the one who adopted her. Norris was more relaxed with Lady than any human being. She brought out the best in him."

"It's funny how dogs can do that."

She drained her glass. "Do you mind if I use your bathroom before driving to the B and B?"

"Right this way." I led her to the half bath, then left her alone. Returning to the family room, I noticed the contents from her purse had spilled onto the floor. Lipstick, keys, passport, leather wallet, and a pack of spearmint gum.

What in the world? Why did Ivey have her passport? Was it normal to carry it around if you didn't plan to leave the country? I didn't think so, but I rarely left Heyward Beach.

I hurried and knelt beside the items to get a better look. There were two passports. Not one. I opened each book and confirmed they belonged to Ivey and Norris.

The muted sound of a toilet flushing led me to drop the items and scurry across the room.

Ivey reappeared. "Thanks for helping me tonight."

I faced the older woman. "Were you and Norris planning to leave the country?"

Her complexion grew pale. "Why would you think that? I was in Savannah for a family vacation."

"I didn't mean to pry, but your purse had tipped over and I noticed your passport has fallen out. Ivey, what's going on?"

Sunny stood and glanced back and forth between us.

"Look, if you think I killed Norris and planned to skip the country, you're wrong. We planned to travel. Together." With shaky hands, she held up both passports. "See? Two."

"Yes, ma'am. I see them." Weird though. "Where'd you plan to go?"

"Bali."

Interesting. "Why?"

"It's none of your business, Andi Grace." She grimaced. "If it's still okay with your friend, I'll head to the bed-and-breakfast."

"Sure." Sunny and I followed her down the wide hall, and I opened the front door. "If you need me to do anything, just let me know."

"Keep your eyes open for Lady." It wasn't a request. Her tone commanded me to watch for her dog.

"Absolutely."

She walked down my steps and soon drove off in her gray Lexus SUV.

"Come on, Sunny. We're going to my office to see what's in Bali besides beaches."

Chapter Six

BALI, A BLUE MINI COOPER, AND A MISSING SCHNOODLE were my clues to solving Norris Gilbert's murder.

Jungles, volcanoes, wellness retreats, and wild nightclubs were all available on the Indonesian island. Surfers and ecotourists were drawn to the province, at least according to my online research. Bali appeared to be a safe country, but expensive.

Wellness retreats? Had Ivey's cancer returned?

My phone buzzed, and Marc's face appeared. He'd been visiting Lincoln, and I swiped the screen. "Hey, whatcha doing?"

"I'm heading your way with supper from Tony's Pizzeria. He misses you."

My heart squeezed. Tony had been a good friend watching out for my family ever since my parents had died. "I need to visit him next week. It's been too long." I jotted down a note to remind myself.

"That's what he said."

"How'd it go with Lincoln?"

"Really good. I'll update you over dinner."

"Okay. See you soon." I left my research notes in the office and darted into the kitchen. I pulled out plates and glasses. Cokes and pizza seemed like a perfect combination. Who cared that I'd had a soft drink earlier? Actually, I'd had multiple Cokes throughout the day. After finding a dead body and discovering a dog had been nabbed, I needed the indulgence. I'd do better tomorrow.

The doorbell rang, and I hurried to let Marc inside.

Chubb greeted Sunny and me with a bark.

I kissed Marc, who held an extra-large pizza box with a smaller box on top. When the kiss ended, I focused on the food he carried. "Wait, no salads?"

He winked. "I wasn't feeling in the mood for salad. In fact, I ordered tiramisu for dessert."

"Whoa, that must've been some meeting you had with Lincoln."

"Yes, it was." His smile lit the room. "We're celebrating tonight, and I'll get back on track after this holiday weekend."

We joined the dogs in the kitchen. While filling their bowls with kibble and water, I wondered how Lady was. Were the mean dognappers treating her kindly? Did she have food and water? I shook my head. There was nothing I could do until we heard from the cruel people who'd taken the schnoodle.

By the time we fixed our plates and drinks, the dogs had finished their food. I pointed to the back door. "Shall we eat outside?"

"Yep. It's not too humid, and it'd be a shame to waste the nice evening."

The dogs ran down the porch stairs and played in the backyard.

I nibbled on my food and tried to ignore my fears regarding Lady. Marc devoured his food, then leaned back in his chair. He stretched out his long legs and smiled. "You ready for this?"

"Shoot." I sipped my drink and pushed my plate to the side.

"Lincoln is going to make an offer on Piney Woods Apartment Complex."

"Why?" The place was in a great location near the marsh, and it was an easy walk to the beach. A person could make a fortune tearing down the old apartment complex and building expensive homes.

"He didn't grow up wealthy. I told him about our past experience there, and when he learned the place was for sale, he was intrigued. He wants to make it nice for the low-income residents, but he also knows he doesn't have time to oversee a project like that."

"What does that mean? He's going to forget about the place?"

"Far from it." Marc continued to smile. "He hasn't been able to quit thinking about it."

"Boy, do I know how it is to get something on your mind that just won't go away."

Marc laughed so hard the dogs ran up and checked on him. He rubbed their heads.

"So, what is Lincoln going to do with the complex?"

"I introduced him to Griffin Reed."

"Oh, is Lincoln going to hire him to update the place? Juliet will be so happy to have her brother in town for a long-term project." I leaned forward and tapped my fiancé's knees.

"Don't get too excited yet. Griffin isn't officially on board, but he's inspected the property. Like I said, Lincoln's going to make an offer, and then we'll move forward."

"Okay, but Griffin is in town to convert the storage building at the old HOSE into living quarters for Ike Gage." Ike was my sister's biological father, and he'd decided to live in Heyward Beach and run a beach store in order to spend more time with Lacey Jane. None of us had known of my mother's affair leading to my sister's existence until the past year. Once Ike had met his only child, he'd decided to plant roots in Heyward Beach.

"It's almost ready, and Griffin even helped with a few projects in the store." Marc squeezed my hand. "Lincoln offered to let Griffin live on-site, rent-free."

"That's great." I'd consulted with Griffin earlier to convert my front room into an office for Marc. I'd need to confirm he hadn't forgotten me. "It sounds like y'all have thought of everything."

"We've tried to look at the pros and cons. It may not be a moneymaker, but it'll be good for our community. How about going for a walk?"

"I've got a better idea. There's supposed to be a live band at the pier parking lot to kick off Labor Day Weekend. Are you up to dancing?"

"If it means I get to hold you in my arms, you bet." His gray eyes sparkled. "We can also keep our eyes open for Ivey's dog."

"You're right. It's possible she escaped from whoever who took her. Give me a few minutes to get ready."

"Take your time."

It didn't take long to get ready, but I did slip into a sundress and pull my hair into a smooth bun. I was ready to focus on Marc only. Not Norris or Ivey Gilbert. Not any kind of murder. The rest of this night was going to be devoted to having fun with my fiancé and keeping my eyes open for Lady.

Chapter Seven

MARC AND I WALKED HAND IN HAND from my home to the pier. Heyward Hoots was the band playing and music floated on the ocean breeze.

Marc whistled along with the song.

I glanced up at my handsome fiancé. "I haven't seen Heyward Hoots perform in years. This is going to be fun."

"They sound good despite the distance. What's their story?"

We stopped at the end of Crab Street, waiting for a break in the traffic cruising up and down. "They got famous and outgrew us years ago. After a while a couple of the guys got in a disagreement and split. Recently they decided to try getting back together and see what happens."

"How old are these guys?"

"A little younger than Norris and Ivey. I'd guess they're in their fifties."

At last, a truck stopped, and we crossed Ocean Drive and headed toward the pier.

Marc said, "I hope it works out for the band this time."

"Me, too."

"Hey!" An angry masculine voice yelled. "Don't you know it's a crosswalk?"

I turned at the commotion.

The car honked.

The pedestrian punched the hood of a blue Mini Cooper. "Try that again and see what happens."

The driver pulled a U-ey and escaped the angry guy.

Cars in both directions honked.

I elbowed Marc. "Hey, did you see that?"

"Yep. Looked like a man driving that blue Mini."

"That's what I thought too. Any chance we can—"

"No, there's no possible way to run and catch the car."

"Aw, man."

He laughed and slipped his arm around my shoulders. "Let's just enjoy the dance."

"You're right. No more thinking about murder." How many times did I need to remind myself? We strolled to the pier.

The parking lot had been roped off, and many couples danced to the beach music. More people stood around, talking to each other.

The tempo of the music slowed, and the Heyward Hoots transitioned to a romantic song.

"Now that's what I'm talking about." Marc moved his arm and took my hand in his. He led me to the makeshift dance floor and pulled me close.

All stress exited my body, and I swayed in time to the music with Marc.

"If you ask me, October can't get here soon enough."

"I agree. I can't wait until we're married." A gentle ocean breeze drifted over us. My phone vibrated in the pocket of my dress, but I ignored it. The night was glorious, and I didn't want to be distracted. I snuggled closer to Marc.

My phone stilled, but a moment later Marc stepped back and reached into his pocket. "This could be important. I had it set on silence except for a few select people on my favorites list. You know. Ice."

"Ice?"

"Yeah, the people on my in case of an emergency list." He looked at his phone. "It's your sister."

"Oh." No doubt she'd been the one trying to call me.

"Hello." Marc nodded but didn't interrupt whatever Lacey Jane was saying.

I leaned close but couldn't hear over the band. "What's wrong?"

Marc shook his head. "Try to stay calm. We'll meet you at the sheriff's office."

I gasped. "What's going on?"

Marc leaned close to my ear and spoke in a low voice. "Ike's been taken in for questioning."

"Questioning for what?"

"The murder of Norris Gilbert."

Chapter Eight

LACEY JANE, MARC AND I stood in the empty waiting room at the sheriff's department. My back was to the glass entry door and check-in window. We spoke in hushed tones. Ike was innocent. No doubt about it. The man hadn't spent years waiting to meet his only child just to turn around and commit murder. No, siree.

Marc made eye contact with me. "I'll be right back."

I gave him a thumbs-up. My fiancé had been here often in his official capacity as a local attorney. He knew his way around the place.

Lacey Jane's pale complexion concerned me. I reached for her arm. "Let's sit."

"No." She shook her head. "I can't relax until the sheriff releases Dad."

"The stress can't be good for you or the baby. This tile floor is hard to stand on. You should sit." I rubbed her shoulder, but my sister didn't budge. "What does David say? Being a deputy and having your father-in-law questioned is probably stressing him out."

Lacey Jane shook her head then began pacing. "David isn't taking my calls, but he did text me saying we'd talk later."

"Okay, that makes sense. David knows Ike, and I'm sure he doesn't believe your dad is guilty of murder."

"Yeah. David spent time helping Dad with the remodeling of his new business. He also helped convert the shed in back of the building into nice living quarters. They get along fine."

"See? It'll be okay."

She turned on the toe of her white tennis shoe and walked in the opposite direction of where I stood. "I wish I felt your confidence."

"What possible motive could there be to suspect Ike?"

Marc reappeared, carrying vending machine snacks and soft drinks. "I can answer your question." He motioned for us to sit in the corner of the still-empty room.

Lacey Jane sat and opened a package of peanut butter crackers. She bit into one. "They argued about me, right?"

"Why would Ike and Norris discuss you?" I stared at Lacey Jane. "You barley know the Gilberts, and Ike's new to the area. What am I missing?"

My sister opened a water bottle. "One afternoon I was standing in the parking lot at HOSE. I'd brought food for the guys who were working on the remodel. Norris pulled up next to me in his fancy Lexus. He mentioned he could help me sue Ike for back child support."

I gasped. "That's not fair. Mom didn't want Ike involved in our lives."

"You're right. The letters Mom wrote to Dad prove it."

"How did you respond to Norris?"

She took a drink before answering. "I told Mr. Gilbert that I only wanted a relationship with Dad."

Marc leaned closer, resting his forearms on his thighs. "Norris went behind your back and approached Ike. Norris flat-out lied and told Ike you planned to sue him. Then he suggested your dad just go ahead and pay him. He even had a figure in mind for how much it should be. Norris assured Ike he'd manage the money for you."

Lacey Jane choked on her water.

I patted her back and looked at Marc. "What did Ike say that got him brought in for questioning?"

"He warned Norris to stay away from Lacey Jane. He also added that he and his daughter would work out any financial compensation on their own." Marc rubbed his hands together. "The conversation grew heated. No offense to Ike, but he's used to men obeying his commands. Even though he's a softie around Lacey Jane, he knows how to hold his ground."

Lacey Jane groaned. "Great day in the neighborhood. How can this be happening?"

My heartbeat increased. "There must have been a witness to their conversation, because it's not like Ike would turn himself in."

The white paneled door at the far end of the room opened, and David joined us. "Marc, Ike's asking for you to join him."

Marc stood. "I'm not a criminal defense attorney."

"I know, but his request for legal representation forced Wade to stop asking questions."

Lacey Jane hopped up. "This is terrible. Marc, please help us."

Marc's gaze darted from Lacey Jane to me. "It's going to be all right. Have a little faith."

My sister reached for her husband's hand. "David, is my dad okay?"

David leaned over and kissed his wife's cheek. "He's a warrior who's more anxious about how you're dealing with this than anything else."

She lifted her chin. "Tell him I'm fine."

Marc and David left us sitting alone.

I opened the app on my phone to take notes. "Do you know Ike's alibi for this morning?"

"You can say he was with me." She took a bite of another cracker. Orange crumbs fell onto her lap.

I pointed at her. "Lacey Jane, listen to me. Ike is innocent, and we're not going to lie just to get him out of here. That's a crime, and you don't want to deliver your baby in prison."

My younger sister turned and squeezed my arm. "Andi Grace, I need you to catch the killer."

Marc and I were scheduled to get married in six weeks. There wasn't time to complete my wedding to-do list and solve a murder.

"Please? Ike is the only grandparent my baby will have on our side of the family." A tear ran down her cheek.

I hugged Lacey Jane. "Well-played, baby sister."

"Hey, that's my prerogative as a little sister. I'll use emotional blackmail or whatever I can to protect my family."

"Touché. I'll try to catch the killer, but you need to promise to take care of yourself."

"Yes, ma'am." She pulled away and ate another cracker. "Who's on your suspect list?"

"How do you know I already started thinking about it?"

She laughed. "You found the body, so of course you're curious."

"You got me there."

"And?"

"I never considered your dad might get dragged into the murder investigation. Ivey is an obvious choice, and there's a person in town who drives a blue Mini Cooper." I explained why the driver interested me.

Her eyes widened. "You should talk to Erin, because I've seen a car like that at Daily Java."

"Good to know. I can ask Dylan to take over walking the dogs on my morning schedule. That'll allow me to go by the coffee shop and begin my investigation into Norris Gilbert's murder."

Lacey Jane finished her crackers then started on a candy bar.

I texted Dylan then looked on social media for accounts by Norris and Ivey.

Norris didn't appear to post much, but his picture was all over social media. If there was a public event or community fundraiser, Norris must have been in attendance. He could be seen smiling, drinking, and schmoozing with all the movers and shakers in the Low Country on other social media accounts. Ivey was in some of the photos, but not all. Although, she'd spent time fighting cancer.

Ivey's pages and posts revolved around her job as a real estate agent.

The door opened again, and I turned off my phone.

Marc and Ike joined us.

"Oh, Dad!" Lacey Jane hugged the man. "I was so scared."

He patted her back. "I'm sorry to have worried you."

Marc said, "Let's get out of here."

"Why don't we go to my house? You two can update us." They all agreed, and except for a few stray orange cracker crumbs, we left the room as we found it. Cold and empty.

Chapter Nine

SATURDAY MORNING, I headed to Daily Java in serious need of a strong cup of coffee. After Ike's release the night before, we'd all gone to my house to discuss the murder. Ike had insisted the authorities would believe in his innocence. Even though Lacey Jane's husband was a deputy, she'd dragged me into my home office and begged me again to help prove Ike's innocence.

Lacey Jane was a newlywed and expecting her first child. What choice did I have?

I pulled into the parking lot and scanned the area for a Mini Cooper. No luck, but it was still early. I backed my SUV into an empty space, then rubbed my German shepherd's head. "I'll be right back, Sunny."

She barked then sat tall in the passenger seat.

Despite Lady having been dognapped, I felt safe leaving my German shepherd in the SUV with the windows down. If anyone approached, she'd bark, and I'd see her from the coffee shop. I rubbed her one more time. "You're a good girl." I left and watched for any signs of danger as I strolled into the coffee shop.

"Good morning, Andi Grace," Erin greeted me. As owner of Daily Java, she worked almost nonstop.

I smiled at her. "Morning. What's your special coffee today?"

"There's the Labor Day Latte. It's a Low Country roast teamed with vanilla and a dash of cinnamon."

"Sounds interesting. I'll try it."

"Hot or cold?"

"Hot, please." I reached for my money. "And extra-large."

"I've got fresh scones with blueberries and cherries. You interested?"

"It sounds good, and patriotic too."

"That was my intention. Whatcha got going on today?" She rang up my purchase.

"I'm looking for the owner of a turquoise-blue Mini Cooper." We exchanged money, and I dropped a couple dollars in her tip jar.

"Yeah, he's a regular. He's into saving the planet." She reached for a scone. "For here or to go?"

"I'll take it with me. Sunny's in my SUV. How do you know he wants to protect the planet?"

"He saw me drive my Prius to work one day, and we discussed the importance of environmentally friendly vehicles." She placed my scone in an eco-friendly brown paper bag. "He also always brings in a reusable cup for me to serve his coffee in." She handed me the bag. "I'll let you know when your latte is ready."

"Sounds good."

Despite the early Saturday morning hour, there were quite a few older gentlemen in the coffee shop. Even though they sat at different tables, they talked back and forth about college football. A few men wore Clemson hats, and the others wore random gear supporting their favorite teams.

I skirted around them with a nod and a smile, then chose a small table near the window. I adjusted the chair to face the parking lot. If the environmental guy drove up before I went outside, I'd spot him.

"Mind if I join you?" Juliet's brother, Griffin Reed, shot me a smile. His blue-green eyes lacked their usual sparkle.

"Of course you can join me." I pushed the empty chair back with my foot. "How are you doing?"

"Can't complain." He sat, then dumped a packet of sugar into his black coffee. "You working a case? Let me guess. The Norris Gilbert murder." He stirred his drink then lifted the mug to his lips.

"Uh, yeah. How'd you know?"

He hitched a shoulder up. "It seems like the last couple of years, if there's a murder in Heyward Beach, you're involved."

"Lacey Jane's biological father was questioned by Sheriff Stone, and she begged me to prove he's innocent. He's also going to walk me down the aisle in October."

"You're not asking Nate?" He hit is forehead with a fist. "Stupid question. He can't walk you down the aisle. It's a double wedding, and your brother is marrying my sister."

"You nailed it, and you're walking Juliet down the aisle." We'd all grown up together, and it'd be easy to shift into becoming a family. At least I hoped it'd be a smooth transition.

"So, why are you hanging out in the coffee shop?"

"I'm hoping to meet a man. Like a specific man who might know something about the murder."

Erin arrived with my latte. "Here you go, and the environmentalist just pulled into the parking lot."

"Oops, I got distracted with wedding talk. Thanks, Erin."

She walked back to the counter.

"The environmentalist? Do you mean Rhett Alton?"

I met his gaze then shifted my focus to the front door. "Does Mr. Alton drive a blue Mini Cooper?"

"Sure does. Why are you looking for him?"

"He was seen driving near the Gilberts' home the morning of the murder, but I didn't know his name."

"Why don't we play it cool? I can invite him to join us."

I'd meant to approach him outside, but an introduction would be smoother. "How do y'all know each other?"

The man I'd been waiting for entered the shop and stood in a short line.

Griffin said, "I may take over management of Piney Woods Apartment Complex."

"Yeah, I heard that. Congratulations."

"Thanks. If I take the job, it needs to be done right. Mr. Alton and I have discussed some drainage concerns. Do you want me to invite him to join us?"

"Definitely."

Griffin walked to the line and spoke to the man in question. They shook hands and talked for a few seconds before Griffin pointed to our table. The other man nodded.

I sipped on my Labor Day Latte. The vanilla and cinnamon were noticeable without overwhelming the taste of the coffee.

Griffin sat down. "He agreed. You sure it's the right guy?"

"He drives the right kind of car, so it seems possible. Some hunches pay off, and others fizzle." I took another drink and tried to ignore my shaky hands.

"What's Marc up to this weekend?"

"He's packing some of his belongings to move to my place. If you take over running the apartment complex, will you still have time to convert my front room into an office for Marc?"

Griffin ran a hand over his dark, neatly trimmed beard. "Let's jump on it next week before life gets too hectic."

"I love it. Thanks."

The environmentalist approached, carrying a turquoise insulated travel mug. It matched his car.

Griffin pulled over a chair from an empty table. "Have a seat."

"I appreciate the invite."

"Rhett, this is a friend of mine, Andi Grace Scott. Andi Grace, this is Rhett Alton."

"Nice to meet you." I shook his hand.

"Likewise, but I hope I'm not interrupting." He wiggled his eyebrows.

My face grew warm. "Oh, no. Griff's sister is my best friend, and Griff is my friend. We're not a couple. In fact, I'm getting married soon. But not to Griff."

Griffin laughed. "Take a breath, Andi Grace."

I inhaled deeply and counted to ten in French. How embarrassing. "Sorry. I don't know why I got so flustered."

Rhett leaned back in his chair. "It happens. You look familiar. Have we met before?"

"Not officially, but I think I've seen you driving on the island. Do you have a turquoise-blue Mini Cooper?"

His eyes narrowed. "Yes. Why?"

"Can I be completely honest?"

"I find honesty saves time. What do you want to know?" He bobbed a tea bag up and down in his cup.

"Yesterday you were seen driving on the street of a murder victim. Do you know Norris Gilbert?"

"I don't appreciate being ambushed, Griffin." He pushed the top down on his cup and stood so fast the chair tipped back and fell clanging to the floor.

Conversations around us ceased.

Griffin also rose. "Look, man, we're not trying to ambush you. There was a murder in the area where you were seen, and we were just curious if you saw anything unusual."

"Did you?" I remained seated so he wouldn't feel threatened by me. "See anything unusual, that is."

Griffin shook his head. "We didn't mean to insult you. Sorry, man."

"Yeah, I'm sorry too. Would you like my scone as a peace offering?" I lifted the bag. "Erin made it."

"There's no need to bribe me, but I have no intention of answering your questions. Have a good day." Rhett stalked away.

I stood and touched Griffin's arm. "Sorry about that. I hope I didn't make things difficult for you."

"Forget about it. He's always been talkative and friendly. Of course, we've always discussed his favorite topic."

"The environment?"

"You got it. Be careful around him, Andi Grace."

The men around us went back to talking sports.

"I'll stay alert. Let's get out of here."

"Staying alert isn't the same thing as being careful." We walked to the door, and he held it open for me. "Don't make me rat you out to your brother."

"Lacey Jane begged me to help prove Ike is innocent. If you mention this to Nate, you'll be putting me in a bad spot between my brother and sister."

"If it keeps you safe, I don't care. Do you promise to be cautious?"

"I'll do my best, but after that little tantrum, Rhett Alton is officially a person of interest. See you later, Griff." I walked to my SUV, pondering my next move.

Before the encounter with Rhett, I'd been curious. Nothing more. Ivey Gilbert had been my top person of interest. If Rhett had used good manners, I probably wouldn't have given him more than a fleeting thought. His rudeness changed everything, and I planned to learn more about Rhett Alton and see if he had a connection to Norris worth killing him over.

Chapter Ten

AFTER THE FIASCO WITH RHETT ALTON, I drove to Kennady Bed and Breakfast to check on the dogs boarding at Stay and Play.

Dylan King and Melanie Bradshaw were scheduled to take care of the animals for the weekend. Both of my employees lived on-site and cared about our canine guests.

I parked under an old oak tree, then Sunny and I walked toward the barn.

"Morning, boss." Dylan waved from the outside play area. "I'm squeezing in an obedience for Captain and Pumpkin."

I detoured to the section where Dylan stood with Phyllis Mays's two big dogs. Captain was an Australian shepherd mix, and Pumpkin was a pure German shepherd. Phyllis loved her dogs, but she never disciplined them. It was the primary reason I got so many dog-walking appointments with her. Whenever Phyllis had a group of church ladies coming to her house, she'd ask me to take care of her dogs. Phyllis was our local pastor's wife, and she kept herself busy with meetings and functions. "Great. They need all the help they can get."

"I know. It beats me why she won't pay for a dog-training program for both of them. The dogs and the family would all benefit."

I shook my head. "I can't explain it, but it's good to work with them every chance we get."

"Watch this." Dylan turned to the dogs and held out a hand. "Sit."

Pumpkin obeyed first, and Captain followed suit.

"Good job." Dylan gave each shepherd a treat, then he showed me more commands. Stay, roll over, and walk. "They've been staying all week, and I can already tell a difference."

"I'm impressed. Are you sure you don't want to work with me forever? You don't really want to get back into construction, right?" I propped my arms on the fence, and Sunny sat by my side.

"Sorry. I had a blast working on the little house for Mr. Gage. It's my calling. What can I say?"

"I understand." Dylan had become like another brother to me over the past couple years, and he deserved to follow his passion. "Next week, I'll begin a real search for your replacement."

"Thanks, boss" He ran a hand through his dark hair. "I met a girl, er woman, at a party last weekend. She's looking for work around here. Her name's Cheyenne, Cheyenne Marther. Would you like me to ask her if she's interested?"

"Sure, but I'll need references."

Dylan grinned. "And you'll want to observe her with the animals."

"You know that's right. Listen, don't mention your apartment comes with the job."

"Why?"

"I don't plan to kick you out until you find a good place to live."

His face grew red. "Thanks, Andi Grace."

"You're welcome, and you're family now. We care about you."

Whatever he mumbled was indecipherable. He turned back to the dogs, and I made my way into the barn.

Lady was a well-behaved dog. If she'd run away on purpose, she must have been terrified. Was it possible the dog's disappearance and Norris's murder were not connected?

I spotted Melanie, my groomer, playing with Chloe, Heinz, and Gus.

Sunny barked and headed down the hall leading to my office and Dylan's studio apartment.

Melanie stood. "Hi, Andi Grace. Your brother and Marc are in the office, and Mrs. Gilbert wants to speak to you about the ransom for her dog. What's going on?"

With as few words as possible, I updated Melanie. "I'll see what the guys are up to before checking in with Ivey."

Nate sat at my desk, looking at the computer. Marc stood with his arms crossed, and Sunny circled Marc's and Nate's dogs. Chubb, Bo, and Sunny sniffed each other. Chubb had belonged to my first murder victim, and Marc adopted him. Nate had rescued his black Labrador retriever years earlier from the pound. Satisfied, the three dogs settled down.

Marc's eyes sparkled when our gazes connected. He closed the distance and kissed me. "Morning."

"Good morning. This is a nice surprise, but I thought you were packing some things."

He wore a navy T-shirt with white letters saying *Whatever Floats Your Boat*. "Chubb and I ran into Nate and Bo when we were out for our morning run. What are you doing here?"

"I really came out to check on the dogs. Melanie just informed me that Ivey wants to discuss the dognapper's ransom demands. How did y'all end up in my office?"

Nate said, "One of my landscapers saw your post on social media about a lost dog. He was riding bikes with his wife near the marsh and thought he saw Lady."

"I'm so confused. If he saw her, did she escape? We need to look in case it really is her. Where did he say he thinks he spotted Lady?"

"Piney Woods."

"I'll text Leroy and ask him to watch for her." Leroy Peck was an older adult friend who'd adopted a murder victim's beagle. We'd become friends over the years, and he lived at Piney Woods Apartment Complex. I paused. Maybe my sleuthing motto should be something like, *If I discover your dead body, I'll find a good home for your pet.* No, that was morbid. I shivered.

"Sis, you've got lots of replies to your offer for a reward. How will you sort them out?"

"If I find the dog, Ivey can decide how to give out the reward money." I shot a text off to Leroy in case Lady was loose. "It sounds like I should speak to Ivey first. Will you print me off a list of people claiming to have seen the missing schnoodle? I'll run up to the main house and look for Ivey."

"Sure. We'll meet you up there in a few." Nate turned his attention to the computer.

Marc said, "If you don't mind, I'll tag along."

"I'm always happy when you're around. Let's take the dogs to the little play area in case any of the guests don't like dogs roaming around." It didn't take long to settle Sunny, Chubb, and Bo, then we strolled over to the main house.

Ivey sat by herself in the sunny piano room with a cup of coffee by her side.

I stopped in the doorway. "May we join you?"

She jerked as if we'd awaken her from a trance. "Yes, please come in. I got another ransom message from the dognapper."

"How? Text? Email?" I sat on a love seat across from Ivey, and Marc sat beside me.

"It was a text message, but they don't want money."

"How'd they get your information, and what are they demanding?"

"It's all rather vague. See for yourself." She swiped her phone, then passed it to me.

If you want to see your dog again, get the records from LC Pain Clinic. Include patients connected to your law firm. Leave the files from both behind Paula's Pickings after dark. That's the only way you'll see your precious little dog again.

After reading the message three times, I passed the phone to Marc.

I stared at Ivey. "What's your connection to the LC Pain Clinic?"

She pursed her lips.

"Ivey, why does the dognapper believe you can provide that information?" My pulse throbbed in my neck.

"There was a building that had been for sale a few years ago. It was one of my listings, but nobody was interested for the longest time."

"So, you got LC Pain Clinic to rent or buy the property. There's no way you'd have access to the records."

Marc's knuckles whitened as he clutched Ivey's phone. "Did Norris introduce you to the people in charge of the clinic?"

She lifted her chin. "Yes, he did. But he wasn't involved with them. It turned out to be a pill mill."

I said, "The dognapper must believe you're tangled up with those people since they are asking for files from both the pain clinic and your husband's law firm. I'm sure Norris's files are confidential. Are they encrypted? How is the information protected?"

"I don't know."

Was it grief or denial? In normal circumstances, Ivey was too smart not to understand the gravity of the situation. "Ivey, listen to me. If the person behind the ransom note is the same one who murdered Norris, we need to find the information they want. I also think you need to discuss this with the sheriff."

"Ivey, you need to take Andi Grace's advice. Norris has been killed. Your dog is missing. It makes sense you'll be the next person in danger." Marc lifted the phone. "If you don't mind, I'd like to send a copy of this message to myself."

"Go ahead."

I stood. "Is there any chance you recognized the phone number attached to the text message?"

"No." She shook her head. "It doesn't belong to any of my contacts, but I didn't expect it would."

Marc passed the phone to Ivey. "Which one of us is going to call Sheriff Stone?"

Ivey slumped in the seat. "I suppose it should be me."

I almost patted her shoulder, but she probably would've recoiled. "When you talk to Wade, ask him when you can get back into the house. Meanwhile, we may have a lead. I'll let you know if I find Lady."

"Then I don't need to call the sheriff just yet."

Marc frowned. "No. The dognapper may have killed your husband. If you don't contact the authorities, I will."

She shooed us off with her hand. "Go find my dog, and I'll make the call."

Marc and I left Ivey Gilbert sitting in the piano room. She must have been aggravated with Norris for getting her tied up with an illegal pill mill. An unanswered question loomed over the situation, and it was a biggie. Was Ivey mad enough to have viciously murdered her husband?

Chapter Eleven

MARC PARKED HIS TRUCK in front of Leroy Peck's duplex at Piney Grove Apartments. "No sign of his truck. I bet he's at the pier fishing."

"No doubt he's catching more than enough for his dinner. Let's walk around and see if we can find Lady." I slid out and met Marc on the road leading to the apartments. "Lincoln and Griffin will have their work cut out for them if the sale of this place goes through."

Marc laughed. "Linc won't be doing much of the physical labor, but he'll show up regularly to keep an eye on progress. Do you think Leroy will stay in the duplex or move to one of the apartments?"

We walked along the potholed blacktop. "If Peanut is allowed in the apartments instead of the duplex, I think Leroy will fit in better with the other renters. Jeremiah may be his only friend here." Jeremiah Prichard was ex-military and had such bad PTSD that his family had rejected him years earlier. He was a quiet man, but he'd helped Marc and me save Leroy's life a few months earlier.

"I agree. Wait, do you hear a dog?"

I stopped moving. There. "It's to our right." I darted into the wooded area. Sunshine filtered through tree limbs.

"Andi Grace, it might not be Lady." Marc was close behind me.

"Yeah, but it might be her." I batted away spiderwebs and twigs while walking toward the sound.

Marc followed. "Wait, look over there."

I stopped to see what he was pointing at. A redheaded woman was moving through the woods, looking down at the ground. "Let's go ask her if she's seen Lady."

Marc's nostrils flared. "I don't feel too good about this. Let me take the lead."

In my excitement, I closed the distance between us and the redhead without waiting for Marc. "Hey!" I waved at her.

Her eyes widened, but she waved back. "Hi."

We were close enough to see freckles on her pale skin. "Can we ask you a question?"

"I need to catch my dog." She continued to move to the west at a fast clip.

"I'm not going to let that stop me," I muttered, only loud enough for Marc to hear.

Movement appeared in the brush ahead of the woman.

"Looks like she really is chasing her dog. I'll try to cut them off." Marc took off in a different direction.

I kept my sights on the lady tramping after the unseen animal.

The woman dove and disappeared from my view. A dog yelped. "Gotcha."

Briars scratched my shin and ankle, but I beelined it to the commotion.

The redhead stood about the same time Marc reached her. She held a scruffy black-and-white schnoodle.

I stopped in my tracks and fought a wave of dizziness.

The dog struggled in the woman's arms.

Marc said, "Is that your dog?"

"Um, yes." She kept her eyes on the canine.

"You don't say. Andi Grace, she claims this is her dog. What do you think?"

I wiped away the sweat under my eyes, then reached out to the nearest tree to steady myself as dizziness hit me. What was going on? "What's your dog's name?"

"None of your business." Her voice squeaked.

Marc moved to me. "You okay?"

I nodded. "Just a little lightheaded. I probably should've eaten that scone earlier."

Movement caught my attention. The redhead was walking away from us. The dog barked.

"Lady, come here." I watched for a reaction from either the dog or the redhead.

The schnoodle barked and struggled to break free.

"Marc, you've got to stop her. I'll be fine."

"Okay." He left me leaning against the pine tree.

Marc closed the distance between them and cut off her escape. "I don't believe that's your dog. In fact, I'm pretty sure the dog in your arms belongs to a man who was murdered yesterday. Why don't we call the sheriff? He'll help get to the bottom of this."

"No!" She stepped back. "It's not my dog. I just found her."

"You just said she was your dog. It makes me think you're the murder victim's dognapper." Marc pulled out his phone.

"Honestly, I found the mutt. I saw on the news there was a reward for finding her, and I thought I might get lucky. Will I still get the money? I could really use it, mister."

I felt steady enough to walk the short distance to Marc and the woman. "Why did you claim she was your dog?"

She hung her head. "I didn't want to split the money with you two."

Her excuse seemed plausible. "What's your name?"

"Cheyenne Marther." She struggled to calm the dog.

Whoa. The same person Dylan wanted to take over his position? "Interesting. I just heard you're looking for a job. Why don't you give the dog to me?"

"No, I found her first. You're not going to steal the reward money from me." She cradled the dog closer to her chest.

Lady struggled to get free.

"Cheyenne, I know the dog. Let me have her." I held my hands out. "I won't take the money from you. In fact, I can call Mrs. Gilbert and tell her you found Lady."

"You'd do that for me? Why?"

"Lady is my main concern. You and Mrs. Gilbert can work out the reward details." Something bothered me about the woman, but I couldn't put my finger on it.

Cheyenne stepped closer, and the schnoodle leapt to me. The woman's forehead crinkled, and her jaw went slack. She blinked and seemed to recover from the dog's action. "So, you'll call Mrs. Gilbert?"

"Yes." Lady calmed in my arms, and I rubbed her head. "Good girl. Let's take you home and get you a bath. You're probably hungry too."

"I'll make the call. How can we get in touch with you?" Marc faced us.

"I live in an apartment here, but I don't have a phone."

"We'll figure something out."

Cheyenne speared me with her gaze. "Did you say something about a job? How'd you know I need one?"

"Dylan King works for me and mentioned your name this morning. We can discuss it later."

She gripped my arm, and the little dog bared her teeth and growled.

"You're scaring the dog." Her actions weren't doing much for my nerves either. "How'd you find Lady?"

"Uh, you know. I was just out walking and saw her from a distance. I'd heard there was a reward for a little black dog. So, I took a chance and followed her. What kind of job do you have for me?"

"I haven't officially posted it. When I do, there will be interviews and background checks, but I'll keep you in mind."

Marc rejoined us. "The owner is thrilled you found Lady. She'll write you a check."

"Is it possible to get cash?" Cheyenne's forehead crinkled again.

Marc rubbed his chin. "Well, it's Saturday, and Monday is a holiday. If you can wait until Tuesday, it'll be a cash reward."

"I guess that's okay." She crossed her skinny, freckled arms.

Marc nodded. "Tuesday it is."

The three of us walked through the woods to the apartments in an awkward silence.

Cheyenne said, "You're not going to stiff me, are you? I didn't even get your names."

"I'm Marc Williams." He removed a business card from his wallet and handed it to the redhead. "You can stop by my office on Tuesday for the money."

"I'm Andi Grace Scott. I'm a dog walker, and Lady is my primary concern. You can trust us."

Bloodshot eyes. Trembly hands. Dirty hair. She wore a silver necklace with interlocking circles. Each had a name engraved. I made out the names, Olivia and Lucia.

We parted ways. Once we were inside Marc's truck, I cuddled Lady near my face. "What's your story, sweet girl? Did you run away from home? Or did you escape your kidnapper?"

Marc reached over and ruffled Lady's ear. "If you weren't dognapped, who was trying to extort a ransom from Ivey Gilbert?"

"Good question. What'd you think of Cheyenne?"

Marc cranked the engine, and cool air blew out of the vents. "She's not in good health. In fact, she looks anorexic. She was awful concerned about the reward money, and the dognapper wanted files. I'm not sure what's going on. Are you considering hiring her?"

"Dylan is going to work for Griffin, and I'll need to replace him. He met Cheyenne at a party and thinks she might be a good fit, but I'm not so sure. I only want reliable people to work with the animals."

Marc drove away from the apartment complex. "Yeah, you definitely need to do a background check on Cheyenne before you offer her Dylan's job."

"I mentioned the same thing to her, and she didn't flinch. Let's hope that's a good reaction."

"Sounds promising. So, where to?"

"Let's go to Stay and Play. Lady needs a bath, and we need to discuss the reward with Ivey. And then there's the dognapper to think about."

"What are you thinking?"

"If Cheyenne isn't the dognapper, and if she innocently found the dog, then who took Lady? And if they lost Lady, it means they lost the ability to get the files from Ivey. What will they try next to get their hands on the files?"

"All good questions. What's your next step?"

"I want to investigate the LC Pain Clinic and the employees. There's also Rhett Alton to consider. He was anxious when I questioned him earlier." My stomach growled.

Marc said, "First you need to eat before you fall out."

My face warmed. "You're right. Lunch, talk to Ivey, then investigate the pain clinic. I'll text Melanie and ask her to get ready to bathe Lady."

The dog had fallen asleep in my lap. I rubbed her side, relieved she was safe. Now if I could only solve the murder before anyone else was harmed.

Chapter Twelve

WE PICKED UP CHICKEN SALAD SANDWICHES on our way out of Heyward Beach. Once we arrived at Stay and Play, Melanie took charge of grooming the schnoodle. We plopped down in my office to eat.

Ivey appeared at my office door in the barn. "Where is she?"

I finished chewing an apple slice. "Melanie's grooming her now, and Lady appears fine. Still, you might want to have Dr. Hewitt check her out."

Marc pointed to the exit. "I'll take Chubb and Sunny for a walk."

I mouthed the word *chicken*, and my fiancé grinned before disappearing.

Ivey came closer to my desk but didn't sit. "You think she's okay though?"

"Yes, but you really should let Doc exam her." I stood and motioned toward the door. "Do you want to walk back to the grooming station with me?"

"Oh, sure. I'm so relieved you found her." In her hurry, she bumped my shoulder, then slowed her pace. "How did it happen?"

Lady barked, and Ivey zipped ahead of me. "Oh, look at you. I was so worried. Are you okay?" She took the damp but clean dog away from Melanie.

The groomer said, "Do you want me to finish drying her?"

"No, but thank you for taking care of her. There'll be a big tip for you."

"I was happy to do it. There were some burrs, and I cut them out."

"Oh, the horrors she must have experienced. Poor baby."

I stared at the scene playing out before me. Ivey hadn't shown anywhere near the same concern for what Norris must have experienced. He'd been strangled, and that couldn't have been painless. Was it possible Ivey cared more about her dog than her husband? Or was this some kind of act? If so, why?

Melanie reached for a tube of ointment from her workstation. "This will soothe the irritated areas. Are you taking her home now?"

Ivey's eyes widened. "I don't know if the sheriff is ready to allow me back in the house yet. What do you think, Andi Grace?"

"I'll check with Sheriff Stone and get back with you." I left the two of them chatting and headed for an Adirondack chair under an old oak tree. I tapped in Wade's number and closed my eyes. A nap would be lovely after the day's drama, but it'd take a miracle to fit one into my day.

"This is Stone."

I opened my eyes and sat straighter. "Hey, it's Andi Grace. Ivey Gilbert wants to know when she can go home."

"I'm glad you called. I need to return to the scene of the crime. Can you and Marc swing by the Gilberts' house this afternoon? I'd like to ask a few more questions on how you found the house. Like what condition it was in."

Really? Wow, I wouldn't miss the opportunity to help Wade. "Sure. We can meet you there in an hour. By the way, we found Lady. I'll tell you about it when we see you." I hung up and informed Ivey it'd be a while longer before she could go home, then I went to find Marc and the dogs.

• • •

Wade met us in the Gilberts' driveway. "Thanks for coming."

We'd dropped Sunny and Chubb at my house on the way to meet the sheriff. "I hope we can help."

Wade talked as we followed him up the stairs and into the house. "Did you recognize the leash used to strangle Norris?"

"No." I pushed my sunglasses to the top of my head. "I've always used a pink monogrammed harness and matching leash when I've cared for Lady. It was a soft pink. If I remember correctly, the leash from yesterday was hot pink with rhinestones."

Marc nodded. "Yeah, it was almost neon pink."

Wade said, "Okay, but that doesn't mean it didn't belong to Ivey."

"True." I avoided looking into Norris's office. "It's hard to believe the killer brought a leash intending to murder Norris."

"Stranger things have happened. I can't figure out why the culprit would bring a leash when other weapons would've been easier. You've been here before, Andi Grace. What else did you notice?"

I walked to the far wall and looked out the window at the beach. "When Ivey asked me to stop by, we didn't know for sure if Lady would be here or not. Marc and I were focused on finding the dog. Lady's food, treats, and toys were here." My throat tightened.

Marc said, "We discussed the possibility of Norris having additional dog supplies in his car." He touched my shoulder, and I leaned into him.

"Why did you enter the office?" Wade's tone was curious, not accusatory.

I turned to meet his gaze. "We weren't going to leave until I knew for sure Lady's wasn't anywhere in the house."

"Okay. Did you notice anything strange in the office?"

I shook my head and gulped in air. "Nothing besides Norris."

"Would you mind walking in there and looking around with me? See if something seems off?" Wade's relaxed posture didn't fool me. His eyebrows dipped down, and he clenched his jaw.

"Is there a specific item you want me to focus on?"

"Just give me your general impression first." His gaze darted to Marc. "You, too, but I assume Andi Grace has been here more often to walk the dog. Y'all ready?"

I took a deep breath to calm my jitters. "Sure."

Marc held my hand, and we trailed Wade into Norris Gilbert's home office.

The room was dark and masculine. Bookshelves looked decorative instead of functional. They were painted a dark gray and filled the far wall behind Norris's desk. There were framed sketches of his college, sailboats, and historic Charleston.

I let go of Marc's hand and examined the books on the shelves. "Most of these are about South Carolina history. I guess his law books are at his real office."

Wade moved closer to me. "We're working to get a subpoena to search the law office."

Interesting. Norris was the victim, not a person of interest. "Why? Do you want to see if you can discover a motive?"

"Yea. Divorce cases can be messy. It's possible a disgruntled client came after Norris."

On the next shelf were two artificial potted plants. Artificial, like the man himself? There wasn't a speck of dust on the faux caladium or the fern. "Have you looked into Rhett Alton?"

"Who?" Wade's voice squeaked.

I explained who the man was, then I described his weird reaction to my morning questions.

Wade wrote in his notepad. "Environmentalist, you say? I believe there's a rally at the pier today about ways to protect the beach from erosion and litter. Can you give me a description of Mr. Alton?"

"My best guess is he's around fifty. He's shorter than you guys. Brown hair, blue eyes, tanned, and he looks to be in good shape." I didn't touch any items on the shelves, but one book caught my attention. "Wade, did your deputies look through all the books?"

"They were supposed to. Why?"

I pointed to a large book with a lighthouse statue on it. "There's a wrinkle in this spine. I only find it odd because a decorator probably designed this room right down to the last detail."

Marc moved beside me. "I see what you mean. This office seems more for show than getting real work accomplished."

Wade slipped on disposable blue gloves. "Let's take a look." He opened the book and flipped through the large, thick, yellowed pages.

"Wait, go back. I think I saw something." I pointed to the book.

He turned the pages one at a time until he came to a page with a white envelope taped on it. "You're right. What do we have here?" He placed the book on the desk, keeping it open with a wooden pencil-holder.

Marc and I stood close to Wade and watched as he used a pocketknife to cut the envelope off the page. Marc said, "It's easy to see why your people missed this."

"Nope. It was careless." He removed the envelope and opened it.

Marc whistled. "Look at all those numbers. They could be Swiss bank accounts or crypto currency."

"Hidden money?" My pulse leapt at the potential clue. "I've heard if you don't remember your Bitcoin password, you'll lose your money. Although to be perfectly honest, I'm not positive how it works."

"We don't know for sure these numbers are tied to money."

Marc said, "I think the dollar signs are a pretty good clue."

Wade folded the paper and shoved it back into the envelope. "Keep this to yourselves."

I backed away from the sheriff and crossed my arms. "I know how to keep a secret. I guess you're aware Norris was behind the pill mill moving to our area."

"The Low Country Pain Clinic? I'm aware."

Drat. What other useful information could I share?

"Let's focus on the task at hand." Marc rubbed my shoulder. "What else catches your eye in here?"

"Ivey mentioned that Norris kept long hours. Many nights he'd come home late. If that's true, why have a home office?"

Marc paced. "I work from home on the days I leave the office early, and I sometimes leave early if it's a beautiful day. My assistant knows to schedule as many appointments as possible before lunch unless I have to be in court."

His words confirmed my desire to create a home office for him was a good idea.

Wade clicked his pen open and shut to some unknown tune. "I don't have the luxury of setting my schedule. Case in point, here I am on the Saturday of Labor Day Weekend. The last unofficial weekend of the summer. So, why did Norris have the need for a home office?"

"My staff consists of Rylee Prosser, Lacey Jane Scott, er, make that Lacey Jane Wayne, and I have a cleaning service come in early in the morning twice a week. I trust all of them. I've been to Norris's law firm. His staff is much bigger, so if he wanted to keep something private, he might work from home. For instance, hiding those numbers in the book."

"Why not keep it on a jump drive? It's possible he has other secrets hidden in this room." I looked around. "Wade, are you sure your deputies dug deep? I mean, you could hide notes, money or drives with records. Oh, I just remembered something."

He motioned his fingers in a circular motion, indicating he wanted me to hurry up and state my point. "Don't keep me in suspense."

"Friday night, Ivey had passports in her purse. They accidently spilled out. And before you ask, I didn't riffle through her purse. They fell out all by themselves. Ivey seemed flustered when she realized it. She claimed she and Norris planned to go to Bali after the big family vacation."

Wade scribbled in his notebook. "Bali is a popular place to go and disappear." He glanced at his watch. "I need to head to the pier if I hope to catch Rhett Alton. Rest assured I'll send a couple of deputies back to perform a more thorough investigation."

"I'd be glad to help."

"No, thanks. I've got it under control."

"But—" Did he?

"I'm not going to argue with you, Andi Grace, but thank you for coming by today." Wade turned his attention to Marc. "As much as I appreciate your assistance, I don't want to see you two at the pier for the next couple hours. Understand?"

"It'd be a lie to say I'm not disappointed, but I do have a wedding to plan." I reached for Marc's hand. "Um, Wade, despite the fact I'm a little irritated with you, if you need me to walk Duke, I will."

"I appreciate the offer and will text you if he needs attention. You two be safe."

Marc said. "See you around."

We left the sheriff locking up the Gilberts' house. The gated community was quiet even though the town was flooded with vacationers. "It probably won't be a good idea to drive through the neighborhood this time."

Marc chuckled. "Yeah, Wade would probably catch us. What would you like to do?"

"The pier is definitely out of the question. Let's go to Ike's store and see if he's around."

"Sounds like a plan." Marc drove below the speed limit and slowed more as we approached the beach crowds in public areas.

Questions swirled through my mind. Who hated Norris enough to kill him? Ivey? Had she grown tired of him humiliating her? I'd need to investigate Norris to create a list of suspects.

In addition to finding a person with a strong enough motive to kill Norris, I needed to figure out if the original goal had been to dognap Lady or murder Norris.

Chapter Thirteen

COOL AIR HIT MY FACE when we walked into Beach Mart. "Hello."

Ike disengaged a box cutter and set it on a counter. "Welcome. What are you two doing today?"

I gave him a quick hug. "We just saw Wade."

"Did he ask you about me?" Ike crossed his arms, looking every bit like the commanding officer he'd been as an active Marine.

"No, but I still can't believe he questioned you in the first place. Your relationship with Lacey Jane is solid. Norris couldn't have persuaded my sister to do anything that would hurt you."

"Thanks. I believe David agrees with you, but the sheriff is his boss and in charge of the investigation."

"Let's hope he only wanted to rule you out. By officially questioning you, it won't look like he showed any favoritism."

"If you could've seen him grill me, you would know there was no sign of favoritism." Ike walked over to a single-door soft drink refrigerator. "Can I offer you a drink? I seem to remember you like Cokes."

Marc laughed. "It's one of her weaknesses."

"I hear ya." Ike passed me a soft drink in a plastic bottle. "Marc, what can I get you?"

"Water sounds good."

I took a sip of bubbly deliciousness, then moseyed around the shop. "It's really coming together."

"Yeah. The workmen are focused on converting the shed now. I'd hoped to be up and running by this weekend, but there's more to opening a business than I expected."

A display of oyster knives caught my attention, and I picked up one. The utensil had a stainless-steel blade with a bent tip and an ergonomic handle. "Ike, did you know I saw a knife like this in Norris Gilbert's front yard?"

Ike's eyes narrowed. "Wh-what are you talking about? I haven't sold any yet, and I'm the only business licensed to sell them in this area."

Yikes. That could be bad news for Ike, but Beach Mart wasn't open for business yet. How could anyone have gotten a fancy oyster knife like the ones Ike was going to sell?

Marc said, "Stay calm. There's no way the killer bought it from you. There are probably other stores in South Carolina who sell them."

Ike paced with his hands behind his back. "The manufacturer gave me a sample to try, and mine disappeared a few weeks ago. Am I being set up?"

"Do you remember the last time you had the knife?" I forced myself to speak in a calm voice so my nervousness wouldn't increase his anxiety.

Ike stopped moving in front of the display. "Leroy took Frank Hoffman and me to the river. We culled, pulled, hammered, and replaced wild oysters. Leroy joked that it was a young man's job, but he wanted us to experience it once."

Marc picked up a fancy oyster knife. "And you used one of these when it was time to eat your harvest?"

"Yes." He rubbed his jaw.

"Ike, I'm so sorry for bringing the knife to the sheriff's attention. I never dreamed it could be connected to you. I mean, you're innocent."

"The sheriff's department is bound to test it for fingerprints. If they find mine, it'll add to their case against me."

My eyes watered. "Won't it be circumstantial evidence? I mean, what else do they really have?"

"The last call on Norris's phone was to me." Ike paced again. "On another occasion, I was overheard arguing with the man. I wanted him to leave Lacey Jane alone. I'd be happy to work out a system of paying her all the child support I should've given your parents. I wasn't trying to be cheap, but your sister didn't need the stress of a lawsuit."

My sister was the result of a short-lived affair. "You're right. Lacey Jane isn't having any problems with her pregnancy, but stress isn't good for her health or the baby's safety. Besides, Mom asked you to stay out of Lacey Jane's life, and you honored her wishes. It wasn't like you shirked your responsibility."

"Norris didn't see it that way." Ike glared at the display of oyster knives. "It looks like the sheriff can add my knife to the argument and phone call. Marc, I may need to retain you to represent me."

"I'm happy to help, sir, but if they seriously arrest you, we need to find an attorney who specializes in murder cases."

I shook my finger at Marc. "Wait just a minute. What happened to innocent until proven guilty? Ike is innocent."

Ike shook his head. "Yeah, but how do we prove it?"

"Here we go." Marc chugged his water.

"The best way I know to convince the sheriff that you're innocent is to catch the real killer."

Ike blew out a breath. "I have no doubt Lacey Jane talked you into helping me, but it could be dangerous. Plus, you have a wedding to plan."

"That's right, and I have every intention of you walking me down the aisle." I walked around the shop and found a bin of beach-themed notebooks. I picked up one of them and a fat pen. "Put these on my tab. It's time for us to get serious if we're going to investigate the murder of Norris Gilbert. The first suspect will be his wife." I wrote Ivey's name at the top of the first page.

Marc said, "Be sure to add the guy who drives the Mini Cooper."

"Right." I skipped a few pages and wrote down Rhett Alton's name. "Ike, the man's a visiting environmentalist. Let's take a deep dive into his life. What would be his motive for killing Norris?"

"Is his car blue?" Ike's eyebrows rose.

"Yes, why?" I met his gaze.

"Can you describe the man?"

"You bet. The guy's got light brown hair and blue eyes. I guess he's around fifty. Not too tall. He's in good shape." I didn't mention his irascible personality.

Marc held out his phone for Ike to see. "That's him."

Ike pulled a pair of reading glasses out of the pocket of his short-sleeve plaid shirt. After adjusting them on his nose, he studied the picture. "Yeah. That's the man I saw with Norris. They had a disagreement one day in the parking lot of Daily Java. It was early in the morning. I'd gone over because the electricity didn't work at my little place in back."

"How do you know?" Marc accepted the phone back from Ike.

"You mean besides the yelling?" Ike lifted an eyebrow. "That guy, Rhett, turned red in the face and stormed away."

"I've experienced his irrationality myself." I described my encounter from the morning. "He's definitely a person of interest. I don't guess he's been involved in the improvements to your property."

"Not that I'm aware of. Why?" With crossed arms and feet shoulder length apart, he looked like the spitting image of what I imagined a military leader would look like.

"The missing oyster knife concerns me. If Rhett had been on one of the work crews, we could accuse him of stealing your knife and planting it in the Gilberts' front yard."

"Time out." Marc made a T with his hands. "Don't worry about the knife until the authorities test it for fingerprints."

"Of course you're right." I smiled at Marc.

There was a knock on the glass door, and Griffin entered the building. "Hi, Ike. If it's okay with you, I'd like to work on the kitchen cabinets in your place."

"Sounds good. I'll be here setting up displays if you need me."

"Marc, that's our cue to shove off." I gave Ike a parting hug, then we spoke to Griffin on the way out.

Griffin walked us to my SUV, chatting with Marc about college football.

When the conversation ended, I said, "Griffin, there's no way Rhett Alton was one of the construction workers on Ike's store or tiny home, is there?"

"No, he doesn't work construction. He consults on projects, and Piney Woods is the only project I've consulted Rhett about. Why?"

"Just curious." If he hadn't been here to help with the renovation of the store or the conversion of the shed, I didn't see how he could've gotten the oyster knife.

Griffin pulled a paint tarp out of the back of his truck. "I can't imagine Rhett killed Norris, but there's no way Ike is guilty. Keep working the case, Andi Grace." He left us standing in the parking lot.

Marc opened the door for me. "Time to research Rhett Alton?"

"Absolutely, and we need to investigate Norris. If we determine the motive, it'll lead to the killer." I clutched the notebook and pen in my hands.

"Then let's swing by my office, and I'll pick up a laptop."

I gave Marc a quick kiss. "Divide and conquer. I like the way you think."

He pulled me close and kissed me until my knees grew weak. Oh, baby. I needed to help find the killer fast, so I could enjoy more earthshaking kisses.

Chapter Fourteen

MARC AND I SAT AT MY KITCHEN TABLE. He had taken the task of studying Rhett, and I researched Norris.

"Good night, Norris had plenty of enemies." I opened the blue notebook with pink sea turtles I'd gotten from Beach Mart.

"The key is finding who was mad enough to kill him. They also needed to be depraved enough to follow through on their desire."

"I hear you, and that's tougher to figure out. What are you finding?"

"Rhett has been arrested for climate change protests. He also participated in online demonstrations. His parents took part in organizing the first Earth Day observance. So conservation has been a lifelong goal." Marc folded his arms on the table. "It's important for us to protect the environment, and he's not wrong in some of his views. The problem is he has a history of taking extreme measures."

I added the information to my notebook. "You mentioned his parents. Does he have more family?"

"This is the tragic part of his story. Rhett had a younger sister, Eve Alton. She had asthma and went Upstate to protest the emissions from a fertilizer plant. In the process of protecting innocent people near the area, her asthma grew worse and she died."

"Oh, that's terrible. Poor Rhett." What an emotional day. "I haven't come across any controversy between Norris and nature. Do you know who owned the company that Eve was protesting against?"

"Yeah, it's the Froing Fertilizer Plant. If there's a link to Norris, it's not obvious. I'll dig deeper though." He turned his attention to the computer screen.

"I'll keep looking for others with a motive to kill Norris." After thirty minutes of searching, I'd gotten nowhere. I took Sunny and Chubb to the backyard then called Ivey.

"Hi, Ivey. How are you and Lady?"

She sniffed. "Lady is resting at the dog barn, and I'm trying to make funeral arrangements. How can I help you?"

I threw an old tennis ball to the dogs, and Chubb raced to claim it. "It occurred to me you'll be able to move home sooner if the sheriff catches the killer. Have you had time to think of any suspects?"

"Yes, dear. It must be a disgruntled client."

Chubb dropped the ball at my feet, and I threw it again. "Can you think of anyone in particular?"

"Norris mostly dealt with divorce cases. There's one that stands out. It's the musician. You know the one. He's a country singer."

Chills popped out on the back of my neck. "Are you accusing Lincoln Zane of murdering Norris?"

"Yes, I believe that's the name."

"Who else?"

"Andi Grace, there's another call coming in, and I need to take it. Bye."

Lincoln was Marc's good friend, probably his best friend. I hurried inside. "Marc, we need to talk to Lincoln."

"Why?"

"Ivey told me she thinks he's the most likely person to have murdered Norris. We need to talk to him before Wade does, otherwise he'll get blindsided."

"I'll text him right now." With a deep frown, Marc tapped out a message on his phone.

"Great. Invite him over. I'll make a fresh pitcher of tea."

It only took a few minutes before Lincoln rang the doorbell.

Marc answered the door then led Lincoln and his daughter to the kitchen. "Hey, man. Sorry to bother you, but I'm glad you were able to come over. Belle, it's good to see you."

"Hi, Marc." The teenager's voice was mature.

I wiped an already clean counter with a tea towel. "Hi, Lincoln."

"Andi Grace, this is my daughter, Isabella."

"Nice to meet you."

She smiled. "Please, call me Belle."

It didn't take long for me to pour glasses of tea, and we went to sit at the patio table. Chubb greeted Lincoln with exuberance, but Sunny was more reserved.

At last Marc began the conversation. "Ivey Gilbert believes Norris was killed by a disgruntled client. When asked for specifics, she gave Andi Grace your name. We thought you should be prepared."

"Oh, Daddy. What else can happen to you?" Belle pulled a band off her wrist and with jerky motions tied back her thick brown hair.

Lincoln reached for her hand. "It's okay, baby. We can handle this. Why don't you go inside and watch TV?"

She frowned at her dad. "I'm seventeen and plenty old enough to listen."

Marc said, "It should be easy enough to prove your innocence. Linc, do you have an alibi for Friday morning?"

"I drove to Charleston to pick Belle up at the airport. She graduated from high school early and is going to spend the fall with me."

Chubb stood next to Marc with his tail wagging. Marc rubbed his head. "You should write down your time line for yesterday before the authorities come knocking at your door."

"The sheriff seemed pretty cool the last time I met him. Do I really need to worry?"

Marc leaned forward. "Here's the big question. What conflict did you have with Norris?"

Lincoln drained the tea from his glass before answering. "Norris was power hungry. He approached me multiple times about my divorce settlement."

Belle gasped. "I thought you and Mom were only separated."

"No papers have been filed, but your mother insists she doesn't want to stay married to me." Lincoln grimaced. "I hope the time apart will change her mind."

The girl paled. "I think maybe I will go watch TV."

"Come on. I'll show you where it is." I stood and took her into the family room. "Here's the controller. Can I get you anything else?"

She sniffed and looked at the coffee table instead of meeting my gaze. "How about some friends and a job."

"How do you feel about dogs?" It seemed like I should give her the opportunity to apply for Dylan's position. The only risk would be if she wasn't a good employee. I probably should've kept my mouth shut until I had discussed it with Marc. If I had to fire Belle, it'd put a strain on the friendship between Marc and Lincoln. No. I was going to think positive thoughts. She seemed like a good girl.

"Man's best friend." She attempted to smile, but it flatlined. "I actually love dogs. I have a corgi, but he's with my mom."

"Talk to your dad about it first. If you're interested, we can discuss the job description."

"Yes, ma'am."

"Make yourself comfortable, and try not to worry about your parents." I hadn't been much older than Belle when my parents died in a car accident. It'd be hard on her if Lincoln and Savannah divorced, but at least they'd be alive. Working with me and the animals might be a great step in her healing process. I opened the door, and Sunny walked inside as I walked out. No doubt she'd try to comfort Belle. My German shepherd had a keen sense of knowing when a person was in emotional pain.

Lincoln said, "Sorry to dump our family problems on you."

"We're your friends, and we'll do anything we can to prove you're innocent. Uh, Belle asked if I knew of any job openings. I actually need a person to work at Stay and Play." I described the duties. "And I mentioned it to her. I probably should've discussed it with you first."

He shook his head. "She's growing up, and I'm glad she's looking for work. If she sat around the house all day while I struggle to write new songs, we'd most definitely get on each other's nerves. With my personal life on the skids, this could be my saddest album yet. If I get arrested, the songs will really get dark."

"Whoa, Linc." Marc rubbed his hands together. "You need to focus on the good things in your life. Did you ever imagine Belle would want to hang out with you instead of getting an apartment with friends? You're living on the beach, and we're on your side."

I said, "Marc's right. If necessary, we'll help prove you're innocent. You've got an amazing daughter. I told Belle to think about the job and let me know. There's no need for you to get involved in the job search if you want Belle to handle it."

"Perfect. It'll be a good opportunity for her to grow and mature. Thanks for offering her a job."

"You're welcome."

"You know what else? I think it's best to get ahead of this thing. I'm going to the sheriff's office and give him my alibi. No sense in sitting around and worrying."

"Hey, if you pick up on any clues while you're there, will you let me know?" I shot both men my best smile.

Lincoln laughed. "No problem."

Marc walked Lincoln and Belle out, but I remained on the back patio. It was nice to have two options for Dylan's replacement. Neither one was perfect, but Dylan had a rough life before I hired him. His mother had deserted him when he was a child, and his dad was in prison. I'd given him a chance, and he'd become like family.

Belle was the logical option. There was something off with Cheyenne Marther, but maybe I could give her a part-time job.

In the meantime, I wanted to enjoy the evening with Marc. Solving the murder could come later.

Chapter Fifteen

THE SATURDAY NIGHT FESTIVITIES HAD BEGUN at the pier. Marc and I stood in line at a food truck, waiting to get drinks. The warm-up band, the Moonbeams, had already performed. As the crowd waited for the Heyward Coasters, there was talking, laughter, a variety of smoke floating in the air, the sound of ocean waves crashing on the beach, and an emcee trying to be heard on the stage.

Marc wrapped his arm around my shoulders. "I was impressed with the Moonbeams."

At the end of the teen band's set, they'd announced they were holding auditions for a female singer. "Do you think Belle might try out for the opening act?"

"You can bet Linc will check out each of the boys. If they're into drugs or any other bad things, it'll be a hard stop from him. She may be seventeen, but she's still his little girl."

"Aw, my dad shielded us from bad things when he was alive. After his death, I took on the role of family protector."

Marc kept his arm around me while we scooted closer to the lady taking orders. "You've done a great job of caring for your siblings, but it's not your burden alone anymore."

I nodded. "Yeah, Lacey Jane has Ike now."

"And Nate's a grown man. They still need you though. Who did Lacey Jane turn to when Ike found himself in a bad spot with the sheriff?"

"Me."

"That's right, but you've got me on your side. In fact, you've got a big old support team."

It was our turn to order, and the conversation ended. Marc was right though. I was blessed with amazing friends, and my family was growing. All three of us kids would be married by the end of October, Lacey Jane was expecting a baby, and Ike cared about all of us.

Marc handed me a drink, and we strolled toward the nearest beach access. People milled around. As we walked over the path, the crowd noise dimmed. The moon shone on the beach, and lights from the parking lot and homes prevented it from being dark. "The sea turtle people won't be happy about all the lights."

"I know that's right, but isn't it why the concert has to end before midnight?"

"Yeah. It was a compromise between the festival promoters and the people wanting to protect the sea turtles. I'm sure you know the moon isn't what causes the babies to hatch."

"Uh-huh. The reflection of the moon on the beach is brighter than the moon itself, and they go toward the light."

I sipped my Coke from a recyclable cup without a lid and no straw. Not too far from our spot stood a group of people, and one looked like Rhett Alton. "Marc, do you see who's over there?"

"If I'm not mistaken, it's your conservation man."

I elbowed him in the ribs. "He's not my anything, but let's see if we can get close enough to hear the discussion."

"Fine, but you really need to come up with a solid motive in case he accuses you of eavesdropping." He kicked off his leather flip-flops. "Would you like me to carry your shoes?"

"It'd probably save me from twisting an ankle." I passed my cup to Marc, then unzipped my turquoise wedges and removed them. The shoes complemented my sundress, and I loved wearing them. "Here you go." We swapped my shoes for the drink.

"There's enough people on the beach that we shouldn't stick out, but try to blend in."

"It's high tide, and that works to our advantage. It won't seem as suspicious if we walk near them."

"True that." He finished his drink and dumped the ice into the sand. "In case he's watching, let's toss our cups into the recycle bin."

I hurried to drink the rest of my Coke. A small stream dribbled down my chin. I coughed and handed the cup to Marc. My simple cough transformed into a choking spell. Marc tossed our cups in the appropriate bin while I struggled to breathe.

"You going to make it?" Marc patted my back.

"Yeah." Another coughing fit took over, and my eyes watered.

This was no way to be inconspicuous.

A girl from Rhett's group approached. "Do you want my water? I haven't opened it yet." She held out a plastic water bottle.

"Thanks." I accepted her offer but couldn't get the cough under control enough to take a drink.

"Here, hold your arms up like this." She took a firm grip on my wrists and lifted my hands high. "This should help. By the way, I'm Leah Bland. Don't try to talk. Focus on breathing. In through your nose, and out through your mouth."

My face warmed. *Mortified* was the best word to describe my feelings. Yet, there was less pressure on my chest.

Rhett and the others ran over and watched. He looked at Marc. "Did she choke on something?"

"I think she got strangled on her drink."

"Okay, so we don't need to do the Heimlich." Rhett continued to watch me. "Or do we?"

I shook my head, and met the girl's gaze. "It's better."

She flashed me a toothy smile. "I'm a freshman at the college, and we learned about choking this week. Perfect timing, don't you think?"

"Yes, I do." I lowered my arms. "Thank you so much, and if you need me to brag to your professor, I'm Andi Grace Scott, local dog walker. It'll be easy to find me." I took a long drink of water and it soothed my windpipe.

"Cool."

Marc introduced himself to Rhett, who looked like he wanted to leave. Instead, Rhett used good manners and introduced us to his little group. I focused on breathing and not coughing. It was nice to watch my fiancé interact with the others. He was smooth and charming, and it was no wonder I'd fallen in love with the man. Rhett's posture relaxed, and he explained how he'd been a guest lecturer for a class at the college.

"Will you be in town for the entire semester?" Marc smiled.

Rhett said, "I'm renting a condo on the mainland. In fact, I've begun advising some local builders and construction companies on ways to incorporate environmental pollution control systems. In the Low Country, it's important to have storm water systems in place. I believe builders need to do more than required by law. It's also important to have strategies to survive hurricanes and tornadoes with minimum damage. With global warming, flood lines will shift. Builders need to design more homes with features to survive these massive storms."

In the distance, the band started playing.

Leah squealed. "They're starting. Bye, Dr. Alton." She and her friends laughed and raced through the sand toward the parking lot.

Rhett stuck his hands in his pockets. "Thanks to the band, tonight's lecture is officially over. I'll shove off too."

"Nice to meet you." Marc smiled.

"I'm sorry about offending you this morning. I only hoped you might have seen something." My chest grew tight, and I breathed through my nose.

"Forget about it." He left us standing in the shadows.

Once he was out of sight, Marc looked at me. "I don't care if he is a professor, he's too old to be hanging out with college students. If it was your sister, I'd question somebody on staff at the college or contact law enforcement. I guess I don't have a dog in that fight though. Still, it's worrisome."

I shivered but didn't say anything.

"How do you feel? Do you want to dance or go home?"

"Let's enjoy the band." A coughing spell wasn't going to ruin our romantic evening.

We made our way to the makeshift dance area and slipped on our shoes. Ethan and Violet Seitz joined us. Ethan said, "Hey, can you talk a minute?"

"Sure." The four of us walked to the street corner, where it wasn't so loud. "What's up?"

"The dude with the Mini Cooper is here, and something came to me." Ethan frowned. "It's not good."

"Should we go to my place where we can discuss it in private?" A few people wandered about, but most were at the show.

Violet wrapped her hands around her husband's arm. "Ethan, you'll be more comfortable if you know nobody else is listening."

"You're right. Where do you live?" Ethan glanced right and left with jerky movements. The pharmacist had always seemed calm and composed before tonight. Whatever he needed to share must be terrible.

"It'll be quicker if we walk. Follow me." It appeared Heyward Beach's most recent murder was doing it's best to interrupt my love life, but I couldn't risk missing a good clue.

In very little time the four of us sat on my back patio. Sunny and Chubb moved around in the yard.

"What's on your mind?" My pulse throbbed in my neck as I waited for Ethan to reveal his big secret. Was it possible he was about to reveal the killer? I leaned forward, anxious to hear his secret.

Chapter Sixteen

SECONDS TICKED BY as I waited for Ethan's revelation. The night was humid, but an ocean breeze made it bearable. The ceiling fan helped too. Outside lights and the moon made for a comfy setting. Too bad we had to discuss something so serious we shouldn't be overheard.

Ethan crossed a leg, propping his ankle on the opposite thigh. His wavy dark hair was frizzed. "Was the man you were speaking to on the beach Rhett Alton?"

I tucked a stray lock of hair behind my ear. "Yes, he owns the blue Mini Cooper, and he's an environmentalist."

"That's what I thought." He swiped a hand over his mouth. "He followed Norris into the pharmacy one day. It was deliberate, and Norris was furious. Their discussion got so heated, I asked them to leave."

I clicked my pen and opened the new notebook. "What was the argument about?"

"Rhett accused Norris of insurance fraud, and Norris threatened to sue him for slander. Who knows? Maybe there is a lawsuit in the works. The accusation about insurance fraud confused me. I've tried to wrap my head around it but can't figure it out."

Marc tapped the arm of his chair. "Norris had a connection to the LC Pain Clinic."

Ethan's mouth dropped open. "You've got to be kidding me. It didn't take long to figure out the place was a pill mill. After a couple weeks, I grew uneasy and refused to fill prescriptions from Dr. Rich. When the clinic was shut down, the woman committed suicide. How is Norris connected?"

I said, "Ivey Gilbert was the listing agent in charge of selling the building. Norris was behind the clinic coming to town."

"Interesting. I spoke to some of the patients about my concerns. They paid cash for their appointments. Dr. Rich saw patients in groups of ten, and she'd write prescriptions for multiple painkillers and benzodiazepines."

Violet touched Ethan's arm. "Not everyone knows what benzodiazepines are."

"Sorry. They are for anxiety, and they're addictive. Add them to narcotics, and they are highly sought after by drug abusers. It didn't take long for patients to get hooked. Never does, I'm afraid. I tried to convince them to seek help, but it was like talking to a brick wall. I finally put a sign in the window and on the counter stating that I wouldn't fill prescriptions from Dr.

Stephanie A. Rich. Once word got around, my life became easier, and the doctor quit sending me electronic prescriptions."

Violet rubbed her husband's shoulder. "During those weeks, Ethan had nightmares and lost weight. I was so relieved when he made the decision to drop those patients."

Sunny climbed the stairs and lay at my feet. I patted her side. "Let's think about this. Rhett is all about the environment. What could his beef be with the clinic?"

"It makes no sense. They didn't give drugs there. No shots. No pills. No patches. All they did was write prescriptions." Ethan fisted his hands. "Most prescriptions are now given electronically, so Rhett couldn't even complain about wasted paper. I'm just telling you, the insurance fraud accusation makes no sense. Their operation was cash only. There were rumors the mob was behind the pain center, but I can't imagine the mob is active in our area."

"Dr. Rich was really nice." Violet looked at Ethan. "It doesn't seem possible she had mob connections."

"You're right." Ethan turned his attention back to Marc and me. "She came by the pharmacy one day for ibuprofen and joked about being a pain doctor and treating herself with over-the-counter medications. I wonder if she got tangled up in something too big for her to get away."

Violet said, "She was a little thing. I'd guess she was close to retirement age, so it really didn't make sense to end her career on a bad note."

Nobody spoke for a few minutes. Muted strains of beach music drifted to us from the concert. I looked at Ethan. "Why did you want to talk in private?"

He shrugged. "Dr. Rich died at her own hand. Norris was murdered. The last time I saw Norris was the day he argued with Rhett. I don't know who's safe and who's dangerous. It just seemed prudent not to have this discussion where we could be overheard."

"Do you know Ivey Gilbert very well?"

Violet's head bobbed. "I'm on the welcome committee at church with Ivey. She's nice, but reserved. We take food to newcomers as well as literature about opportunities to participate at church. One time we visited a young family living in an apartment. Ivey mentioned she's in real estate and offered to show them around if they were looking for a home. Don't you think that's tacky?"

I laughed. "Tacky? Yes. Do you two think she could've killed her husband?"

"No. He's way bigger than her, and I heard he was strangled with a dog leash. You remember how I used to struggle to attach a leash to Yoyo's collar? Can you imagine trying to fight a man as big as Norris to strangle him? I just don't see how it's possible." Her thick red hair bounced when she shook her head.

Ethan glanced at his wife. "She could've hired a person to kill her husband."

Violet tilted her head. "I guess that's true."

Chubb growled, and Sunny's ears pointed up. Marc's dog raced to the side gate and barked. Sunny took off with more energy than she'd exhibited in a while. I started down the stairs, but Marc snagged my hand. "Let me. You call the sheriff."

Ethan joined Marc, and the two crept toward the gate.

I returned to the porch and called Wade. Music blared in the background.

"Hey there, it's Andi Grace. I think someone is trying to get into my backyard. The dogs are agitated and barking."

"I can hear them over the music. Are you alone?"

"No. Marc's here as well as Ethan and Violet Seitz."

"I'm on the way, but you should head inside where it's safe."

I hung up and looked at Violet. "The sheriff's on the way. Let's look out the front window. Maybe we can see something."

She patted her crossover mini purse. "I've got my gun if we need it."

"Whoa, keep that thing in there. If anyone is going to shoot, it should be Wade."

"Don't worry, Ethan is carrying too." She shrugged. "Being a pharmacist isn't the safest profession in the world."

"Hmm. Well, come on." Despite the fact I'd had some close calls solving murders, I'd never felt the desire to buy a gun. I opened the door, and we walked through the kitchen and family room, down the wide front hall, and slipped into the room Griffin would convert into office space for Marc. I didn't turn on a light, and we peeked out the window.

Ominous shadows gave me the chills. From my vantage point, I saw bushes, vehicles in driveways, and palm trees.

The sheriff appeared in his new official SUV. It was tan on top and black on the bottom with letters spelling out it belonged to the sheriff. Wade parked his Tahoe in front of my house. He jumped out and ran to the side yard. No doubt the barking dogs gave him a clue where to begin his search.

Seconds ticked by.

A high-pitched scream sounded, and if Violet hadn't been with me, I would've run outside to check. I didn't want her to overreact and shoot someone, and I definitely didn't want Wade to shoot at us if he saw Violet's gun.

My heart raced.

Violet whispered, "Can you see anything from your angle?"

"No." It was killing me to be stuck inside while the action was in my yard.

The back door opened. "Andi Grace, come here."

I hurried to see Marc. Violet was close behind. "What?"

"It's that girl we met this morning, Cheyenne Marther."

I gasped. "What's she doing here?"

"She claims she rang the doorbell, and she wanted to talk to you about the reward for finding Lady. I warn you though, she's been drinking. Do you want to talk to her?"

"Yeah. Let's see what she has to say."

Marc pointed to the front of the house. "Wade said to meet him at his vehicle. Maybe the dogs will calm down."

Violet said, "Where's Ethan?"

"He's with the sheriff and Cheyenne."

The three of us hurried back through the house and met the others at the sheriff's SUV.

"You!" Cheyenne roared. "You're trying to cheat me out of the reward money for that dog. Well, sister, you better watch it. I know where you live." Venom laced the slurred words.

"That's enough." Wade removed his cuffs and read Cheyenne her rights as he restrained the girl.

"It's not fair." She sobbed. "That stupid car hit me. That stupid doctor ruined my life. I lost my precious babies. And now you're robbing me. None of it's fair." Her sob morphed into a wail.

I kept a safe distance away. "Cheyenne, you will get the reward money, but how'd you find me?"

Her shoulders hunched forward. "I'm gonna be sick."

Wade led her out of the grass and uncuffed her in the street. "Don't try anything stupid."

A deputy's car pulled up, and David Wayne stepped out. "Sheriff, I thought you might need some help."

Wade chuckled. "Perfect timing. You can drive this one to the station. Book her for public intoxication and causing a disturbance. Your sister-in-law may want to press charges of trespassing."

Cheyenne fell to her hands and knees and hurled on the sandy street.

David looked toward me. "Andi Grace? Whatcha want to do?"

"I won't press charges, but it'd be nice to know how she found me."

Marc drew me to his side. "People know you, and it probably wasn't hard to learn where you live."

"True. Ethan, you should tell your story to the sheriff. I think it's important."

Ethan's shoulders slumped. "You're right. Sheriff Stone, I don't know if it's significant or not, but I witnessed an argument between Norris Gilbert and Rhett Alton."

"Let's go to my office and chat. Your wife can come with us." Wade turned to David, who stood near Cheyenne. The girl appeared to have quit vomiting. "David, cuff her and I'll meet you at the station." He took off with Ethan and Violet.

David got a limp Cheyenne into handcuffs then helped her into the back of his car. He crossed his arms and looked at us. "I don't want to give her a chance to puke in my car, but Lacey Jane confessed that she asked you to help prove Ike is innocent. I don't want to get between you two, so I'll only warn you to be careful."

"Yes, sir."

After he drove away, I hugged Marc. "I can't believe what just happened."

He held me tight. "There's never a dull moment with you, Andi Grace."

"Before we met, I used to be a dull Low Country dog walker."

He chuckled. "Don't blame it on me." His phone vibrated.

"You appeared when I found my first body. Go ahead and take your call." I collected a water bucket from behind my bushes and filled it with water. I lugged it to the street and rinsed the area where Cheyenne had gotten sick.

"Let's take care of the dogs."

"Who was on the phone?"

"A client, but his issue can wait until Tuesday. I agreed to fit him in my schedule."

"That's nice of you." We held hands and walked inside. The evening's scene had unnerved me. "What do you think Cheyenne meant by losing everything?"

"No idea, but I have faith you'll dig into her background and find out."

I leaned into Marc. "Yeah, you're right."

"So far we know she's desperate for money."

I nodded. Cheyenne had asked me about a job. Running a background check for the position would be a perfect excuse to look into her life. Had she ever stolen a dog before? Maybe she'd had a confrontation with Norris in the past. Had she been involved in one of his divorce cases? Whoa. I needed to remember my priorities. First came wedding planning, then proving Ike was innocent of Norris's death. Then I could check out Cheyenne and see if there was a possibility she'd dognapped Lady. If not, I'd find a way to help her.

Chapter Seventeen

THE SCREAM OF A SEAGULL WOKE ME WITH A START on Sunday morning. It was barely light outside, and Sunny snoozed on the floor beside my bed. Since the first day when she'd come into my life, my German shepherd had slept on the floor beside me. I rolled to the other side of the bed and tiptoed to the bathroom. As Sunny got older, she slept more. Still, there was no more faithful companion in the world.

I brushed my teeth and splashed cold water on my face. In the bedroom, Sunny was sitting up. "Good morning." I rubbed her head and kissed her nose. "You ready to start our day?"

She stood then headed downstairs.

By the time I'd made coffee, taken care of Sunny, and grabbed a bagel, I turned on my computer. Time to learn more about Cheyenne Marther. My research lasted until it was time for a coffee refill. I moseyed into the kitchen and debated drinking water instead of taking in more caffeine. Dylan was scheduled to walk dogs this morning, and I missed being in the fresh air and playing with the animals.

The doorbell rang. Sunny barked and hurried to the door. When I opened it, I found Marc holding a white paper bag and two cups from Daily Java.

"Good morning, beautiful." He leaned in for a kiss, and Chubb pushed past him to greet Sunny. We wobbled and laughed.

"Morning. Whatcha got there?" We walked to the kitchen.

Marc wore a short-sleeve navy Henley, and his eyes sparkled. "Breakfast sandwiches and Erin's Labor Day specialty coffee. You hungry?"

The smell of bacon and coffee stirred my hunger, despite the fact I'd eaten half of a toasted frozen bagel. "Yes, and I have time to share what I've learned this morning." At church we'd signed up to hand out free bottles of water to festival attendees. We weren't due to be at the booth for an hour.

Marc let the dogs out back, and we sat at the table. "Spill. What'd you turn up?"

"Cheyenne married her childhood sweetheart when they graduated from high school. They had babies right off the bat. One day she was walking across the street and was hit by a car. There were multiple surgeries, and Norris was her attorney. He sued the other driver and the insurance company for more than they wanted to settle for. That's public record." I bit into my sandwich. The croissant was full of bacon, cheese, eggs, avocado, and even had a tomato slice.

"What else did you find out?"

"After the surgeries, Cheyenne was still in pain and started going to see Dr. Rich." I sipped my coffee. "She got addicted, and her habit led her to get the family into serious debt. They had to declare bankruptcy, and then her husband filed for divorce. One night she must have shown up at the husband's new place and caused a scene. The neighbors called the cops, and Cheyenne was arrested. There's also a restraining order."

"The pill mill doctor. It can't be a coincidence that Norris was her attorney, then she went to the clinic. While you get dressed, I'll try to see how involved Norris was with the Low Country Pain Clinic."

We finished eating in silence, then I ran upstairs and got ready for the hot day.

On our walk to the festival, Marc shared the information he'd come across. "Do you remember Ethan told us that there were rumors the clinic was linked to the mob? I think it's more than rumors. If it's true, and the clinic was broken up by the feds, the mobsters may have put out a hit on Norris. It depends on the promises Norris made to his connections."

I gasped. "The mob? In Heyward Beach? How can it be possible?"

"Shh." Marc reached for my hand. "Hopefully they left town when the pill mill failed."

The streets near the pier had been roped off. Vendors had booths with a wide variety of items for sale. Pork rinds, boiled peanuts, barbecue sauce, hair ribbons for little girls, coastal photography, and books by local authors were only a few of the festival items available. We found the church's table with coolers of water. It was sandwiched between a booth of volunteers wanting to save the sea turtles, and Rhett Alton sharing information on how to protect the environment.

"Marc, look who we'll be rubbing shoulders with." I pointed to Rhett.

"My, my. Our morning just got more interesting."

We replaced two church ladies manning our booth. In no time, we were greeting visitors and handing out water bottles. During a lull, I approached Rhett. "Good morning. How's it going?"

The man wore vintage shorts and a plaid shirt, probably to make a statement not to get rid of clothes rather than for fashion. "Morning." His red face concerned me.

"Would you like some water?"

He shook his head. "I usually bring my own water in a reusable jug."

A glance at his minimalist space showed no signs of any drink containers. "You look hot. Please, take this. We'll recycle it when you're done." I held the free water bottle out to him.

Marc carried a chair over to us and placed it in a spot under the tent. "Man, you need to sit in the shade before you have heat stroke."

Rhett's eyebrows slowly rose. "It's early."

I twisted the lid off the plastic recyclable bottle and handed it to him. "True, but you're in South Carolina. It's already hot and humid. Please, drink this."

"But I'm not sweating. All right, I can see by the look on your face you've got more to say, and I don't want to argue." He lifted the bottle to his lips and drank it all.

Marc said, "Let's get you in the shade. You won't be able to convince people to save the earth if you pass out."

I gave Rhett another bottle of water, then left the men alone. From a distance I spotted my older friend Leroy Peck. We made eye contact, and I waved.

Leroy cut through the crowd and stopped when he reached me. Cheyenne Marther was at his side. "Andi Grace, I'd like you to meet Cheyenne Marther. She lives at Piney Woods and is looking for a job."

"We met yesterday. Hi, Cheyenne." It surprised me she wasn't still in jail, but I wouldn't embarrass her in front of Leroy.

She looked down at her purple flip-flops with a gash on the side. "Hi. Sorry about last night."

"Forget about it. Would you like some water?" I handed each one a drink. She was probably dehydrated from being drunk last night, and the heat would make it worse.

"Thanks."

Leroy said, "I bailed her out on the condition she find a job and not cause another scene."

Okay, so what game was she playing this time? If she thought she'd take advantage of my friend, she didn't know who she was about to cross.

Marc joined us. "Leroy, it's nice to see you. I need to take our new friend to a place with air-conditioning. Any chance you two would take over our shift here?"

Leroy retrieved his truck keys from the pocket of his khakis. "We'd be glad to. My truck's over yonder. I doubt yours is any closer."

"Perfect. Thanks, Leroy." Marc left us to talk to Rhett.

I squeezed my friend's tanned hand full of age spots. "Text me when you're ready to leave, and I'll return the truck."

"Will do. We've got this covered." Leroy opened a metal cooler and retrieved two bottles.

Marc and Rhett walked toward the truck, and I caught up with them. As crowded as the streets were, it'd be faster to walk. Too bad Rhett didn't appear to have the strength. It took almost fifteen minutes to reach my house by driving the crowded streets. Rhett rode shotgun and cool air blasted him. Once inside my home, I lowered the air conditioner and fixed cool compresses.

Rhett half sat, half lay on my couch, drinking a sports drink. Marc sat in a chair and watched the professor. The dogs kept an eye on my fiancé.

"Here, let me put this on your forehead." I placed the cool, soft cloth on his face. "Would you prefer we call the paramedics?"

"I'm sure this will be fine. Thanks for your help."

I signaled for Marc to meet me in my office. Chubb followed Marc, but Sunny remained with Rhett.

"What?" Marc kept his voice low.

"Are we doing the right thing? Should we call for help?"

"He hasn't had muscle cramps. I feel like we started hydrating him soon enough. Why don't you stay in here and work on the investigation? I'll keep an eye on our guest."

My doubts drifted away. Marc had said *our guest*. Soon this would be our home, and we'd be a forever couple. I kissed him. "Thanks, and who knows? I may even make some wedding plans."

"You can't fool me. Planning our wedding will be a lot more fun after you solve the murder." He and Chubb left me alone in the office.

I texted Griffin about the office conversion, and while waiting for his response on a start date I remembered Ethan had mentioned insurance fraud. So, I searched for cases against Low Country Pain Clinic and Dr. Rich.

Chapter Eighteen

THE SOUND OF MALE VOICES drew me out of my dive into insurance fraud. I walked to the family room and found Marc, Rhett, and Griffin talking.

"Hi, Griff." I hoped he didn't blow my surprise for Marc by showing up unannounced. I glanced at Rhett. "Hey, your color is better."

"I feel better. It's probably time for me to go back to the festival."

"No." Marc's firm reply brooked no argument. "Your body gave you a warning, and you don't need to push past your limits. Next time your reaction to the heat could be worse. Stay here where it's nice and cool. We can watch a baseball game or a movie or something."

"I'll refill your drink, Rhett." I reached for his glass. "Griff, how's your day going?"

"It's good. I stopped by with a couple of wedding questions." He winked at me.

Marc said, "I'll take care of Rhett. You should talk to Griff, unless it's about a bachelor party."

Griff chuckled. "If I plan one of those, I won't be asking your fiancée for advice."

"Why? I'd suggest something like ax throwing, surfing, or fishing."

"Ha, and that's one example of why I'm not asking you. We're not going to have a party so tame that all the guys fall asleep."

"Don't forget, if the grooms arrive to the wedding with hangovers, you'll have to answer to me and your sister."

Griffin's smile faded. "I'd never do anything to hurt Juliet. Now, if I can have a minute of your time."

"Come on. We can talk in the front room." I reached for the TV remote and tossed it to Rhett. "Knock yourself out."

I leaned against the doorframe of the front room while Griff measured it. On the TV, broadcasters announced the lineup for a baseball game and their predictions for who'd win. The sound was loud enough for me to know it was a Braves game.

Griff put the tape measure in the pocket of his faded denim shorts. "Here's a drawing I came up with based on what you shared earlier. I know Marc's office isn't far away, so it makes sense to keep it simple here. A few shelves, a desk, an easy chair for reading boring contracts or whatever he needs to read, and good lighting. If we stick to soft beach colors, it'll add a comfortable air to the room."

"Let me see what you drew." Everything he said struck a chord in me, but I wanted to actually see his drawing.

"Here." He released his sketch of the room. "What do you think?"

His drawing proved he'd listened to my dream for Marc's home office. It'd be my wedding gift to my groom. "It's perfect. The only thing I'd like to add is some artwork."

"Trust me. I've got it covered. If you give me your approval, I'll be ready to start on Tuesday. Can you keep Marc out of here for a few days? It shouldn't take very long, but if you want it to be a surprise, don't let him inside."

"I should be able to keep him distracted and away from here. Thanks so much for taking on this project."

"Yes, ma'am." He winked. "I wanted to do my best for you without distractions. Once I begin work on Piney Woods Apartment Complex, it'll demand all my time." He headed to the front door. "If Marc questions us, what's our story?"

"You wanted to help pay for the wedding and suggested hiring a band, but I told you Lincoln Zane was going to play some of the music. Then you suggested hiring some food trucks, and I nixed that idea. You're still trying to come up with a great wedding present for Juliet and Nate."

"Let's hope I can remember that whopper."

"Details help lies succeed." I needed to remember this theory if one of my suspects gave me too many details.

Griffin laughed. "I'll be here bright and early Tuesday morning. Make sure you're up and decent."

I opened the door. "No problem. See ya."

Marc approached. "Everything okay?"

"Yeah, he's struggling to pick a great gift for his sister and Nate." I wrapped my arms around Marc's waist. "I wish we could enjoy the day snuggled up and watching a movie or something. How's our guest?"

"He's ready to leave. Leroy texted, and I agreed to give Rhett a ride back to the festival. Do you want to join us?"

"May as well. We might stumble across another clue."

"Clue to what?" Rhett snuck up on us.

I took a deep breath. This man had been furious with me once, but could I miss this opportunity to see if he knew something regarding the murder? No way. "Rhett, I don't want to get sideways with you, but is there a possibility you saw anything out of the ordinary the morning of Norris

Gilbert's murder?"

His nostrils flared, but he didn't storm away. "You're not a cop or a reporter. In fact, you're a dog walker. There's no reason for me to answer your question."

The nerve of the man. His tone dismissed my job and it rankled more than a bit. "I found the body and would like to help the sheriff catch the killer."

"I'm sorry for your experience, but there's nothing I can do to help. Norris was a shady character, and I even tried to sue him once. Marc probably told you about that failure."

"No, I didn't." Marc frowned. "Client-attorney confidentiality. I'm not allowed to disclose what we discussed in my office about your case."

"Glad to hear it. If you don't mind, I'm ready to go."

"I'll ride over with you. Let me bring the dogs inside so they don't get too hot." I hurried to let Sunny and Chubb into the house. They had plenty to drink in their bowls, and I grabbed a water bottle for Rhett. No matter how much he'd aggravated me, I didn't want him to pass out in the heat.

We met Leroy and Cheyenne in front of the ice cream shop.

Rhett hopped out of the truck. "Thanks for taking care of me."

Marc said, "I'd suggest you go home where it's cool and take it easy."

Rhett shook Marc's hand then reached out and shook mine. "Andi Grace, you should be careful. You don't want the killer to come after you." He left us standing in the parking lot.

Goose bumps exploded all over my body. Had Rhett issued a friendly word of caution, or was it a threat?

Chapter Nineteen

LEROY CHUGGED AWAY IN HIS OLD TRUCK, and Cheyenne remained with us. Strands of red hair escaped her ponytail. "Um, I'm sorry again about last night. Will you still consider hiring me?"

Her request surprised me. "I've always taken the best possible care of the animals I'm responsible for. Your drunken episode at my place leads me to believe you won't be a good fit. I'm sorry."

"Let me explain."

People walked past us and into the ice cream shop.

"Ladies, why don't we move to a table in the shade? I'll get us some ice cream." Marc pointed to the white tables with bright yellow chairs and yellow-and-white-striped umbrellas.

"Please, give me a chance to explain. Please?" Cheyenne folded her hands in front of her chest.

"All right." The least I could do was hear her out. We settled at a table, and Marc entered the shop.

An uncomfortable silence fell over us. Cheyenne cleared her throat, and she placed her folded hands on the little table. "You probably don't know much about me."

"I'll be honest. Before I hire somebody to work for me, I do a background check. My employees don't have to be perfect, but I do look for signs on how they feel about animals."

"Then I guess you know about my accident." Cheyenne pressed her lips together.

"Yes. I was sorry to learn about the car hitting you and your struggles on the road to recovery."

"Mr. Gilbert was my attorney, and he convinced me to go to the pain clinic where I got hooked on drugs. I've been trying to get clean, but I relapsed last night." Her eyes widened. "No hard drugs, but I had too much to drink at a party."

What had triggered her relapse? "What do you mean by hard drugs?"

"Oxy, fentanyl, heroin." She shrugged. "Last night I smoked some pot and drank more than my fair share of beer."

"Why? Did something happen yesterday?"

Tears filled her eyes. "It was my little girl's birthday, and I'm not allowed to see her unless it's supervised by a social worker approved by the state. Even if I'd gotten the approval, I couldn't get to Greenville. That's where my ex-husband moved with them."

Aw, man. Who knows? In her position, would I have reacted the same way? I patted her hands. "I'm sorry, Cheyenne."

"It won't happen again. Please, I need money to live, and I promised to pay Leroy back for getting me out of jail. In order to see my family, I have to take a bus or hitch a ride with a friend. It all takes money, which I need desperately. Please hire me."

"What about your settlement with the insurance company?"

She shook her head. "I've been asking Norris for it, but he said something about my husband had been paying the medical bills so it's only fair he gets the money. Norris kicked me out of his office so many times, it's why I—"

"Why you what?" Cheyenne didn't strike me as a killer, but had she been desperate enough to dognap Lady?

"Never mind. It's nothing."

I studied her. She was too thin, and her hair was stringy and unkempt. I'd try a different tactic. "How old are you?"

"Twenty-seven."

Whoa. Not much younger than me. "Do you have any idea who may have wanted to kill Norris Gilbert?"

"He was a mean and nasty man. What about his wife? One day when I went to his office to ask about my money, they were arguing."

"What about?"

She closed her eyes. "Um, money. Mrs. Gilbert had a check bounce, and she was mad. Oh, no. Do you think she can afford to pay me the reward for finding her dog?"

"Yes." Ivey and Norris had plans to go to Bali, and that couldn't be a cheap trip.

Marc appeared with a plastic sack under his arm and three cups of ice cream. "Hey, they were having a sale on T-shirts with this year's logo."

I reached for the cup with green ice cream. "Mint chocolate chip?"

"Yes, ma'am. Cheyenne, you have a choice of vanilla or strawberry cheesecake."

"Vanilla. Thanks."

Marc passed her the cup then sat next to me. "I always like a bargain, so I bought shirts for all of us. They even had flip-flops on sale. See what you think."

I pulled out three colorful shirts with pictures of ice cream in waffle cones and white letters advertising Scoop It Up Ice Cream Shop. "Cheyenne, Marc has quite a collection of T-shirts. Most have a boat theme though. These are nice." No doubt my fiancé had noticed the hole under the arm of Cheyenne's dingy white cap-sleeve shirt.

"I can't accept this."

Marc stopped lifting a spoonful of pink ice cream to his mouth. "All sales are final in there, and that won't fit me. It's yours, and please take the shoes."

I took a bite of the cold snack. Refreshing mint mixed with chocolate floated over my tongue. "Yum. Hey, Marc. Maybe you can help Cheyenne." I explained the situation with her insurance money.

He nodded. "Let me look into it Tuesday when I'm back at work."

"Okay, and don't forget Mrs. Gilbert's supposed to pay me on Tuesday."

"Right. You can swing by my office early in the afternoon, and the money will be waiting."

"I don't have a car."

"It's an easy walk from here." Marc gave her directions, then the three of us finished our ice cream.

"Cheyenne, I've already got a prospect for Dylan's job. All of my openings will require you being able to provide your own transportation." Stay and Play was out in what I considered the country, even though the drive didn't seem as long now as it used to.

Her shoulders sagged. "A few years ago, I worked for a car dealership as the bookkeeper. If you loan me a laptop, I can do your financial paperwork."

"I've got that covered." No way would I allow a recovering drug addict who'd driven her family into debt manage my finances. "The tourist season will be winding down after this week, so I doubt there will be openings at gift shops. Is there anything you can do to help Griffin Reed and his construction team? While they work at Piney Woods, transportation won't be an issue." My hopes were high that she'd be hired to do something at the apartment complex.

"That could work. I'll ask him." She stood and reached for her shirt. "Thanks for this and the ice cream."

"You're welcome." Marc waved as Cheyenne walked toward the festival.

"I always knew you were Mr. Nice Guy." I leaned over and kissed his cheek. "What do you want to do next?"

"Let's walk around the festival. You can update me on what you learned from Cheyenne."

I threw away our trash and strolled down the sidewalk with Marc.

"According to Cheyenne, Ivey had a check bounce." I related the details of our conversation to him. We swung by my place and left the shirts inside. "Hey, how come you didn't tell me you'd met Rhett before?"

"I can't tell you who my clients are. If you happen to see someone at the office, it's okay, but I can't just throw names around."

"I admire your integrity. It'd probably be hard for me to keep secrets."

"I didn't say it was easy." He stopped and looked at his phone. "It's Lincoln. He may have some information about the murder."

"Let's go." Lincoln's house was next to the pier parking lot, and we were already walking in his direction. "I'm curious who it could be? Of course I've ruled out Ike and Lincoln, but Ivey, Cheyenne and Rhett are on my list."

Marc glanced at me. "Rhett? Really?"

"He's up to something and very secretive. So, yes. He's on my list of suspects."

"All right. It'll be interesting to see who Lincoln suspects."

I picked up my pace, hoping for a viable suspect to add to my list.

Chapter Twenty

MARC AND I SAT NEXT TO EACH OTHER on a blue outdoor love seat on Lincoln's back deck. He sat opposite us in a matching blue Adirondack chair, and Belle was inside playing a baby grand piano and singing.

The waves pounded on the beach. Fluffy white clouds drifted over and out to sea.

Marc said, "Whatcha got for us?"

"You know the Heyward Coasters, the band playing each night at the festival?"

"Yes." Below the deck and near the water, I spotted Deputy Denise Harris and Deputy Levi Sawyer patrolling the beach. They wore official white polos and black shorts.

"Freddie Fisher is the lead singer. I told him about my plan to invest in Piney Woods and how I hope the improvements will make a positive impact on the low-income population in the area. This led us to discuss the increase in drug trafficking, crime, and deaths. Of course, that segued into Norris Gilbert's murder. Freddie confided to me that Norris had been putting money in Swiss banks. He's not certain where the extra money came from, but he knew Norris was a sleazebag."

Marc leaned forward. "How would a singer know this?"

"Freddie is more than a musician. He's also a golf pro. Not only does he give lessons, but he sometimes plays with members of the country club. Norris was bragging about hiding money from the government and his wife. Freddie suggested other safe ways to hide money, and it led to quite a conversation."

I stood and paced on the deck overlooking the beach. Tree fronds swished in the breeze. "Cheyenne Marther just told us Ivey confronted Norris when a check bounced. Ivey also had their passports the day he was murdered. She claimed they planned to vacation in Bali after their big family vacation."

The door opened, and Belle stepped out. "Dad, we don't have any good food here."

He chuckled. "Do you want to go out to eat? There are lots of food options at the festival. We can go check them out together."

"Awesome. Let me change first." She left us alone.

Lincoln stood. "Trust me, she's more bored than hungry. I need to grab my summer Stetson. When I pull it low and wear sunglasses, not as many people recognize me."

"We can go and let you enjoy the afternoon with Belle, unless you know more." I waited.

"No, that's all I remember. I'll see you around, and Belle is working on a résumé for you."

"Great." After quick hugs, we left and wandered to the festival. Right away we ran into the sheriff. "Hi, Wade."

"Andi Grace. Marc. It's good to see y'all having fun for a change instead of nosing into my murder investigation."

Marc laughed.

"Don't tell me. You're trying to solve the latest Heyward Beach murder." Wade fisted his hands and planted them on his hips.

I shot him the sweetest smile I could muster given his grouchy attitude. "If you're nice, we'll share what we found out."

"I'm listening." He quirked an eyebrow.

"It's going to take a few minutes."

"We were just together last night. How can you have gathered so much information so fast? And for the record, Cheyenne Marther is out of jail."

"Yeah, we've seen her. Do you realize she overheard an argument between Ivey and Norris about money?" When he motioned with his hand for me to continue, I relayed everything I'd learned. "Can you share any information with me? Like were there any fingerprints on the gaudy leash?"

"The killer probably wore gloves because it was clean. There's one more item I'm interested to get your thoughts on, but it needs to stay between the three of us."

"You can trust us." This time my smile was heartfelt.

Wade paused until a group of giggling girls walked past us. "The bloodwork showed Norris had benzodiazepines in his system, but he didn't have a prescription for it. One of the techs found traces of diazepam in the kitchen sink, and it's a benzodiazepine."

Marc placed his hand on my shoulder and nudged me closer to him and Wade. "Are you insinuating Norris was drugged?"

"Yup." The sheriff drew in a deep breath. "The question is why. I'd like to hear who y'all have on your radar."

"Ivey Gilbert is the most obvious. Could she have drugged Norris in the hopes he'd fall asleep driving to Georgia and have a wreck?"

Marc said, "It doesn't explain the leash."

Wade held up a finger. "Unless Ivey needed Norris to be sluggish in order to strangle him. Who else do you think might be the killer?"

"Ivey insists Norris had disgruntled clients, and she accused Lincoln of killing Norris. Of course, I don't believe Lincoln killed him. In addition to some unknown clients from the law firm, there's Rhett Alton. He seems suspicious, and I'm trying to see if there's a connection between Rhett's sister's death at the fertilizer plant and Norris. Then there's Cheyenne Marther. She had trouble getting her insurance settlement from Norris. He told her he gave the money to her ex-husband. If he did wrong by Cheyenne, there are probably other clients he didn't treat fairly."

"I'll try to get a subpoena for his law firm records."

"Hey, Wade. Ethan Seitz overheard Rhett accuse Norris of insurance fraud. I don't understand how because he's not a doctor, but maybe you can make sense of the accusation."

"Sounds like a bunny trail to me, but I'll keep it on the back burner. I almost hate to ask, but do you have more clues?"

I mentioned the Swiss bank accounts, then we parted ways. "Hey, Marc, how would you feel about us going back to my house?"

"I'm down for that. For the investigation, right?" He paused while I nodded. "That's what I figured. I'll look for a link between Norris and the fertilizer company that Rhett mentioned. What are you going to do?"

"I saved the articles on Cheyenne's accident. It feels like the right time to reach out to her ex-husband and see if Norris gave him the insurance money."

Chapter Twenty-one

I HUNG UP AFTER TALKING TO CHEYENNE'S EX-HUSBAND.

"What'd he say?" Marc filled two insulated glasses with ice and poured water into one.

Ugh. "I need something stronger. There should be Cokes in the fridge."

"Coming right up. So, what did he say?"

"His name is Jordan Marther, and Norris did mail him a check. Jordan called the law office to find out why. Norris told him Cheyenne wanted him to have it because she felt guilty for the financial problems her drug abuse caused the family. Also, and this part makes me mad, Norris feared if he gave the money to Cheyenne, she'd blow it on drugs. Jordan was confused but kept the money for the kids."

Marc poured my drink. "It wasn't his place to make such a decision."

I waited for the fizz to settle down. "Cheyenne begged me for a job because she's broke. She needs money for essentials, and she can't afford to visit her family in Greenville. There's no way she asked Norris to send all the money to Jordan."

"There must be an ulterior motive for Norris to give Jordan the settlement."

"Yeah, I'm suspicious about his motive also. Jordan said Norris seemed to be a likeable guy, but he didn't call Cheyenne to go over the situation with her. He believes the less contact he has with his ex-wife the better."

"It's amazing how open he was."

"What can I say? I'm a likeable person." I laughed, then took a drink.

Marc winked. "Yes, you are. I fell for you the first time I saw you standing over a dead body."

"Oh, no, you didn't. In fact, you believed I was the killer." I playfully poked him in the chest.

He took me in his arms and kissed me until I was breathless. "You were so cute trying to convince me you were innocent."

The kiss ended and I pulled my thoughts together. "Speaking of innocent, did you find a link between Norris and Froing Fertilizer Plant?"

"As a matter of fact, there's no obvious connection. Norris wasn't on the board of directors, and he wasn't the CEO, CFO, or COO. It's not a publicly traded company, so there's nothing I can find to link Norris to the fertilizer company."

I sighed and leaned my head against his well-defined chest. "Okay, then I guess it's a waste of time to keep looking at Rhett Alton as a suspect because we can't find a connection. Norris treated Cheyenne poorly, but she doesn't seem strong enough to hurt a flea. You remember she could barely hold Lady the other day?"

"You're right. She was shaking like a leaf." Marc rubbed my back. "It sounds like Ivey moves to the top of your suspect list."

"Yeah, and it's time to give her a call." As good as it felt to be in Marc's embrace, I moved away from his warmth and reached for my drink.

"What will you say?"

The carbonated bubbles tickled my throat and nose. "I'll offer to help her with Lady."

"Okay. How about if I see if Lincoln can introduce me to Freddie Fisher? If we can talk to him about Norris hiding money, we might stumble upon another clue."

"Great idea." I refilled my glass and grabbed my murder journal. To give Marc some peace, I wandered outside with the dogs on each side of me. From my spot on the deck, I could see Marc through the windows in my office. Excitement thrummed through me at the thought of converting the front room to Marc's home office. I couldn't wait to see the expression on his face. I'd also redecorate my bedroom. It was too flowery for him. Together we could pick out a bedspread and maybe a few coastal pictures to hang on the walls. Decorating might not be high on his priority list, but he needed to know this was our home once we married. If he ended up feeling like a visitor, I'd insist we move.

I swiped my phone and dialed Ivey. Once Norris's killer was arrested, I could devote myself completely to working with the animals and preparing to marry Marc.

"Hello, Andi Grace?" Ivey was always polite but never the warmest person.

"Yes. I, uh, how are you holding up?" I sat in a chair by the patio table.

"Better now that Sheriff Stone is going to allow me to return home."

"I know that must be a huge relief. Would you like to leave Lady at Stay and Play? I'd be happy to take care of her for a few days. I can't imagine all the things you need to handle."

"No, I should probably take her home." She sniffed. "Can I call you though if she becomes distraught with a house full of people?"

"Absolutely. You've got my number." If I was going to get a clue on the murder, it was time to ask. "Ivey, have you thought of anyone besides Lincoln Zane who might have wanted to kill your husband?"

"As a matter of fact, yes. Have you considered Freddie Fisher?"

"The lead singer of Heyward Coasters?" The same guy Marc was trying to meet?

"Yes. He gave Norris golf lessons, and they had an ugly dispute. Before you ask, Freddie claimed Norris owed him money. My husband always paid his bills."

I switched to speaker mode and opened the journal to add this information to my notes. "So, Freddie never used Norris as an attorney?"

"Not that I'm aware of, but Norris kept his client list confidential." A door shut in the background. "I need to pick up Lady and head home. There's no telling what mess the deputies left behind, and it'll be easier for my kids not to see crime scene tape in the office."

"Just one more question. Will you still go to Bali after the funeral? I can watch Lady for you." My ears tingled as I waited for her reply.

"I don't truly know what my plans will be, but if Lady needs watching, I'll call you." Ivey hung up.

I sent a quick text message to Dylan and Melanie. *Ivey is coming to pick up Lady. Make sure she pays us. Thanks.*

What had the Gilberts planned to do with their schnoodle when they went to Bali? Would they have taken their little dog because they planned to never return to South Carolina?

Norris was supposed to bring Lady on the big family vacation. Ivey and Norris were going to Bali after their time in Tybee Island. You couldn't just take a dog into a foreign country. There were rules and regulations to be followed. Had they filled out paperwork and been approved? Maybe Norris thought he was above the law in Indonesia too. Had his unscrupulous ways led to his murder? Or was the motive personal?

No matter how much Ivey tried to direct me to people like Freddie and Lincoln, she remained a person of interest to me.

I turned the page and began an updated list of suspects. Ivey for many reasons. Freddie Fisher because Norris owed him money, at least according to Ivey. Cheyenne blamed Norris for sending her to the pain clinic and for giving the insurance money to her ex-husband. Rhett had argued with Norris about insurance fraud and he'd been in the area the morning of the murder. Then there were the unknowns. Norris had tried to talk people into lawsuits, and Ivey claimed he had disgruntled clients. Of all the people on my list, Ivey stood to gain the most from his death. I wouldn't accept the obvious conclusion though. I'd continue to search for clues.

Chapter Twenty-two

LINCOLN STOOD ON THE BEACH IN FRONT OF HIS HOUSE with another man. Despite the heat, Marc and I walked faster to join them.

"Sorry, we're running behind. The crowds slowed us down." Marc slapped Lincoln's shoulder.

"No worries. This is my new friend, Freddie Fisher. He's the lead singer of Heyward Coasters." Lincoln continued the introductions, starting with Marc.

Pelicans flew over in a V formation. A nearby child threw pretzels in the air for seagulls. The birds cawed and swooped to the sand. A crow joined the fight for the food.

Lincoln said, "This is Andi Grace Scott, our local dog walker."

I shook hands with a sturdy man. Curly blonde hair stuck out from his hat with a silhouette of a golfer on the front. "Nice to meet you, Freddie."

"Same. Lincoln says you two have questions for me about Norris Gilbert's murder. We weren't close, but I'll be happy to try to help."

"I'm going to shove off. Belle wants my help on some song lyrics." Lincoln trudged through the sand to the steps of his private boardwalk.

Marc pointed south, away from the activity and noise around us and the pier. "Why don't we walk that way? Fewer distractions and all that."

"Sure. What do you two want to know?" Freddie adjusted his mirrored sunglasses and turned toward the south end of the beach.

I'd already asked Marc to pay close attention to the conversation, because taking notes might prevent Freddie from sharing as much. "Did you and Norris discuss ways to hide money from the government or creditors or anyone who wanted a portion of his earnings?"

Freddie walked between us and scratched his stubbled cheek. "I would never tell somebody not to pay their taxes, but we did discuss ways to invest money. Norris was all about Swiss bank accounts, but personally, I'm not a fan. I assured Norris that cryptocurrency was a better investment strategy. There are risks involved, but if you do your research, it can be profitable."

"How did he respond to your recommendation?" I skirted a wave rushing up the beach from the ocean. The incoming tide forced me to walk closer to Freddie.

"He asked tons of questions. Intelligent questions. I answered them to the best of my ability." He chuckled. "I'm no expert in investment strategies. Music is my jam, and working at the golf club pays the bills."

"Speaking of paying the bills, I heard Norris owed you money." I dodged a crumbling sand castle.

Freddie pulled a golf ball out of his shorts pocket, tossed it in the air, then caught it. He repeated the process a few times. "You probably also know I confronted him. The guy owed me a few thousand dollars. I couldn't afford for him to stiff me. My family depends on my income to survive, and after the funeral, I'll ask Mrs. Gilbert to pay me."

"Good luck with that. She's thinks you may have killed Norris."

"Well, I'll be duffed." His gaze jerked toward Marc. "If she refuses, I may call you to help me begin a lawsuit."

I darted out of the path of another wave. This walk was as challenging as an obstacle course. "What about Ivey accusing you of committing the murder?"

He shrugged and tossed the golf ball again. "I'm innocent, and I trust law enforcement to catch the true killer. Why are you asking me all of these questions?"

Marc laughed. "My future wife can't seem to stop herself from butting into murder investigations."

"Hey, now. I've always had a good reason." I smiled because technically he was right.

Freddie stuck the golf ball into his pocket. "What's a good reason to investigate a crime if you're not a cop?"

"Usually, people ask me to help prove they're innocent." I didn't appreciate Freddie's smart-aleck tone.

"Interesting. Specifically, who is the sheriff questioning this time to lead you to investigate Norris Gilbert's murder?"

"Ike Gage. He's part of our family and walking me down the aisle when I marry Marc." No need to plunge into the dynamics of how Ike fit into our family.

"Most killers have family. Why are you convinced he didn't do it?"

My heart beat faster. Of all the nerve. "Ike is a man of honor, and I believe him. What about you, Freddie? Do you have an alibi for Friday morning?"

The man stopped walking and leaned into my personal space. "I agreed to help you understand Norris better. Don't go accusing me of murder."

Marc wedged himself between Freddie and me. "Hey, man. Cool it. Ivey Gilbert accused you. Not Andi Grace. All you need to do is give us your alibi. Maybe we can prevent Ivey from mentioning your name to Sheriff Stone."

Freddie's nostrils flared. "I was checking in a new shipment of hats at the pro shop."

Marc lifted his hands, palms up. "There you go. Do you have any idea who might have killed Norris?"

"Start with his wife. Norris often booked me to play a round of golf with him. It gave me the opportunity to see him in action and address his weak spots. Mrs. Gilbert sometimes called him. From listening to his side of the conversations, I deduced she's not as nice as y'all believe."

I said, "She was in Georgia Friday morning."

He removed his sunglasses. "Was she really? How do you know for sure? Does she have an eyewitness in Georgia to prove her claim?"

Despite the humidity, chills scrambled up my spine. "No."

"Will you confront her like you did me today? You know what? Forget about it. I need to go." He jogged away from us.

When the sight of Freddie Fisher blurred, I turned to Marc. "What do you think?"

"We need to confirm both alibis. His and Ivey's."

"You're right. Why don't we go to Daily Java and have Erin put together a basket of coffees, teas, and whatever else she has on hand. We can take it to Ivey and figure out a way to prove her alibi."

Marc took my hand in his and we walked toward the crowd. "Is the coffee shop open on Sunday afternoons?"

"Not usually, but I think Erin wants to take advantage of the weekend crowds. I'm sure she'll be there." As we walked, I replayed Freddie's comments in my mind. The man had been rude and condescending. As much as I enjoyed the band, it'd be hard to listen to them with the same enthusiasm after my conversation with the singer.

My next three moves would be to stop by Daily Java, add notes to my journal, and come up with a way to prove Ivey's whereabouts Friday morning. Had she really been in Savannah?

If Ivey was behind her husband's death, had it been a moment of anger? Or was it premeditated? If so, had she planned to strangle him then head to Bali by herself? And what about the drugs in his system? The most confusing part of the plan was the dog. Why had she called me to take care of Lady if her strategy was to skip the country?

Chapter Twenty-three

ERIN TIED A RED RIBBON on the handle of a sweetgrass basket. "You can't buy ground coffee any fresher than this in Heyward Beach. I've also included my homemade pecan-peach biscotti, a variety of teas from one of the farms close to Charleston, chocolate chip cookies, and dark-chocolate-covered espresso beans for a quick pick-me-up."

"It looks perfect." I pulled my credit card out and handed it to Erin. "Did Ivey stop here on the way out of town Friday morning?"

"The last couple of days have been hectic, but I remember her coming in early. She mentioned leaving town and ordered the Labor Day special brew. Extra-large. Why?"

"She told me she was heading to Tybee Island for a family vacation. Did she buy a large quantity of pastries for her family?"

"Sign here." Erin pointed to her new credit card machine. "I think Ivey ordered a fat-free blueberry muffin to go, but that's all."

I added a generous tip and signed my name with the stylus attached to the machine. "I must've gotten confused."

Erin quirked a dark eyebrow. "That seems unlikely, but customers are pulling into the parking lot and I can't ask about what's going on. Thanks for your purchase. Your support means a lot."

"Take care, Erin." I stepped outside and joined Marc at his truck. He'd decided to stay with it so he could keep the air conditioner running. No doubt Rhett Alton wouldn't approve of the extravagance, but the temperature had hit the mid-nineties. At the moment, I didn't care what Rhett thought.

I hopped into the truck and settled the basket on the console. "Erin doesn't remember Ivey ordering a lot of pastries for her family vacation. She said Ivey ordered coffee and a muffin." I opened the pink journal and looked at my notes. "Yeah, it's right here. I understood Ivey to say she picked breakfast treats up here. She purchased other groceries in Savannah. Oh yeah, she also stopped at her favorite deli. If I could figure out what deli it is, that could be a way to prove if she really was in Georgia. Don't you think?"

Marc sighed. "Yeah, but even you will have to be creative to find out the name of the deli. Then you'll need to be more creative to get the employees to confirm if she was there. What's our next step?"

"Let's go see Ivey. We'll take her the basket and try to pump her for information."

Marc pulled out of the parking lot and headed in the direction of Ivey's house. "How do you feel about submarine sandwiches at our wedding reception? Or for the rehearsal dinner?"

"It's not very fancy, but if you want to serve sandwiches to our guests it's okay with me." My fiancé was easygoing and put up with so much from me. There was no way I'd argue over food, no matter how much I preferred something fancier.

Marc glanced at me and laughed. "You should see your face. If we choose to go that route, we can ask Ivey for recommendations."

"Oh, I get where you're going with this. Very smart, Mr. Williams. Very smart."

In less than ten minutes, Marc and I stood in Ivey's kitchen.

She picked up each item in the basket. "Thank you so much. It's very thoughtful of you two."

"We tried to pick a variety to please your family. When do you expect them?"

"My oldest daughter and her family should show up anytime. My son and his family will arrive tomorrow, and my other daughter is more of a free spirit. We'll see her when she's good and ready to deal with her father's death."

"Aren't they all in Tybee Island?" Maybe I'd misunderstood what she'd bought at Daily Java on Friday morning, but I didn't misunderstand when she said the family was all either in or on the way to Tybee Island.

"Of course, but the house was rented for a week. We won't get our deposit back, so it makes sense for them to enjoy it as long as possible." She pulled an electric kettle out of a cabinet and filled it with water. "I can't seem to get warm in here. Thoughts of Norris haunt me. Was he scared? Or did it happen so fast he couldn't react? Had he known his attacker? Or was it a stranger?" She shivered and placed the kettle on its base and pushed the appropriate button.

"Do you think you'll feel more comfortable when your kids arrive?"

"I can only hope." She pulled her red sweater tighter around her thin frame.

"Where's Lady?"

Ivey pointed toward the office. The door was closed, and no light shone underneath. "She's resting in Norris's office. Poor thing doesn't understand he's not coming back. She adored him, and he loved her."

"Oh, I'm so sorry." Dogs were usually a good judge of character. Had Norris fooled Ivey, or was he a different person at home?

Marc said, "How can we help you, Ivey?"

I jumped in before Ivey could answer. "Have you unloaded your car? I bet you have water bottles, probably food, and beach gear. We can help you bring everything inside."

"I have a cooler of food in my Lexus. Marc, would you mind carrying it up? Or you can wheel it into the elevator. I just don't feel like I have the strength to deal with it."

He nodded. "I'll be right back. Is the car unlocked?"

Ivey removed a key ring from the pocket of her black linen slacks. "Mine is the bigger key fob, and I drive the Lexus SUV, not the sedan."

Marc left us standing in the kitchen. Neither of us had been able to ask the name of the deli, but I'd find a way to get the information. I said, "Ivey, why don't you sit down and rest? I can prepare your tea."

She pushed a strand of silver hair behind her ear. "It's best for me to keep moving."

At the B and B, she'd been lethargic, staring into space in the piano room. Maybe being back in the house where Norris was murdered was truly freaking her out. "Hey, there's no shame in going back to stay with Juliet. I'm sure she hasn't booked your room to anyone else this soon."

The kettle clicked, and Ivey pulled out a mug and reached for a box of tea we'd brought her. "If the family wasn't coming here, I'd go back. I'll probably put this place up for sale soon."

Marc returned with a large cooler and set it beside the refrigerator. "Andi Grace, why don't you unload it for Ivey? I'll bring in her luggage."

"Okay." I opened the lid. There were packages of deli meats, cheeses, a jar of dill pickles, and a container of chicken salad. "Oh, my. Looking at all this good food is making me hungry."

Ivey opened the refrigerator. "Juliet kept all the perishables in an extra refrigerator for me while I was at her place. It should be good if you want to eat something."

"No, this food came from your favorite deli, and it should be shared with your family. Thanks though." I placed everything but the pickles in the meat drawer. They went on the top shelf. The container of chicken salad told me the food came from Molly's Deli. Great, now there'd be no awkward questions to achieve the name. "Too bad we don't have a good deli in Heyward Beach."

"It's an insignificant price to pay for small-town living." She bobbed the tea bag up and down in her mug of hot water.

"You're right. I wouldn't trade living at the beach for anything." It was always so hard to read Ivey. Had she insulted me? Probably, if her tone was any indication.

Marc returned. "Where would you like your suitcases?"

"I'll show you." Ivey led Marc away.

I took the cooler to the back deck and dumped the ice over the rail. It hit the sand dune with a soft thud. A gentle breeze kissed my face. There were very few people on the beach. It was one of the perks of living in a gated community.

On the day of Norris's murder, Rhett had been seen driving on the street by Ethan. The killer could've approached the house from the sand though. There were no restrictions on walking the beach even though a guard had to let you enter on the street.

I turned my attention from the beach to the house. Four security cameras were attached to the structure on this side. One on each corner, one in the middle of the house, and the last camera over the door leading inside. My heart leapt. Had the sheriff or his deputies looked at the recordings? If this area had four devices, there had to be more.

Marc joined me on the deck. "Are you ready to go?"

"Almost. We need to ask Ivey about her security system. There's bound to be a clue to lead us to the killer."

His eyebrow quirked up. "Us?"

"Wade and the deputies." I elbowed him. "You knew what I meant."

He chuckled. "I know exactly what you meant. Come on. Let's get this over with."

We entered the quiet house.

Ivey sat on the couch, holding her tea. A blue crocheted blanket covered her lap.

I sat beside her. "I noticed all the security cameras when I poured the ice out of the cooler. Has the sheriff reviewed the recordings?"

"No." She stared at her cup.

"Why not? It seems like it'd provide the best clues."

Marc sat in the leather recliner on the other side of Ivey. He was positioned so I could see him, but Ivey would have to turn her body. It seemed like an awkward seating arrangement, but at the moment it worked for me. With subtle motions, Marc pointed out two little white motion sensors.

Ivey closed her eyes. "We didn't want any interruptions to our vacation.

With my phone app, I disarmed the system on my way out of town. If only I'd kept it activated, Norris might still be alive." Her shoulders shook with silent sobs.

I took the cup from her hands and placed it on the coffee table. "I'm so sorry, Ivey." I wrapped my arms around her and patted her back. "Ivey, if you turned the security system off, how'd you know there was movement in the house?"

"Simple. When Norris didn't answer his phone, I reactivated the system."

Marc stood. "I'll meet you at the truck. Take all the time you need."

I nodded and remained with Ivey.

After a few minutes she pulled away and hurried to the bathroom. Water ran, and I imagined she might be splashing cold water on her face. When she finally returned, there was no sign of smudged makeup, and her skin wasn't red and blotchy. If she'd been crying, it wasn't obvious. Had she faked it? If so, why?

"Andi Grace, don't worry about me. My kids will arrive soon, and Lady is the only issue I might need help with. I'll let you know."

"Okay. Take care." I left her standing at the front door. The question of the delicatessen had been answered. Molly's. Too bad there were so many more questions. Who turns off their security system for vacation? Was there really a family trip planned? It didn't seem like Ivey could've fooled Norris, so was he in on the lie? Why? Was there a link between the murder and the bogus vacation? And how would I begin unlocking all these potential clues?

Chapter Twenty-four

MARC AND I WALKED SUNNY AND CHUBB along the island streets, but we avoided the crowds. I waited as my German shepherd sniffed around the Sullivan Way street sign. "I've shared my concerns about the murder. What did you notice in Ivey's house?"

"For starters, there were no photos of Ivey and Norris but plenty of framed pictures of the kids and grandkids. Just like everything else, it doesn't make much sense."

"Although you could argue they see each other all the time and don't need pictures."

"I guess."

Sunny finished her business, and we crossed the street.

"Heal." Chubb tried to pull on his leash, but Marc remained firm. "I really need to take him for a run to burn off his energy."

"Sunny used to be like that, but old age is creeping up on her. Not that she's old yet, but she's slowing down." I patted her side then glanced at Marc. "Do you want to go for a run on the beach?"

He shook his head. "No. All the people will be a huge distraction for Chubb. I probably should take him home soon, and we can run on one of the paths by the river."

I didn't want Marc to leave, but it made sense. "I can't wait until we're married."

"It's not too late to elope." He waggled his eyebrows.

"Oh, boy, don't tempt me. If it wasn't for fear of hurting Nate and Juliet, I might take you up on your offer." I paused. "Do you think Norris and Ivey had a romantic trip planned? Maybe renew their wedding vows or something?"

"Not a chance. Ivey told you they were going to Bali. My gut tells me they planned to leave for financial reasons."

"Ivey said they'd been in counseling and the marriage seemed better. But you're probably right. France would be romantic." We stopped for a car backing out of a driveway.

"I promise to take you to France one day. In fact, it might not be too late to change our honeymoon trip to Maine." We stepped to the side and allowed a young couple pushing a stroller to go past us.

"Don't change a thing. We're going to have a great honeymoon."

Marc leaned down and kissed me.

Chubb barked, and Marc pulled away. "Quiet, boy."

We continued our walk. "Back to Bali. You said Ivey mentioned a disgruntled client. Freddie said Norris owed him money. Rhett was seen arguing with Norris. I want to ask around and see if there was a pending lawsuit, or even liens, against Norris or his firm."

"I didn't know you could place a lien on a person."

He shook his head. "I misspoke. The lien would be a judgment against Norris's property or other assets."

"I see." What I really saw was how smart Marc was.

"It's possible someone was suing Ivey."

"Why?"

He shrugged. "Real estate agents can be sued for breach of duty, not disclosing a defect, trying to give legal advice, failing to recommend inspections, releasing a client's information, or even a trip and fall during a home tour. Those possibilities are just off the top of my head. I'll swing by the office tomorrow morning and check it out."

"But tomorrow's a holiday." I shouldn't be disappointed. It was my murder investigation tempting him to go into work.

"Let me put it this way. I'll sneak in and not get distracted with my own cases. How about we meet for lunch?"

"I should be through walking the dogs on my schedule by then. There are fewer appointments because of the long weekend." We turned onto Dolphin Drive and walked to my house.

Waves crashed in the distance, and the sound reached us. "I heard there's a tropical storm heading for the Bahamas."

"Yeah, but the weather authorities have so many possible models of the path it's unclear whether we'll get hit or not."

"I vote for not, but if it comes our way, at least it'll be after the festival." I hadn't dealt with a hurricane since living in my current house. "If it does aim for Heyward Beach, I'll need to learn how to work the hurricane shutters. In my old home, we always hung plywood over the windows." I'd lived my entire life on the coast of South Carolina, and I had a healthy respect for the dangers a hurricane could bring.

"Shh, it's going to be okay. If it comes our way, I can help with the shutters and anything else we need to do to protect the house. I assume you'll ride out the storm at Kennady Bed and Breakfast."

"You bet. Even if it's not a Category Five, the island will probably flood."

We reached my driveway, and Marc walked me to the front door. "I'll head home now unless you need anything." Sunny plopped down at my feet.

"We'll be good." I hugged him. "I love you."

"I love you, too." He kissed me until Chubb barked. "Guess that's my signal. See you tomorrow. I'll bring lunch."

After Marc drove away, I went inside and armed my security system. Most nights I felt safe, but Cheyenne had already caused one scene at night, and there was a killer on the loose. It only made sense to use the system.

Sunny lapped up her water, and I refilled the bowl.

Once I got comfortable on the couch, I opened my murder journal and added all the notes from my day, then reviewed the clues I'd recorded.

Diazepam. Wade had confided in me. Norris didn't have a prescription for a benzodiazepine. It made sense Wade would've checked Ivey's medication history too.

How had the medicine gotten in his system? If the killer drugged Norris with diazepam, how long had it taken for him to be so relaxed that he couldn't fight off the killer? Did the culprit sneak inside and drug Norris's drink then wait until he passed out before strangling him? Or had Ivey drugged him, pretended to leave, then returned to kill her husband?

My pulse leapt. What if Ivey drugged her husband and thought it was enough to kill him? She was a small woman, and it was possible she'd miscalculated how much diazepam it'd take to murder Norris. Suppose she expected him to die, so she went home. He was still alive. Ivey panicked and resorted to another method of murdering Norris. Yes. This scenario made the most sense. The thing bothering me all along was the fact it appeared two modes of murder were used.

There was still the possibility Cheyenne was guilty. She'd been furious with Norris. It was possible she'd stopped by the house Friday morning. Maybe she intended to reason with him. She'd arrived prepared, and she was no stranger to drugs. When the conversation didn't go her way, it was possible she slipped the medicine into Norris's drink so he'd be loopy enough for her to strangle him. This same scenario could've been applied by Freddie, Rhett, or anyone else with a bone to pick.

There was still the question of how a killer knew what Norris would drink on Friday morning. Also, how had the culprit gotten the diazepam into the drink without Norris noticing?

Ivey Gilbert remained my most solid person of interest. In my opinion, Cheyenne Marther's motive would be anger because Norris gave her ex-husband the insurance money from the car hitting her. Ike Gage and Lincoln

Zane were innocent. Freddie Fisher was rude and on my updated list. Ivey had given me his name, and she'd mentioned a disgruntled divorce client. Too bad I didn't have that person's name.

I headed to the office and grabbed my laptop. Sunny lay on the cool kitchen floor. I skirted around her and returned to my comfy couch.

Freddie Fisher was the first person I looked for on the internet. A picture of a broad-shouldered man with curly blonde hair appeared. The man was all over social media with his band. His career as a golf pro was nowhere near as visible. For ten bucks, I performed a more thorough search. The man wasn't on a government watch list. Good to know. Neither was he a sex offender. As far as the law was concerned, Freddie had multiple speeding tickets but nothing else. The report I paid for revealed Freddie didn't have much money. If the statement was true, the bank owned his home and his vehicle. Not unusual.

A college website had a little article saying Freddie and another band member, Tucker Wilder, had been in a fistfight. According to the article, it was over a girl. The issue resolved itself, and no charges were pressed. Interesting, but it didn't relate to Norris.

So far, I hadn't exposed anything juicy, or at least worthy of a motive beside money. The alleged fight made me believe Freddie was the kind of person to lose control in the heat of the moment. Norris had been drugged and strangled with a pink dog leash. Slipping Norris the diazepam would have taken planning and effort. The murder had taken place in the morning, so there probably hadn't been time for the men to play a round of golf. What about a lesson?

Freddie claimed he'd been checking in a shipment of hats at the pro shop at the time of the murder. It didn't mean there wasn't a lesson earlier in the morning. How fast did diazepam go into effect? If they'd been together at the golf course, or driving range, and Freddie had spiked whatever Norris had been drinking, would he have been able to drive home?

I looked for the answer on a medical website. Fifteen to sixty minutes before the drug took effect, if taken orally. I added the information to my notes. During my time working at the vet clinic, I'd learned not all drugs can be crushed and achieve the desired outcome.

If that was how the last day of Norris Gilbert's life played out, had he been able to resist Freddie when it came time to strangle him?

It still didn't make sense to me. The country club was in the country. How did he not crash on the way to the island?

I found Ethan Seitz in my contacts and called him.

"Hi, Ethan. It's Andi Grace Scott. I'm sorry to bother you but I have a quick question."

"Okay, shoot."

"If a person was drugged with diazepam at the country club, would they be able to safely drive home?"

There was a long pause. "Are you insinuating Norris Gilbert was drugged? I heard he was strangled."

Uh-oh. "I can't tell you anything definite." There was a bark in the background, and I could picture Yoyo trying to get Ethan's attention.

"Sit. Good boy." Ethan cleared his throat. "Andi Grace, the answer depends on how much of the drug was in his system. You need to take into account when the diazepam was administered and what time Norris, or whoever, drove away. The driver's reflexes would be delayed, and the drive could end up being deadly."

I scribbled Ethan's response on a clean sheet. "Okay."

"If we're discussing Norris, I don't believe he could've been drugged at the country club and driven home safely. Of course, I don't have all the details. It's possible there was only enough diazepam in his system to take the edge off. You know what I mean?"

"I'm still not admitting anything. Hypothetically, how big of a dose would be needed to show up in his system?"

"I'm not comfortable answering your question." He paused.

"Okay, but is diazepam water-soluble? Or can you bake it in brownies like pot?"

"No, it's not water-soluble." Ethan sighed. "Andi Grace, it might not be safe for you to investigate Norris Gilbert's murder."

My blood pressure rose. I understood the danger better than anyone of being an amateur sleuth. More than once, I'd put my life in danger. I took a deep breath. Ethan was only being nice and watching out for me. "Hey, Ethan, can we keep this conversation between ourselves? I don't want to make the sheriff mad."

"I won't mention it to anyone, but I also won't lie for you."

"I'd never ask you to lie, and I promise to be careful. Lacey Jane's biological father is one of the persons of interest in the murder. You probably know she's pregnant, and she begged me to help prove Ike is innocent. There was no way I could say no."

"Just be careful."

"Thanks, Ethan. I'll talk to you later." After we hung up, I studied my notes. If Freddie was the killer, he probably hadn't administered the diazepam at the golf course.

Chapter Twenty-five

MONDAY MORNING. Labor Day. I walked Chloe and Heinz, my favorite Westies, in their neighborhood. They were sister and brother and belonged to two families who were best friends. The owners were spending the day on the Waccamaw River and had asked me to check on the dogs.

After the Westies were settled back at their homes, I headed to take care of Captain and Pumpkin for Phyllis Mays. The rambunctious shepherds greeted me at the front door.

"Well, hello there. How are you two today?" I rubbed on Pumpkin, the German shepherd first. Captain, the Australian shepherd mix barked. "I haven't forgotten you." I loved on him too.

"Hello, Andi Grace? Is that you?" Phyllis called out from one of the bedrooms.

I jumped back from the dogs. "Yes. I'm sorry for barging in. I thought you and Pastor Mays had left town."

Phyllis appeared wearing dark blue jeans, a flowing sleeveless white top, and a red scarf at her neck. She was struggling to secure a tennis bracelet around her wrist. "We were supposed to leave for Charleston, but Ivey Gilbert called us late last night. Can you fasten this for me?"

"Absolutely." I took the jewelry from her. Tiny little diamonds sparkled in the sunlight. "It's beautiful."

"They aren't real, but it is a stunning piece."

I clasped the two ends together. "There you go. Do you still want me to walk the dogs?"

She nodded. "Oh, yes. I don't want to start sweating before necessary. We'll probably need you to come back this afternoon too. Is that okay?"

"Sure. I'll get their leashes and head on out."

"Are you looking for a murder suspect in Norris's death?" Her gaze pinned me.

I stopped moving. "Why? Do you know something?"

"Ivey has been a dear friend for years." She motioned for me to have a seat on one of the bar stools at the kitchen counter.

The dogs circled me, and I motioned with my hand. "Sit."

Pumpkin whined, but both dogs obeyed. The previous week they'd spent at Stay and Play had been beneficial.

"Good job." I gave each one a treat from my pocket.

"You're marvelous with them. I promise one day we'll sign up for obedience lessons. Dylan admitted he worked with them at the farm, and I can tell it made a positive difference." Phyllis took a seat, and I joined her. "Like I started to say, Norris was a pathetic husband for years. It amazes me he never landed in prison, because he'd been part of some underhanded deals. But once they began marriage counseling, Norris became a better spouse. The funny thing is, Ivey became secretive. It was almost as if she turned to the dark side like her husband. Pity."

"Dark side?" Phyllis had a gambling problem, and it was one reason her husband had gifted her with the dogs. His plan was for her to be too busy to gamble. Little did he predict how often she'd hire me to help with the dogs.

"I'm sure you've heard rumors about the mob and the pill mill. Ivey handled the real estate deal. In fact, Norris introduced her to the director of Low Country Pain Clinic. Ivey also met Dr. Rich, the clinic's physician." The pastor's wife folded her hands together. "I met Dr. Stephanie Rich at a funeral once. She was very pleasant and not the monster I'd imagined. It's a shame she committed suicide."

I'd think harder about Dr. Rich later. "Tell me more about Ivey's dark side."

"She became irritable and snappy. If we had a meeting and she got a call, she always excused herself to take it. In the old days, she'd ignore a call until we concluded our get-together. In June, our book club was at my house, discussing the latest cozy mystery by our favorite author. Ivey had suggested the book, but she got a phone call. She stepped out to the back patio and stayed outside so long that I took her a glass of water. I heard her mention Dr. Rich."

"Could it have been an innocent conversation? Maybe she was helping Dr. Rich find a house in Heyward Beach."

"No, the doctor had a place in a nice subdivision near the river. I'm not certain if—"

The front door opened and Larry walked in. The dogs barked, and he let them into the fenced-in backyard. "I take it they haven't walked yet."

I laughed. "We're about to start. I hope you two have a nice day."

Phyllis said, "Did you discuss funeral details with Ivey?"

Larry shook his head. "They plan to cremate the body and sprinkle the ashes in the ocean. No funeral and no memorial service of any kind."

I gasped. "Really? Have all of the children arrived?"

"Yes, and they presented a united front. I offered for the church members to bring them food, but they turned me down flatter than a flitter."

Phyllis reached for her phone. "That's utter nonsense. We need to support the family during this time."

With a gentle touch, Larry took the phone out of her hand. "Honey, the best way you can support Ivey is to honor her wishes."

Phyllis's shoulders slumped. "If that's what you believe is best, I'll agree."

The tense atmosphere between the couple led me to find the leashes. "I'm going to walk the dogs, and I have your house key if you leave before we get back."

In unison they thanked me, and I joined the dogs in the backyard. While we walked through the neighborhood, I replayed the conversation with Phyllis in my mind. I couldn't think of a suspicious reason for Ivey to talk to Dr. Rich, or talk about her. It could be something as simple as a question about the building where the clinic was located.

My focus needed to remain on Norris Gilbert's murder. Dr. Rich was gone, and if she had family, my heart broke for them. However, Norris had been murdered Friday morning. I didn't see how there could be a connection between the doctor's suicide and Norris's homicide. I'd keep my eyes on Heyward Beach's latest murder.

Chapter Twenty-six

ON THE WAY HOME from taking care of Captain and Pumpkin, my ringtone sounded. I pushed the button on my steering wheel to answer.

"Hey, it's Wade. Can you walk Duke this afternoon?"

"I'd love to." The mutt was a little bit beagle, a little bit collie, and a little bit of a mystery. "I'm sure you're up to your eyeballs working the murder case. Have you questioned Freddie Fisher, the local golf pro and the lead singer of Heyward Coasters?"

"I know who he is, but why question him?" Irritation laced his tone.

"Norris died owing Freddie money. He claims to have been checking in a shipment of golf hats the morning of the murder."

Wade growled. "Andi Grace, I can't save your hide every time you cross a killer."

Un, deux, trois. I better talk fast to the sheriff while I had the opportunity. "People just tell me this stuff. I happened to see Pastor Mays this morning. Before you ask, I was scheduled to walk his dogs. He and Phyllis were delayed leaving town by a call from Ivey this morning. The Gilbert family plan to cremate Norris and spread his ashes over the ocean. I'm not convinced the family had all converged on Tybee Island for a vacation. It sounded like they were coming here from different places. So why pretend to go on vacation?"

"Take a breath, Andi Grace. I'll look into your concerns, but I have other clues to track down first."

"Okay." His response was better than nothing. "I'll take care of Duke this afternoon. Anything else?"

"Stay out of trouble, if that's possible."

"Ha, ha. Very funny. Bye." I pushed the button to end the call. My conscience was clear. I'd updated Wade on what I knew.

Too bad I felt stuck. If I leafed through my journal much more, I'd wear out the pages. Two families stepped onto the painted crosswalk, and I stopped my vehicle. Maybe if I went to the festival I'd find another clue. One could only hope.

• • •

The first people I crossed paths with at the pier were Cheyenne, Leroy, and Griffin. Interesting trio. "Hi, y'all. What's up?" I hugged the men and shook hands with Cheyenne.

Leroy said, "We ran across this young fellow. There's a rumor floating around that he may take over management of Piney Woods. If it works out, he and I will be next-door neighbors. Best of all, he's agreed to keep us a pet-friendly community."

Griffin smiled. "Let's not get ahead of ourselves. There are a couple hurdles needing to be jumped."

"I'm just a gonna pray you're hired, then there'll be all kinds of improvements at the complex."

Cheyenne's eyes widened. "You'd pray about him getting the job?"

Leroy tilted his head and studied the young woman. "Let's take a seat in the shade and I'll explain what I'm talking about." The two of them left Griffin and me standing alone near a booth of paintings.

"This isn't the first time Leroy has looked out for a stray. So you'll allow him to keep Peanut?"

"Yep. I met the beagle, and he's a cutie."

"Don't forget when you're settled, I'll help you find the right dog."

"I regret there's not enough time these days to take proper care of a dog."

"How about a cat?" I didn't have one in mind, but the shelters closer to Charleston probably had plenty needing to be adopted.

"Why don't we discuss the office project at your place? I went over my list of supplies, and I'm good to get started tomorrow."

"So soon?" My spirits lifted.

"Yeah. It'll give me something to do while Lincoln handles the paperwork for Piney Woods."

"Awesome. How early will you come over?"

"Six o'clock."

My heart dropped to my feet. "That's pretty early."

"True, but there'll be fewer people around to watch me unload supplies. You don't want a nosey neighbor to spill the beans to Marc."

"You're right. I'll let you inside, then Sunny and I will get out of your way." I pointed to a food truck down the way. "I need something to drink. Come on. My treat."

We walked the short distance and each ordered homemade lemonade with mint. I took a drink and my mouth puckered. "They didn't short us on tartness."

"You're scaring me." He took a sip. "Woo-wee. I might havta let the ice melt some before I drink any more."

I laughed. "Good idea. I know you've worked all sorts of places from here to Charleston and all the way up to Wilmington. Have you ever done business with Ivey Gilbert?"

We walked along the makeshift row of vendors. A breeze drifted over us and blew up some of the tablecloths on display tables.

Griffin said, "I placed a bid on the LC Pain Clinic building a few years ago. The job went to a company from Jersey. I still don't understand how they could've underbid me. I kept the costs as low as possible so I'd be able to hang around Heyward Beach."

"They would've needed to bring a crew and house them and ship in some of the equipment. You're right. It doesn't make any sense." I stopped walking and looked toward the Atlantic. "Unless—"

"Unless what?"

I leaned close and lowered my voice. "Have you heard any rumors that the mob backed the clinic?"

"Shh. If that's true, you don't want to say something to the wrong people." He slurped down his drink then tossed the cup into the nearest recycle container. "I'm serious, Andi Grace. You can't go all over town making accusations like that."

"I trust you. Did you have any uneasy feelings about the building?"

"Nope. I went inside, checked the electricity, the foundation, the water, well, you get the picture. I assessed the damages and problem areas and drew up an estimate within twenty-four hours. Your brother has run into problems with landscaping bids. It's part of doing business. You win some and lose some."

"Who did you give the estimate to?"

"Ivey Gilbert."

"Have you noticed any changes in her personality?"

"Look, Andi Grace, I barely know the woman." He led me to the walkway leading to the beach.

I swigged more of the lemonade, then tossed the ice into the sand. Once we left the crowds, Griffin faced me. "I don't know anything about the mob or if the Gilberts were involved in underhanded dealings. I keep my head down and work hard, but my head would have to be buried in this sand not to know Norris Gilbert was up to no good. Will it do any good to ask you to ignore your curiosity?"

I tossed my cup into another recyclable container then met Griffin's gaze. "Lacey Jane asked me to look into the murder, and I gave her my word."

"There's one piece of gossip going around town, and maybe it'll wake you up to the possible dangers swirling around Norris and his murder."

My heart may have flipped in my chest. "What did you hear?"

"The doctor at the clinic may not have committed suicide. Her death could've been murder too."

How had I not known this? Had I been too busy focused on the wedding, my business, and my family? Wait, could you ever really be too focused on friends and family? No.

My sister's request had plunged me into solving another murder. I'd give it my attention, but after this, I needed to quit solving murders.

Norris had been drugged with diazepam. Had the killer meant for it to appear to be another suicide? If so, something must have gone terribly wrong. Why else would the killer resort to strangling Norris?

Chapter Twenty-seven

MARC ARRIVED AT MY HOUSE with Italian sandwiches from Tony's. Before he opened the paper bag, his gaze seared mine. "I saw you at the beach talking to Griffin."

"Yeah, I bumped into him at the festival." Marc didn't look jealous, but his expression reminded me of a hurt little boy. His face drooped, and his eyes lacked spark.

"Why were you two talking on the beach?" He stuffed his hands into his pockets, looking even more like a child afraid of getting scolded.

I longed to wipe the wrinkles off his forehead. He'd been abandoned as a little boy when both parents died. He'd only formed an attachment with one foster family. It was where he'd learned to build boats. When the father had a heart attack, Marc was shuffled to another family. I understood he had abandonment issues, and I never wanted to hurt him. "Griffin wanted to tell me something about Norris, and he didn't want our conversation to be overheard. He's worried I'm in over my head."

"Honestly, I'm concerned too." His tone was even and calm. "What did Griffin tell you?"

"I was shocked to hear there's a rumor going around that Dr. Rich may *not* have committed suicide. Did you know that was a possibility?"

"Honey, if I'd known, I would've mentioned it. After lunch, why don't we see what we can learn about her death?" He opened the bag of food, and I poured drinks.

"Let's eat inside today, I got hot walking the dogs and hanging out at the festival. Wait until you hear what else I discovered." I sat at the end of the table, and Marc sat to my right. "Ivey isn't having a memorial service or anything for Norris." I updated him on the news I gathered during my morning. "What did you learn?"

"There have been quite a few people who tried to sue Norris, but the lawsuits were always settled out of court."

"That seems unusual." I bit into my tuna sandwich loaded with pickles, lettuce and tomato. "Does that mean we don't know how much money was involved?"

"In these specific cases, yes." His voice was flat. "I can just picture Norris acting contrite or even being a bully in order to convince the people their lives would be easier if they settled out of court."

"Do you remember when he intimidated me a long time ago?" It had involved another murder investigation.

"Yep." He stared at his roast beef sandwich.

Something was wrong. I reached for Marc's arm and wrapped my fingers around it. "Hey, what's going on with you today?"

"Nothing." One side of his mouth slid up but slipped right back down, as if a smile was too much effort.

"I don't believe you. Is there something about this case that's bothering you?"

"Not exactly, but we both could've been killed when you looked into Dirk Cutter's death." He placed his sandwich on the wax paper and met my gaze. "Do you believe we're going into this marriage on equal footing?"

"Of course." My heart thundered like a herd of scared horses. If anything, I was still surprised Marc had fallen in love with me. He was so smart, handsome, kind, and funny, and how'd I get lucky enough for him to fall in love with me? "Why?"

"I'm not sure how to say this."

Uh-oh. "You're not dumping me, are you?"

His eyes widened. "No, but are you having second thoughts?"

"Never." I squeezed his arm. "Please, tell me what's wrong."

"Here goes. You don't need to ask my permission to grow your business or spend time with your family. But it would be nice if you'd consult me once in a while."

"I thought I was doing a good job including you in our wedding plans."

"That's not what I mean." He placed his other hand over mine. "I may sound like a jerk, but it would've been nice if you'd asked my opinion before agreeing to investigate another murder. I also realize it was your sister who begged for help. But we're about to get married, Andi Grace. It just seems to me like we should consult with each other before putting our lives at risk."

My nose tingled. "Oh, Marc. I'm so sorry. You're right, and you've been great at helping me every step of the way on this case. I guess there were so many years when I made family decisions and helped my siblings without consulting anyone else. You're going to be my family—"

"Hold up. Nate and Lacey Jane will always be your family. It's honorable how much you love them and put their needs ahead of your own. I'm not asking you to turn your back on your siblings, but it'd be nice to be included in the decision-making process."

"Of course. I thought I was doing better." This conversation proved I'd slipped into old patterns of behavior. "My dream is for us to be partners in life. I love you so much, and I want to be a good wife to you. Just say the word and I'll tell Lacey Jane she needs to trust the authorities to prove Ike is innocent."

He shook his head. "We've come this far. May as well move forward with your investigation."

I freed my hand and leaned forward to kiss him. "I love you, Marc Williams."

His hands went behind my head, and our lips met. Lunch and murders were forgotten. I loved this amazing man, and I refused to cause him anguish by my actions. No murder investigation would trump Marc.

Chapter Twenty-eight

MARC LOOKED UP FROM HIS LAPTOP. "According to this article, Dr. Stephanie A. Rich lived in Blueburg, South Carolina. I don't know any law enforcement personnel there."

"Me, either. I guess she commuted to work." I reached for my journal and added the information.

"It'd be less than an hour to drive here, so it's doable." He rubbed his chin. "It takes me over thirty minutes to drive to work, and I don't mind. Once you get used to the distance, it's not a big deal."

"Hey, that's a perk to us living here. You can even walk to work."

One side of Marc's mouth shot up in a half smile. "Yeah, it's a perk but not the primary reason for us to live in your house after we get married."

I met his gaze. "It's going to be your home too. If you're not comfortable here, we'll move."

"It's your dream house. We're not going to live anywhere else."

"I love you more than any house. As long as we're together, I don't care where we live."

His eyebrows lowered. "I appreciate that, but there's no need to worry. When I was in foster care I moved a lot. It's no big deal."

His words convinced me to work harder to make this house feel like home to him. "Are you sure you don't want me to ask Ivey to look for a different house?"

"The only conversation we need to have about Ivey is in regards to her husband's murder. What do you think?"

"All right." In the days ahead, I'd keep my eyes open to how Marc settled in and bring the topic up again if needed. "She sells real estate in our area, but Blueburg is the next county over. All of her listings seem to be around Heyward Beach."

Marc nodded. "Go on."

"Ivey had cancer a while back, but I never heard about her dealing with pain problems. To our knowledge, Dr. Rich wasn't involved with ownership of the clinic. So, what was the connection between Ivey and Dr. Rich? Old friends? Relatives?"

"Have you looked at Ivey's social media?"

"Yes. She mostly posts pictures of properties for sale. There are a few pictures of Ivey and Norris at social functions with our local movers and shakers." I swiped my phone. "There's one other thing I can try."

Marc twirled a pen between his fingers. "We don't know much about Dr. Rich. It's possible her middle name is a family name, like Andrews. I'll see what else there is on the pill doc."

Minutes ticked by. Sunny snoozed in a sunbeam in my home office. I scrolled through images on the internet.

Marc whistled. "I'll give you fifty bucks if you can guess what the *A* stands for."

"That's a lot of pressure." I laughed. "It's surely not Andi, like me. It could be Allison. Allie for short."

"Take another guess."

"Ariana? Ariel? Alina? Alexa?" He shook his head at every one of my guesses. "It could be her maiden name. Albright? Abbot? Atkins? Austin? Andrews?"

"Nope. Give up?"

"Yeah, I'm never going to get it." I leaned forward. Sunny's snores filtered through my office. "Tell me what her middle name was."

"Alton, as in Stephanie Alton Rich." Marc gave me the first genuine smile I'd seen from him all day.

"Alton, like Rhett Alton?"

Marc's eyes sparkled. "Exactamundo."

I stood and paced. "Now the question to ponder is are they related?"

"Or is it a coincidence?" Marc turned his attention to the laptop.

"Ethan overheard Norris arguing with Rhett. Suppose Dr. Rich's death was a suicide. Why would Rhett be mad at Norris?"

"Norris brought the clinic to town. Let's suppose the pressure from the government to shut it down led to her suicide. There's no reason to believe she was murdered."

"Unless she agreed to testify for the government against the mob."

"Honey, now you're thinking about two rumors. The mob." He held up one finger, then another finger. "And that Dr. Rich was murdered. We need to keep our focus on Norris's death."

"You're right. Norris was slain, and I want to prove Ike is innocent." I smiled at my fiancé. "We should talk to Rhett. Face-to-face. It'd be good to watch his reaction to our discovery."

"Again, we don't know if there is a connection for certain."

"I hear ya, but it still seems like we should ask him."

"Okay, fine. We'll try to find Rhett and question him." His tone was grumbly.

"Why don't we take Sunny with us? After we talk to Rhett, we can go to your place."

"It's a disaster with all the packing."

"Then I'll help you pack." I wrapped my arms around his neck and stretched to kiss my handsome fiancé.

His lips met mine, and thoughts of murder and mayhem disappeared.

At last Marc pulled back. "Instead of packing, maybe we should do more kissing."

"I like the way you think." I smiled, then reality slapped me upside the head. "Oh, man, I need to make a quick stop to walk Captain and Pumpkin. Wait, I also need to take care of Duke."

"It sounds like a normal day in the life of Andi Grace Scott. Why don't I go with you to find Rhett, then we can head our separate ways for the afternoon?"

I didn't like him using the word *separate*, and Marc still seemed a little off. "Are you sure we're okay?"

"It's all good." He gave me a quick kiss. "Let's go find Rhett Alton."

We each took our own vehicle and found Rhett in a parking space by his condo. He was struggling with a stack of white poster boards attached to wooden sticks. The man looked like he wanted to disappear when he saw us approach. He stuffed the signs into the back of the car and slammed the door.

I parked my Highlander behind his Mini Cooper and hopped out. "Hey, Rhett. I thought you were going to take it easy after your heat episode."

"I feel better."

Marc joined us. "Hey, man. You should be inside resting."

Rhett crossed his arms. The man was closer to my height than Marc's, but it was obvious he worked at more than lifting protest signs. "Is it safe to assume you two are not just here to check on my health?"

Marc pointed to a crepe myrtle. "If you refuse to invite us inside your place, let's at least have our discussion in the shade."

My attention shifted from Rhett to Marc. The sharp tone of his voice showed me how out of sorts he was.

Rhett moved to the shade. "What do you need to say?"

Marc spoke first. "Were you related to Dr. Stephanie Alton Rich?"

Rhett's head jerked back. "I assume you already know the answer. She was my aunt."

The environmentalist sure did a lot of assuming. "Did you argue with

Norris Gilbert over your aunt's death?"

"You may have saved me a trip to the ER, but I don't owe you an answer. If you'll excuse me, I'm heading inside. Alone." He stomped off as well as anyone could wearing flip-flops.

Marc walked me to my Highlander and opened the door. "I'll call you later."

I kissed him. "You know I love you more than anything. If you decide this case is too dangerous, we'll discuss it. I can walk away from solving this murder, but I can't walk away from you, Marc."

"Good to know, because I don't want to lose you." He gave me a knee-shaking kiss, then we went out to conquer our own agendas.

Before walking the dogs, I texted Lacey Jane. *We need to talk. Face-to-face. Can you meet?*

Her reply was immediate. *Yes. Where?*

I sent her an answer and drove to Wade's house to walk Duke.

Chapter Twenty-nine

I TUGGED A BASEBALL CAP ON and pulled my ponytail through the back before hopping out at Wade's house. The wind had picked up, and I didn't trust my ponytail to last without reinforcement.

An empty rocking chair on Wade's front porch swayed back and forth in the breeze. I unlocked the door and entered the family room of the small house. "Hey, Duke. Where are you?"

The mutt appeared from the kitchen. Wade had named his rescue dog for his hero, John Wayne.

I held the back of my hand out, not wanting Duke to feel threatened by my presence. "Hi, boy. Did your person tell you I'd be coming?"

Duke sniffed my hand, and I rubbed the furry black, white, and brown dog. "Let's go for a walk."

There was a knock at the front door. "Andi Grace, it's me." Lacey Jane appeared. Her baby bump had transformed into more of a melon shape.

"Hey, sweetie. This is Duke." I attached the leash to his collar. "Are you up to a walk?"

"Let's go. I can't wait to hear what's on your mind. Did you find the killer?"

"Not yet." We went outside, and I locked the door. "How does your husband, Deputy Wayne, feel about you asking me to help?" I put strong emphasis on the fact David was a deputy.

We walked to the corner of the street and paused to let Duke sniff the ground.

"David has to be politically correct, and he understands I want to prove Ike is innocent. I don't keep secrets from my husband. If you don't know who killed Norris, why am I here?"

"Something about this case is weirding Marc out. I'm not exactly sure what's going on, but I want you to know that if Marc asks me to drop the case, I will."

She reached for her necklace and touched her wedding ring. "My fingers are swelling. So are my feet." She pointed to the yellow flip-flops on her puffy feet.

Duke moved, and I followed his lead. "Is that all you have to say?"

"I didn't think you'd appreciate me telling you to hurry up and catch the killer before Marc makes you stop." Her bottom lip popped out.

"Marc would never make me, but if he asks me to walk away for safety reasons, I will."

Lacey Jane's shoulders drooped. "I'm sorry. I don't want you to be in danger either. This pregnancy causes me to have mood swings, and it's hard to control my emotions."

"I've heard that's a thing." I was clueless on what it was like to be pregnant, and it was hard to believe my baby sister was the first of us to get married and have a baby.

"Tell me what you know about the murder."

We turned onto another street. "Ivey Gilbert is my top suspect, but I'm also looking at Rhett Alton and Freddie Fisher. I've also met Cheyenne Marther. Norris wasn't fair with her, but was it enough to be a motive for murder?"

"Tell me more." Lacey Jane panted.

I slowed the pace of our walk, and Duke didn't tug on the leash. By the time we circled the block and arrived back at Wade's house, I'd relayed the information I'd gathered.

Lacey Jane hugged me. "I appreciate your help. I'm going to stop by and check on Dad."

She'd called Ike dad without a blip. "Sounds like y'all are growing close."

"Yeah, he's pretty great. You know how much I want a dog?"

I nodded. "Are you ready to adopt one?"

"Not until we move out of our apartment and into Marc's house."

"Your house."

A big smile broke out on her face. "That's right. My new home. Anyway, after we get settled, it'll be time to adopt a puppy. Maybe a cat too, so keep your eyes open. Can David and I go play with the dogs at Stay and Play this afternoon? We can walk them or whatever needs to be done."

"Absolutely. I'll let Melanie and Dylan know to expect you."

"Thanks. I'll see you later." She waved and took off.

I got Duke settled with fresh water, then I brushed his hair. "You're a good boy. Maybe you can come to Stay and Play one day soon. You're probably lonely when Wade's on a big case, and the death of Norris Gilbert is huge." After giving the mutt plenty of care and attention, I left and drove to look after Captain and Pumpkin.

On the way home an hour later, my phone rang. I answered it with my car system.

"Andi Grace, it's Wade. Thanks for helping out with Duke. What do you think about scheduling him for a visit to Stay and Play?" He cleared his throat. "You know, because I'm so busy with this murder investigation."

A chill shook me. "Were you in the house while I was talking to Duke?"

He chuckled. "No. I saw you on the security system, and I have indoor cameras."

"Wade, I have to say that's a little creepy. Do you always watch the feed?"

"If I receive an alert, I check. It'd sure be embarrassing for the sheriff to have his house robbed and he didn't even look at the security library. The press would have fun with that."

I turned onto the causeway that ran over the marsh and onto the island. "Do you find it odd that Ivey and Norris turned off their security system when they left town for vacation?"

"Just between us, I haven't figured out why anyone would do such a crazy thing. I mean, why have a security system if you're not gonna use it?"

"Good point. And you know when she couldn't get Norris to answer his phone, she turned it back on. She called me because she claims there was motion in the house. Ivey is at the top of my list of suspects." Whoops, I was talking to the sheriff. "Not that, well, you know what I mean."

"Is there anything I need to be aware of?"

"Like Rhett Alton's aunt was Dr. Stephanie Rich?"

Wade sighed. "Perhaps you should give me a full update."

"Hold on. I'm about to pull into my driveway." After I parked, I unloaded all my clues on the sheriff.

By the time we finished our conversation, it was time for me to walk Captain and Pumpkin. I ran inside, got Sunny, and together we went to check on the dogs.

I didn't hear from Marc, so after taking care of the dogs I texted him. *Heading your way.* We only stopped to pick up salads from Tony's Pizzeria. It took longer than it should have because my friend Tony wanted to catch up. When I returned to my SUV, there was no reply from Marc. Odd, but he'd been in an unusual mood all day, starting with our conversation about Griffin and me on the beach.

I ran my hand over Sunny's head. "It's time to find Marc and Chubb. He's going to be your brother soon. What do you think about that?"

My German shepherd tilted her head and looked at me as if I was crazy.

Marc's place was located next to Kennady Bed and Breakfast. His land had been parceled off from the original homeowner's acreage years earlier. Marc had a little house, a boat shed, and most important, a dock on the river. It'd been perfect for my boat-loving fiancé. Marc had suggested we give his house to Lacey Jane and David as a wedding gift, and I'd agreed.

Ouch. We had agreed. Marc had made the same point with me earlier. To have a good marriage, we needed to make big decisions together. There'd been many times when I'd made a decision and moved forward without consulting him. Agreeing to help solve Norris's murder was a perfect example.

Where did that leave me on surprising him with the home office? What if he'd like a darker room? A different desk? Carpet instead of the wood floor? I signaled and turned onto River Road. I needed to let Marc and Griffin design the new office, even if it caused us to run behind schedule.

Sunny barked and crawled over the console to the backseat.

A glance in the rearview mirror showed a fast-approaching pickup truck. The driver came close to my bumper and honked.

Sunny woofed again.

My heart raced, and I stomped on the accelerator.

The black truck pulled closer and tapped my bumper.

Sunny's agitated barking didn't help my nerves.

I swerved and tightened my grip on the steering wheel. The current speed would lead to a crash. I slowed, keeping my eyes forward. No sign of the truck. Where had he disappeared to?

I reached for my phone and squeezed it. "Call Marc."

The truck vroomed into sight behind me.

Again, Sunny barked.

I glanced in the mirror. The truck came closer and honked.

"Hey, sorry I didn't pick up earlier. I was out in the kayak."

"Honey, I'm on River Road. There's a truck trying to run me off the road." My voice wobbled violently, making it hard to speak.

"On the way. Don't hang up."

"Okay." I dropped the phone into a cup holder while continuing the frantic conversation on the SUV's system. "Marc, I'm scared."

A door slammed in the background. "It's okay. Come to my place, not the B and B."

"Right." I white-knuckled the steering wheel. My pulse pounded in my neck.

Sunny continued to bark like crazy. She might have some age on her, but her desire to defend me hadn't diminished a bit.

Now if I could only protect us with my driving skills. I zipped past the bed-and-breakfast. The turnoff to Marc's wasn't far away. Would the driver rear-end me when I turned? I slowed more.

The other driver decreased his speed, but he remained on my tail.

This wouldn't be like a big-city chase scene where the lead car escaped his pursuer. I signaled, hoping he wouldn't kill us all. Marc's turn was just ahead. I slowed more. The Highlander skidded. I executed the move onto Marc's property without wrecking. The only problem was, the truck made the turn too.

Chapter Thirty

SHADOWS, CURVES AND BUMPS slowed my progress. At last, I made it to the clearing in front of Marc's home. He stood there with a fierce frown. He motioned for me to go past him. I drove away from the house and toward the boat shed, skidding to a stop.

Sunny howled and moved to get a better view of the maniac who was on our tail.

The black truck roared up the private drive.

I grabbed my phone, disconnected from Marc, and called Wade.

He answered on the first ring. "Andi Grace, David's on the way. What's happening?"

"Some jerk driving a black truck tried to run me off River Road. He followed me to Marc's place. What should I do? Marc's standing in the clearing and ready to take on the driver."

Sunny pressed against the passenger window and growled.

"Let Marc handle it. You'll just be a distraction. David will be there soon. He's playing with dogs at your place, and I'm on the way."

"Fine." With trembling hands, I disconnected the call. Sitting here while Marc fought my battle was out of the question. I swiped to my camera app and hit the video button. I leashed Sunny, and we slipped out of the Highlander. Sunny growled again, and I motioned for her to be quiet as we ran to the shadows of the woods lining Marc's driveway.

The truck driver slammed on the brakes and leapt from the big black truck. The vehicle lurched forward, and the man jumped in and shifted to Park before leaping out again. Freddie Fisher approached Marc with aggressive strides. He stopped inches away and poked Marc in the chest. "Where is she? You can't protect her."

Marc reached for the man's wrist and pushed his arm away. "Freddie, you need to calm down."

Never had I been prouder of Marc. Calm and collected in the face of his enemy. I recorded the confrontation.

Chubb's frantic barks could be heard from the house.

The singer-slash-golf-pro jerked his arm away and fisted both hands. He looked right and left, then turned in a circle. "Andi Grace! Where are you?" the man screamed.

Sunny tugged on the leash.

"Stay. You can't hurt him. Unless he punches Marc, then he's all yours."

Marc said, "I understand you hit her vehicle on the road. Have you lost your mind? All of you could've been hurt. In fact, she may be injured. I don't know yet. What I know is you need to cool it."

An unseen vehicle rumbled up Marc's drive.

Freddie cursed. "Why did your girlfriend tell the sheriff to investigate me? I'm just trying to get by and survive. Norris owed me money, and I want it."

An official Charger appeared with the sheriff's department logo emblazoned across the door. The siren blipped, and Deputy David Wayne stepped out of the car. He wore a ratty T-shirt and cargo shorts. His hand hovered near his gun. "What seems to be the problem?"

If David was here, and Freddie didn't appear to have a weapon, it must be safe for me to walk over. I kept a tight grip on Sunny's leash and headed to the men.

"He tried to kill me on River Road." My legs trembled, and my voice shook.

Freddie turned and darted toward his truck. David was faster. He cuffed him and read him his rights.

I leaned against Marc. "I was terrified he was going to kill me."

He wrapped his arm around my shoulders and kissed my temple. "Your call shook me up. I can't tell you how relieved I am that you're all right."

Chubb continued barking from inside the house, and Sunny whined.

Marc said, "Why don't I take Sunny and Chubb to the fenced-in area? Maybe they'll settle down if they're together."

"Sounds good." I gave him the leash, then watched David talk to Freddie.

"My truck is still running." Freddie's tone sounded like a pouting toddler.

David put the man in the back of his cruiser before shutting off the truck. He came over to me. "Are you hurt?"

"Who knows? I'm flying high on adrenalin. Do you want to look at the back of my Highlander? He rammed me, but it wasn't hard enough to send me careening off the road and into the woods."

David held my elbow, and we walked over together to inspect the damage. Black streaks and a dent on my fender testified to Freddie's actions.

"Oh, no." I ran my hand over the destruction.

"It can be fixed. Focus on the fact that you and Sunny are okay." He patted my back.

"You're right." I sighed. "David, I'm glad Lacey Jane is married to you."

"Thanks." He removed his hand and reached for his phone. "Andi Grace, do you know why Freddie Fisher came after you?"

"He mentioned something about me siccing Sheriff Stone on him." I shrugged. "And to be fair, I did tell Wade that Freddie was mad at Norris about money."

"Can you be more explicit?"

I caught him up on as many details as I knew.

Marc appeared with four water bottles. "I thought we could all do with these." He passed them to us, giving David the extra one. "I figured Freddie must be thirsty too."

While David took the water to his cuffed prisoner, Marc embraced me.

I held tight. "It seems like this could be a good time for us to discuss my involvement in Norris's murder."

"Honey, there's no telling how many years you scared off my life today. It's not your fault though that Freddie flipped out."

I clung to Marc's strength. Despite the heat and humidity, we stood that way until Sheriff Stone arrived in his new Tahoe. "It looks like the real questioning is about to begin."

"No doubt about it."

"I wonder if Wade traced the mysterious numbers we found hidden in the book in Norris's office."

Marc groaned. "And just like that, I realize you can't drop your investigation."

"Oh, man. I'm sorry."

"Your curiosity and determination make you Andi Grace Scott. It's okay with me if you want to continue looking for clues. You don't need my permission."

His response surprised me. "But?"

"We'll need to come up with a plan to keep you safe while trying to solve the murder."

I hugged him tighter. Nobody understood me better than Marc. "Thanks for understanding."

"Of course. We're a team."

Wade and David stood by the Charger talking. When the conversation ended, David met my gaze, nodded, then took off with Freddie Fisher riding in his backseat.

Wade strolled over. "Happy to see you're alive and kicking."

"Yeah, me too." I shivered.

He inspected the rear of my Highlander. "You lucked out today, but next time could be a different outcome."

I gasped. "Hopefully there won't be a next time."

"The best thing you can do is quit butting into my case." Wade crossed his arms.

I met his glare before turning to Marc. He gave a slight nod, and I turned back to the sheriff. "I'll be more careful. More discreet even. But there's no way I can just forget about it. Will you question Freddie now?"

Wade took pictures of the front of Freddie's truck and the back of my SUV. "I'd left a message with him on his cell about his relationship with Norris. It could be the reason he came after you."

"Aha. It's your fault. Freddie was furious with me. He claimed it was because I ratted him out to you."

"I'll question him about today's incident and the murder charges. Try to be cautious and stay out of my investigation. Don't touch his truck. We'll get it towed away then go over it with a fine-tooth comb. We might get lucky and find something to connect him to the murder." The sheriff looked back at my Highlander. "See you around."

"Bye." I waved to his retreating figure then turned to Marc. "We should check on the dogs, and I brought supper."

"Really?"

I opened the back door of my SUV. Lettuce, carrots, cucumbers, and tomatoes were strewn all over the floorboard. "Sunny must have stepped on our salads. Sorry."

"That's the least of our worries. We can scrounge around my kitchen and find something."

"Sounds good." I didn't have much of an appetite anymore, but maybe eating would make me feel stronger. I also needed to think clearly if I intended to help catch the killer.

Chapter Thirty-one

AFTER MARC AND I ATE DINNER, I'd calmed down enough to drive over and pick up Lacey Jane from Stay and Play. She and David had been there playing with the dogs earlier when Freddie had tried to run me off the road. David's quick appearance had left my sister stranded, but it was no problem to drive her to town.

Lacey Jane rode shotgun in my Highlander, and Sunny snoozed in the very back. I drove with a higher level of anxiety than I'd ever experienced behind the wheel. My hands shook and my vision blurred. It appeared I wasn't as calm as I'd believed.

My sister sighed. "You don't have to drive so slow on my account."

"Sorry. I just feel kinda shaky."

"Do you want me to drive? I'm sorry about needing a ride home, but David's still questioning Freddie."

"No, I'm glad to take you home. It gives us a chance to visit."

"Except you're as nervous as a plump turkey in November. Honestly, I'd also be in a dither after almost being run off the road. Are you going to quit your investigation?"

"It would probably be the smartest thing to do. Marc and I even discussed it, but I'll keep trying to discover who killed Norris. What does David say about Ike? I can't believe he's still a suspect."

Lacey Jane rubbed her belly. "He's not saying much, and I know he'll tell me when Dad isn't a person of interest."

I slowed for a curve. "All they can possibly have on Ike is the fact he and Norris argued over you. And, oh yeah, there's the oyster knife."

"What knife are you talking about?"

I relaxed my grip on the steering wheel, then retightened it. My palms were damp, but that mean old Freddie Fisher wouldn't take away my ability to drive.

"Andi Grace, are you sure you don't want me to switch places with you? I bet you're dealing with PTSD, and there's no shame in that."

"I'm fine." My answer wasn't one hundred percent true, but I would be fine. Maybe not tonight, but eventually.

"Hmph. I don't believe you." Her voice sounded like our mother's voice more and more every day.

I kept my eyes glued to the road. "Why?"

"You never answered my question about the oyster knife."

"Oh. Ike had an oyster knife, and it disappeared. Meanwhile, a knife just like his appeared in the Gilberts' front yard."

She slunk in her seat. "That doesn't sound good. See why I need you to keep looking for the real killer?"

The road ended, and I turned onto the main highway and moved into the slow lane. "Yeah. I get it, but are you sure my investigation won't cause a rift between you and David?"

"He understands I believe Ike is innocent, and I understand that he can't keep me updated on the investigation. Do you think Freddie Fisher is the killer?"

"Maybe." I glanced in the rearview mirror. A black truck appeared barreling up the road in my lane, and I yelped.

"What's wrong?" Lacey Jane sat straight and looked behind us.

"Freddie's back." I mashed the accelerator.

Sunny barked.

The truck drew closer. It switched lanes and roared past us.

"Calm down, and slow up. It's not Freddie. He's being questioned by David, and the truck is somewhere being examined."

My heart raced faster than the vehicle that had flown by.

"Andi Grace Scott, snap out of it."

My sister's command pulled me back to reality, and I returned to a reasonable speed. "Sorry about that."

"You need to pull over at the next gas station and let me drive."

"Man, you sound like Mom." I could picture our mother reacting the same way.

Lacey Jane sighed. "There's a convenience store on the corner."

I signaled my intention and pulled up to a gas pump. "May as well fill the tank while we're here."

Sunny paced in the back, looking out each window before resettling on the shaggy fur dog bed.

The sun had begun its descent, and clouds filled the sky to the south of us. Shadows played on the surface of the parking lot. Faces of people around me were obscured. Who was who? I shivered despite the humidity. By the time I'd finished fueling my SUV, Lacey Jane was sitting in the driver's seat. Not desiring an argument, I walked to the passenger side. Deep down I was grateful.

Lacey Jane drove onto the highway. Country music played on the radio.

Before I realized what was happening, the vehicle came to a stop. I looked at my sister. "I must've dozed off. Sorry about that."

She shut off the engine then shrugged her slender shoulders. "David will probably have a very late night, and I thought it'd be fun to spend the night with you."

"I guess that's code for you think I'm too scared in my present state to stay by myself." Sunny climbed over the seats and plopped onto my lap. I hugged my German shepherd. "You're not the right size to be a lap dog, but I love you."

"Let's go inside. I need to use the bathroom. Part of my pregnancy is the urge for frequent bathroom breaks."

"Thanks for staying with me tonight." I'd survived scarier experiences, and I didn't understand why Freddie had unnerved me so much.

"That's what family is for. Now get moving."

Once we were inside, my sister beelined it to the bathroom. I set the security system and fixed us herbal tea.

Lacey Jane joined me in the family room and sat on the other side of the couch. She propped her swollen feet on the coffee table. "I'm ready to hear your answer about Freddie Fisher."

I held the blue mug of tea in both hands absorbing the warmth. "He scared me half to death, but he claims he wasn't trying to kill me. I never saw a weapon in his hands. It's possible he's a hothead and only intended to frighten me. He also had an argument with Norris."

"So do you think he yells at whoever he gets mad at then gets over it?"

"Yeah. Maybe." I sipped my tea. "It'll be interesting to see what David and Wade learn from questioning Freddie."

Lacey Jane reached for the TV remote. "We need to find a good romantic comedy to watch. No more talking about the murder."

"I like your plan." Tomorrow would be soon enough to think about murder and mayhem.

Chapter Thirty-two

TUESDAY MORNING, David appeared early to pick up Lacey Jane. He looked exhausted and in no mood for questions. I hugged both of them goodbye and they left as Griffin arrived. I took off after letting Griffin inside to start work on the home office for Marc. Somehow, I'd forgotten to bring up the subject with my fiancé, so I let the men get to work on our original plan.

After I finished walking the dogs on my morning schedule, I drove to Ivey's house. Two little boys wearing swimming trunks answered the door. They told me they were twins, and they yelled for their grandmother to come to the door. Once Ivey appeared, they whooped and ran out the door leading to the back deck.

"Dear me. Those boys have so much energy. The rest of the family is on the beach, but those two got in a fight. They were sent up here for time out, and I came with them to make sure they behaved." Her smile faded. "Why are you here?"

As much as I wanted to ask about the secret numbers we'd found in an envelope in Norris's office, Wade had told us not to mention them. "Would you like me to deliver the reward money for finding Lady?"

Her eyes widened. "Yes, I'll write a check. What's her name?"

"It's Cheyenne Marther, and she was one of your husband's clients."

"How nice." Ivey disappeared and returned with a pen and checkbook.

"Cheyenne needs cash because she doesn't have a bank account."

"Really? How does one survive without one?"

"Lots of poor people get by. It's probably why there are so many check cashing businesses. If you'd like to make the check out to me, I can cash it. Please write Cheyenne's name on the memo in case the IRS questions me later."

"Oh, yes. We mustn't upset the Internal Revenue Service." Sarcasm dripped from her voice. "I also owe you for taking care of Lady because I didn't pay your employees last night."

"Yes, ma'am, but I can send you an invoice from the business." If she fled the country or was arrested for Norris's murder, I'd probably regret my decision. Although, I had to be fair and I didn't know the total of what she owed.

"Whatever suits you best." She wrote the check for the reward money.

After slipping it into my pocket, I said, "I know you sold the building to the LC Pain Clinic."

She cut me off. "That's public knowledge."

"Did you sell Dr. Rich her house?"

"I only work in Heyward Beach. Stephanie bought a home in Blueburg."

Aha. They had been on a first-name basis. "Were you two friends?"

"Norris and I had dinner with her a few times, when he was trying to convince her working for the clinic would provide her a comfortable retirement."

I'd read articles on the woman's death. "She was seventy-two. Why was she still working?"

"I can't answer your question. Now if you'll excuse me, I'd like to enjoy the beach with my family." Ivey turned and walked to the same door her grandsons had used. "You can see yourself out."

"Thanks, Ivey." I moved toward the front of the house, but when the door shut behind Ivey, I tiptoed into Norris's office.

The room was empty. No desk. No books on the shelves. No chairs. If we hadn't found the envelope of numbers when we did, it'd be too late now. Had we missed anything else?

Lady greeted me in the main room, and I knelt. "Hey, girl. Howya doing?"

The schnoodle licked my face.

I laughed. "You've got a house full of company. Are you having fun?"

Her answer was another face lick.

I lifted Lady and held her close. "Are you getting enough attention? I bet you miss Norris, but his family does too." Looking for family pictures, I circled the room then crept up the stairs. Bare walls and closed bedroom doors.

The doorbell rang.

My heart lurched, and I ran down the stairs snuggling the little dog.

Ivey walked into the house just as my feet hit the floor.

"Andi Grace, I thought you left."

The doorbell rang again.

"I was just about to go but Lady appeared, and I couldn't help but playing with her." I passed the little dog to Ivey. "See you later."

A pizza delivery boy stood at the door. "Hi, it'll be fifty-seven dollars. That's before tip."

"I'm sorry, this isn't my house. Here comes the owner now." I raced down the stairs and got into my Highlander, leaving the premises before Ivey could question me.

My next stop was the sheriff's office. I needed to find out what was going on with Freddie.

• • •

I sat across the battered desk from Sheriff Stone. "You let him go?"

Wade rocked back in his black mesh chair. "The only thing we could charge Freddie with was the attack on you. His arraignment was this morning, and the judge granted him bail. Somebody posted the money, so he is out until the trial. I'm sorry. It was out of my hands."

I leapt from my seat and paced. "That's not fair. He tried to kill me."

"Freddie claims he glanced at his phone and accidently hit you. He followed you to Marc's place to make sure you were okay."

"That's a bunch of baloney. You should've heard what he said. Freddie was irate because we mentioned his name to you." I reached for my phone and opened the camera app. "I'm going to forward what I taped yesterday. It's Freddie yelling at Marc."

"Why don't you sit back down?" Wade pointed to the chair, and I returned to it. "If it'd been up to me, Freddie would be in jail. He doesn't have a criminal record though. His wife and kids showed up for the arraignment. The judge trusts him to behave."

I sighed. "Do you think I'm safe?"

Wade nodded. "We were able to prove his alibi for the time of the murder. He didn't kill Norris. His attorney promised the judge he'd start anger management therapy. To answer your question, I do believe you're safe from Freddie. It doesn't mean you're safe from the killer."

"I promise to be more cautious. By the way, how did you prove Freddie was taking inventory of a shipment of hats at the pro shop?"

"Come again?"

"You know. His alibi was he was working at the golf shop."

"That's not the story he gave me. Freddie was giving a secret golf lesson to a woman who wants to impress her boss. When she interviewed for her job, she claimed to be a golfer, and now she needs to learn the sport."

"Wow, doesn't anyone tell the truth these days? Freddie wasn't honest about his alibi, and the woman lied to get a job."

Wade leaned forward and propped his forearms on the desk. "Unfortunately, I get used to people being dishonest."

"That's one more reason I enjoy working with animals. They never lie. Have a good day, Wade." I left him sitting in his office.

"Andi Grace, wait up." David caught me in the hallway. "I'll walk you to your vehicle."

"Thanks." I studied my brother-in-law. Dark half-moons under his bloodshot eyes and messy hair concerned me. "Did you get to nap at all after you picked up Lacey Jane?"

"Afraid not. I'm glad Lacey Jane spent the night with you. She mentioned you probably have a case of PTSD." He opened the building's door for me, and we walked outside into oppressive humidity despite the wind.

"Yeah, the incident with Freddie unnerved me."

He slid on his sunglasses. "I'm aware my wife dragged you into investigating the murder because of her biological dad. In case you don't know, I fell in love with Lacey Jane the first day we met. She's sweet, kind, loving, smart—"

"Hey, you don't need to convince me she's amazing. Where are you going with this?" I pushed the button on my key fob to unlock my Highlander. I opened the driver's door and allowed the heat to escape.

David rested his bicep on the SUV's roof. The muscles strained the sleeve of his official polo, and it wasn't hard to believe he'd played football in college. He looked at me. "If your family hadn't been in turmoil over Ike and the past, Lacey Jane may not have fallen for me so fast. She was conflicted about her feelings for Ike compared to the man who raised her. She poured her heart out to me, and we grew close faster than we probably would have under normal circumstances. One of the reasons we eloped was Lacey Jane didn't want to deal with additional family conflict. She believed you and Nate would try to persuade us not to marry so soon."

"I'm sure we would have, considering the short amount of time you two had known each other." I decided not to push him to make his point. He'd get there when he was ready.

"I appreciate how you've welcomed me into your little family."

"It's obvious how much you love my sister, and I've always wanted what was best for her."

David rubbed his bottom lip with his thumb. "I do too, and that's my problem. The sheriff's department will catch the killer without your help, no offense. Lacey Jane is worried Ike will be arrested. It's not that she doesn't trust us, but after you lost your parents, she's terrified she'll lose her biological dad too."

My chest hurt at his confession. "I'm so sorry she feels that way, but it makes sense."

"The thing is, I'm more concerned about your safety. I have faith in our ability to catch the real killer, and I don't believe it's Ike. I have no plans to interfere in a promise you made to Lacey Jane, but if you continue your search for the guilty person, you might be the next victim. Losing you could be a loss Lacey Jane won't recover from."

Chills danced up my spine despite the humidity. "Marc's working with me, and I'll try to be more discreet when looking for clues. Thanks for caring, David."

He pushed off the vehicle and hugged me. "Take care of yourself."

"I intend to do just that." I got into the SUV and started the engine, cranking the air conditioner to high.

My next plan of action was to cash Ivey's check, pick up cold drinks, and head to Piney Woods Apartment Complex in search of Cheyenne Marther. I texted Marc and decided to stop by my friend Leroy Peck's place in Piney Woods. Layers of protection would help me stay safe.

Chapter Thirty-three

I PARKED IN LEROY'S DRIVEWAY behind his old truck. He sat on the front porch talking to Jeremiah Prichard, a man who still dealt with PTSD after returning home from war decades earlier. He rode a bike everywhere, lived in Piney Woods, and used a metal detector on the beach to supplement his modest income.

I carried three Cokes from the convenience store and joined them. "Good morning. It's a scorcher today."

Jeremiah nodded. "That's for sure."

Leroy winked at me. His hands rested on his belly. "Good to see you."

I passed a soft drink to each of the men. "I was thirsty and hoped to see y'all."

Jeremiah said, "Thank ya kindly. Would you like my seat?"

"No, thanks. I can't stay."

Leroy took a long swig of his drink. "This sure enough hits the spot. What brings you our way?"

"I'm looking for Cheyenne Marther. Have you seen her this morning?"

"Poor thing was dumpster diving early this morning. Do you think you're going to have a job for her?" Leroy's gaze seared me.

I sipped on my drink. Bubbly deliciousness filled me and cooled me too. "I need to think about it more, but I've got her reward money for finding Lady. I'll walk around and see if I can find her."

Leroy told me which apartment she lived in, and I strolled in that direction.

The low-income housing complex was in desperate need of attention. If Lincoln bought it and Griffin took over as manager and contractor, maybe Cheyenne could work for them. The idea of her working with my animals didn't seem like a good one, especially after the scene she'd caused at my house the other night.

Each building had eight apartments. Four were on each floor, and I found Cheyenne's place. After a quick knock, the door swung open. "Hi, Cheyenne."

"Do you have my money?" She stuck out her hand.

The redhead had gotten a sunburn since I'd last seen her. "Oh my goodness, you're burned. What are you using to heal it?"

"I can't afford anything." She wore faded shorts, a thin T-shirt, and the flip-flops Marc had given her.

"I've got something in my vehicle you can use, but I'm parked at Leroy's place."

"It don't matter. I just need the money."

"Can I come inside? It might not be safe to pass the reward money to you in this open hallway."

Cheyenne opened the door wider and waved me into the apartment.

The place was bare-bones. Sparse. There was a bar stool at the kitchen counter, a clock radio that had seen better days, and a pallet in the family room. Near the pallet of sheets and a skimpy pillow lay a dirty brown backpack. "Oh, Cheyenne."

"Hey, I don't need your pity."

I dug the money out of my pocket and handed it to her. "Five hundred dollars. You should count it."

In a whisper the redhead counted the fifties, twenties, and tens, placing them on the kitchen counter. She counted the money twice, then rolled the bills up and stuck them in her bra. "Thank you."

"Cheyenne, how desperate are you for money? Is there any possibility you dognapped Lady?"

"No."

"I mean, it'd be understandable. Norris put you in this predicament—"

"No. I've got to claim ownership for my drug abuse problem. If I'm going to be angry at anyone, it's the driver who ran over me. His actions led to the accident, the surgeries, the pain meds, and then the addiction. But I was upset with Mr. Gilbert for giving my ex-husband the insurance money."

"Cheyenne, you need some furniture."

"That'll only happen if I can find a job. Will you hire me?"

"Stay and Play is too far away for a person without a car, but I'll keep you in mind if I hear of a job opening. Have you tried applying at Daily Java, Donut Dreaming, or the ice cream shop?"

"Mr. Peck introduced me to some people at the festival, but I haven't officially applied anywhere. Tourist season is over, so it probably won't be easy to find work."

I leaned against the counter. "We have quite a few tourists in the fall, so you might find something. What do you plan to do with the reward money?"

"Pay rent and buy groceries." She touched her chest as if to reassure herself the cash was still there.

"I might be able to help, but you need to be honest with me. Cheyenne, did you steal the dog?"

She walked over to a window and looked outside. "I found the dog running around the day Mr. Gilbert was murdered. When I read the collar, it seemed like fate was giving me a chance to make some money. Too bad the dog ran away."

"What about the ransom?"

"Even though the dog ran away, I decided to try to make some of my money back. It was a gamble, but I created the ransom note and stuck it on your car."

"How did you know to single me out?"

"You're the dog walker, so it seemed like a safe hunch." Her back remained toward me.

"You asked for files. Why?"

"Easy. Blackmail. I'm convinced Mr. Gilbert was blackmailing his clients."

"What was your plan if Ivey paid the ransom and you didn't have the dog?"

"My plan was to skip town with the files. It probably wasn't the smartest idea, but I was desperate for money. Lucky for me I found the dog."

From the looks of things, she was in dire straits. "Listen, I've got time to take you to the community church. They have a food bank and a clothing ministry."

"I doubt I can afford to buy clothes after rent and food. What I really need is a bike so I can get around."

"Cheyenne, the food and clothes are free at the church. I've got a dog to walk soon, but I can drop you off on the way. I'll also bring you back here after my appointment."

"What have I got to lose?" She followed me to the Highlander.

On the drive to church, Cheyenne didn't say much. I ran inside with her and introduced her to the lady in charge of clothes.

As I drove to my next appointment, I tried to make sense of Cheyenne Marther. Yeah, she'd had some bad luck, but blackmail? And demanding ransom for a dog she claimed to have found? What was that? Extortion? There was also the night she got drunk and showed up at my house. The entire experience had been frightening. Maybe I should've taken her to the sheriff's department instead of the church. But except for drunk and disorderly, had she actually committed any of the crimes?

When my parents died, we'd found ourselves in dire straits. Compared to Cheyenne, it hadn't been so bad. For the moment, I'd give her grace. Maybe she only needed to catch a few good breaks in order to turn herself around.

It'd be easy to help her find assistance and possibly a job, but there was no way I'd hire her to work with animals. In case she couldn't turn her life around, I wouldn't risk her dognapping a pet in my care.

Chapter Thirty-four

WHEN CHEYENNE AND I RETURNED to her apartment complex, Lincoln, Griffin, and Marc stood in the parking lot near Cheyenne's place. I parked near her building. "I'll get the sunburn cream and help you carry the supplies inside."

"Those church ladies were so nice to me. They even gave me toiletries. I've been brushing my teeth with hand soap to save money, and there's a big tube of toothpaste in here. Can you believe it?"

"That's great." With full arms, we carried the bags into her apartment and placed them on the kitchen counter.

Cheyenne stepped back. "I've got it now. Thanks for your help today."

"You're welcome. If I hear about a bike or a job, I'll be sure to contact you." I let myself out and hurried to catch Marc before he left.

He met me halfway and kissed me. "I appreciate your text telling me about your plans."

"Safety first and all that. What are you guys doing here?"

"Lincoln's offer was accepted, and he's now the proud owner of Piney Woods Apartment Complex. It's a cash offer, and the paperwork shouldn't take too long. Griffin has officially been hired as manager and contractor. Soon Griffin and his team will make the necessary updates for this to be a good place to live."

"I'm relieved to hear that. I was in Cheyenne's place. She is practically homeless except for the fact she has a roof over her head." I shared my impressions with him.

"Does this mean you've taken her off your suspect list?"

"I'm afraid not. She took advantage of Lady when she put the ransom note on my SUV. It was just shear luck that she actually found Lady, and either way, she planned to carry out the ransom scheme." My heart sped up. "She gave me the impression she knew Norris was out of the picture. No, wait."

"It's a small town. Maybe she'd heard about the murder."

I replayed the conversation in my head. "I can't figure out what made me think she knew. Probably an overactive imagination."

"I believe your imagination is the reason you're so good at solving murders. You consider all the options."

Griffin motioned for us to join them.

Marc reached for my hand. "Duty calls." We walked to the men.

"Hey, Andi Grace. Can you believe this place will belong to me in a few days?" Lincoln laughed.

"I don't think you'll get rich here, but there's a whole lot of good you can accomplish. I'm proud of you." I patted his shoulder.

"Thanks. We're going to keep my connection on the down-low for various reasons."

Griffin said, "We don't want anyone price gouging us because they believe Lincoln has deep pockets."

The men discussed the first project to tackle.

I quit listening to their conversation and looked around the property. Until a few days ago, I hadn't known Cheyenne. How had she ended up at the local pain clinic? Why not a place in Charleston or somewhere closer to her kids? I was also curious how she'd picked Norris to be her attorney. Had someone at the clinic referred her to Norris because of his ties to them? How deep was that connection?

A trickle of sweat ran down my face. Norris had helped the owners of the pain clinic find their building. Ivey was the agent in charge of the sale, meaning the Gilberts had profited from the transaction.

If injured people needed pain treatment, and they went to the pain clinic, did the staff always refer them to Norris if there was a possibility of filing a lawsuit? Nice plan to benefit Norris, but did the scheme work in both directions? Had Norris sent his clients who'd suffered an injury to see Dr. Rich?

A dark cloud floated over us, giving relief from the sun's heat.

It was easy to imagine Norris being in cahoots with the pain clinic. The old arrangement of you scratch my back and I'll scratch yours.

The day was blazing hot, and I needed something cold to drink.

Cheyenne was furious with Norris for giving her settlement money to her ex-husband, and she was upset with the clinic for enabling her to get hooked on narcotics. Cheyenne had faced a lot of obstacles to reclaim her life. Was Norris one of the obstacles she'd decided to confront? How? She was tiny. It didn't seem possible she'd be strong enough to strangle the attorney.

Ivey wasn't a big woman either, but she'd had years of anger. Had marriage counseling helped her forgive his unfaithfulness?

White spots danced before my eyes. I needed to get to some real shade. I turned and headed for the coolness of the woods surrounding the apartment complex. It seemed so far away, but surely I could make it.

Fingers circled my arms. "Andi Grace." The voice belonged to Marc. He lifted me off my feet and carried me to his truck.

"Is she okay?" Griffin questioned my fiancé.

"Do you have anything to drink and food? She probably didn't eat breakfast."

"Be right back."

Lincoln hollered, "My truck's already cooling off. Bring her here."

I understood the fuzzy voices but didn't feel strong enough to reply.

Marc slid into the passenger seat of Lincoln's Chevy pickup with me still in his arms. Cool air blasted from the vents. Marc slammed the door shut. "Please tell me you've had more than coffee and Coke today."

"I've been busy."

Griffin tapped on the window, and Marc lowered it. "Water, sports drink, and an energy bar. What else can I do?"

"Thanks. You and Lincoln continue making plans. I'll rejoin you in a bit."

"Take your time." Griffin patted the windowsill then rambled off.

Marc handed me the sports drink and closed the window. "How about starting with this? You'll be cooler if you're not sitting in my lap. Be right back." He hopped out of the truck but was soon sitting in the driver's seat.

I finished the watermelon-flavored drink then picked up the food bar. "I'm embarrassed."

"What in tarnation was so important that you couldn't stop to eat?"

I took a bite of the peanut butter energy treat. "I know better, but there was so much to do. Time got away from me."

"We agreed you need to continue looking at the murder, but I believed the only danger you would face was making the killer angry. It never occurred to me you wouldn't take care of yourself."

He made a good point. "You're right. I always carry dog treats with me, and it looks like I should keep snacks in the car for myself too."

"I don't think these guys need me anymore. It was more of a courtesy that they included me. I'll tell them we're going out to lunch."

"Sounds good, but I'll stay here where it's nice and cool until you wrap it up." I finished the snack and drank the water.

If I ruled out Cheyenne and Freddie, I was left with Ivey, Rhett, and an unknown divorce client. Before I could delve farther into the case, I needed to eat.

Chapter Thirty-five

MARC AND I SAT IN THE COOLNESS OF DAILY JAVA. Between drinking a glass of water and the fruit smoothie, I'd be lucky not to float away. I bit into my veggie sandwich.

"Let me get this straight. Freddie is out of jail?"

I wiped my mouth with a paper napkin. "For now."

"Wade also told you Freddie has a witness, so he didn't kill Norris."

"Yeah, but he gave Wade a different alibi than he gave me, meaning he is a liar." I sipped on the smoothie.

"True, but it doesn't make him a killer." Marc lifted his empty glass. "I need a refill. Be right back."

I ate in silence until Marc returned. After he sat, I said, "We need a clear time line for Friday morning. Norris had an early golf lesson. Later, Freddie worked with a secret client so she could impress her boss. The appointment led the sheriff to believe Freddie didn't kill Norris. There were also the benzodiazepines found in Norris's body at the autopsy."

"Yep." Marc sighed. "Don't forget the crime scene techs found traces of diazepam in the kitchen sink."

"Right, and that makes us think Norris was probably drugged at home. It's hard for me to picture Norris inviting someone into his home, offering refreshments, and then he ends up being the one who is drugged." I wadded my napkin and dropped it on the remains of my sandwich. "Is it possible Norris meant to drug the other person but he messed up the switcheroo? Don't answer that question. I can't imagine he'd be so careless."

Marc tilted his head. "Yeah, Norris didn't get rich and powerful by being careless. May I offer two explanations for the residue in the kitchen sink?"

"Absolutely." I crossed one leg over the other and leaned close.

"Is it possible that Ivey takes diazepam? If so, she might crush it up and swallow it with yogurt or oatmeal or whatever she eats."

"I learned you're not supposed to crush it. Plus, it's not water-soluble. What's your second suggestion?"

"The killer may have arrived with drinks and offered one to Norris. The drink could've been laced with diazepam before the killer arrived. Then after Norris died—" Marc ran his hands through his blonde hair. "Norris was strangled. He didn't die of a drug overdose. Man, I led us down a rabbit hole. Sorry about that."

"It makes so much sense in theory, but we need to focus on who is strong enough to strangle Norris. It'd be nice to find out where the leash came from." I stood. "You've got to go back to work. Do you want to drive me to my SUV?"

"More time with my beautiful fiancée? You bet." He gave me a quick kiss. "Let's roll."

As we walked to the truck, the sky grew cloudier. "I need to look at the forecast. The island will flood if the storm hits us during high tide."

"The storm is one danger we can take off your list. We'll prep your house, and you'll be able to leave as soon as the authorities make an announcement." He opened the truck door for me. "I searched for lawsuits against Norris again. In my opinion, there's nothing worthy of murder."

When Marc pulled up to Leroy's house, there wasn't a soul in sight. "What do you have planned this afternoon?"

"I've got a few dogs to walk later, and I have some bids to go over for the equipment for the doggie play area. It's Dylan's dream, and I want his input before he begins to work full-time for Griffin."

"Take care of yourself. I'll call you later." He leaned over and kissed me.

"Marc, there's something we need to discuss tonight, and it's not related to the murder."

"I'm intrigued, unless I need to be worried."

"Nope, it should be a fun conversation. Love ya!" I gave him a quick kiss and hopped out.

He waited for me to get my vehicle started, then he followed me out of the apartment complex.

On the way home, I stopped at Ike's new business. He was standing at the side of the building, breaking down boxes and stuffing them into the recycle container. "Hi, Andi Grace. What brings you by Beach Mart this afternoon?"

"I wanted to check on you. Has the sheriff questioned you again?"

The trim, military man crossed his arms. "No, ma'am. It's been a pleasant surprise."

"Good." Tension fled from my tight shoulders. "Any chance you found your oyster knife?"

"Afraid not, and that concerns me a bit. I'm not a careless person, especially with an item that could be potentially dangerous."

"I believe you. Hey, could we go inside for a minute? The heat's been getting to me today."

"Sure. You can even reach into the back of the soda refrigerator and find the coldest Coke."

"Perfect." I followed him through the back door and beelined it for the drinks. "Do you want me to grab one for you too?"

"May as well. Thanks." He pulled two old bar stools out from behind the cash register, and we sat. "Is there anything else you need to ask me?"

The drink bubbled down my throat with tiny bits of ice. Perfection. "It seems like the primary reason the sheriff questioned you was because of an anonymous tip. Someone overheard you and Norris argue. Do you have any idea who it might have been?"

"Norris came by here one day when I had a work crew converting the shed into a tiny house. One of them could have reported me. I also went to his office after Lacey Jane told me he suggested she should sue me for back child support. In my life, I've turned a lot of young men into war heroes. It doesn't happen by asking nicely. I know how to get loud, and I didn't use my indoor voice when I showed up at his office. But I never lifted a hand to the attorney."

"I can't imagine you would." I looked around the beach store. "I don't think it's a coincidence that this is the last place you saw your oyster knife, and you argued with Norris while there was a work crew here."

"And somebody reported the argument to the authorities." He stood and paced. "I'll see if I can get a list of who worked on the house."

"Sounds good. I better let you get back to work." We exited the building together. "Hey, there's a young lady living at Piney Woods in need of an inexpensive bicycle. If you come across one, would you let me know?"

"Sure thing. You be careful, Andi Grace."

I hugged the Marine. "I will. Lacey Jane is going to need us to help when the baby arrives."

"You got that right. I wasn't allowed to be a father to my only child, but this grandbaby is going to be a different story. I will be active and loving. See you later."

On the way home, I debated whether the oyster knife was significant. Norris had been strangled, not stabbed, and there were no slits. If Ike had lost a neon pink dog leash, I'd be worried because he was certainly strong enough to strangle a man, with or without a leash.

Chapter Thirty-six

DYLAN STOPPED BY MY HOUSE to discuss Stay and Play's new fun area for the dogs. He'd become like a brother to me, so it was easy to mention his shaggy hair when we finished talking about work. "You're in desperate need of a haircut. I used to do Nate's to save money. How about if I trim yours?"

"Cool."

"Make yourself at home, and I'll get my supplies." I gathered a comb, scissors, towels, and a spray bottle of water.

Dylan was on the kitchen floor playing with Sunny when I returned.

"She'll sleep good tonight." A glance at my watch assured me there was plenty of time before my next dog-walking appointment. "Have a seat in this chair."

He settled into the dining chair. "I heard you met Cheyenne. What do you think about her?"

I wrapped the towel around his shoulders and combed his wavy dark hair. "To be honest, I don't trust her with the animals."

"Why? She seemed excited to learn I spend my days with pets."

"The other night, she showed up here. Drunk and disorderly. She caused quite a scene and was taken to jail."

Dylan gasped and jerked around. His gaze met mine. "Are you kidding me?"

"No, and it's one of the reasons why I don't trust her with the animals." With a gentle touch I turned his head to face forward. I began snipping his thick unruly hair. "You must've seen something worthy in her if you suggested she work at Stay and Play."

"Well, yeah." He threw his hands up. "Cheyenne seemed sweet and innocent. I thought she'd be gentle with the dogs. She told me about her husband moving away with her kids, and I felt sorry for her. She wants to save up enough money to visit them."

I paused the hand motions needed to work on his hair and patted his shoulder. Dylan's mom had run away with him and kept him away from his dad when he was little. I wasn't sure if it'd been months or years. She'd had enough time to brainwash Dylan, telling him his dad didn't want anything to do with him. When the authorities finally caught up with her, Dylan was returned to his father. It'd taken years for the dad to build trust with his son. "I guess it brought up some sad memories for you."

"Kinda. Despite my dad's flaws, he loved me. I hope Cheyenne's ex-husband isn't telling their kids lies about her. The kids will suffer more than the parents." He pressed his lips together.

Poor Dylan. I resumed cutting his hair. "I'll admit Cheyenne has a lot to overcome, but she's also made some bad choices. I'm not saying I would've made better decisions in her situation—"

"You gave me a chance to turn my life around when I messed up."

I didn't want to cry or embarrass him. "True, but there was something so endearing about you. How could I help myself?"

"I am known for my charisma." Dylan lifted his chin and laughed.

"Oh, yeah. You're smooth. Say, are you still dating Kylie Black? I haven't seen her around in a while."

His smile dimmed. "Naw, she met some dude from The Citadel. It's okay though."

"You'll find the right woman at the right time. Look how long it took me to meet Marc. I cringe to think how different my life would've turned out if I'd married my high school sweetheart. He did me a favor by dumping me."

"Bullet dodged. I hear ya."

I exchanged the scissors for clippers and used short scooping strokes on the back of his head to blend it with the rest of his hair. "Did you help Griffin work on the tiny house for Ike Gage?"

"Yeah, but only when I wasn't scheduled for you."

"I trust you, and I'm not accusing you of anything wrong. What I need to know is if you saw anyone with an oyster knife. Ike had one with a turquoise blue handle and it disappeared."

"I can't help you." He shrugged. "Sorry."

"It was a long shot. Did anyone seem shady to you?"

"That dead attorney came by once and got into an argument with Mr. Gage. There was also the guy who wants to protect the environment. He had a conversation with Griffin. They seemed to get along fine. One of the reasons I want to work with Griffin is because of his interest in protecting the earth. All the other people are regulars. Nothing to fear from them as far as I know. We all work hard and go out for beer on Friday nights."

I paused.

"Don't worry, I'm of legal age."

"You caught me doing the math on your age." I set the clippers to the side and ran a comb through Dylan's hair. "Go to the bathroom and see what you think. We can go shorter, but you have such nice hair. You'll catch the eye of more girls this way."

"Hey, that never hurts." He walked away and returned before I'd folded the towel. "Looks great. I'm heading back to Stay and Play and can place the order on the items we agreed on."

"Perfect. Thanks."

He gave me a quick hug and spent a minute loving on Sunny. "Thanks for the haircut. See ya later."

"Bye, Dylan." I grabbed my notebook and added his comments to my notes.

As I reviewed them, it hit me. Dylan had a specific type of woman who caught his attention. When he'd met Kylie Black, she'd been a murder suspect. Cheyenne Marther was only a person of interest to me. Both women needed to be rescued, and Dylan had responded to their needs.

The information wouldn't help me solve the murder, but it was interesting. I might need to keep my eye on Dylan to make sure nobody took advantage of his kind nature.

Chapter Thirty-seven

I PARKED AT HEYWARD BEACH'S DOLLAR STORE and grabbed my phone. Oops. I'd missed a call from Lacey Jane. I tapped my cell and returned her call.

"Andi Grace, Sheriff Stone and a deputy went by Dad's place and questioned him again." My sister sounded out of breath.

"Stay calm. Anxiety isn't good for you or the baby. Did they take Ike with them? Did they handcuff him or read his Miranda rights?"

"No. They only talked to him at the store. The grand opening has been delayed for multiple reasons, and Dad's there all the time. If they arrest him, the store may never open. His reputation is at stake. Worse, his life is at stake."

I leaned back in my seat, watching customers come and go. "Is the sheriff still there?"

"No. I stopped by to see how much progress has been made at the store, otherwise I doubt anyone would've told me."

"Look at the bright side. Wade asked questions and left. That's good news, right?"

"Yeah, but I wish they'd leave him alone."

"I know, sweetie. Don't let it get you down. I actually had a conversation with Ike earlier, and I'm now on my way to look for a clue. You should try to relax. Leave the worrying to me."

"Okay, but if I wasn't pregnant, I'd be right there with you. Be careful, Andi Grace."

"I will." I ended the call and hopped out of my SUV. People needed to quit telling me to be careful. I had no intention of acting reckless.

Ahead of me a lady walked into the store with twin boys. They were Ivey's grandsons. It couldn't hurt to keep an eye on them.

I wandered to the pet supply aisle.

The twins were inspecting the wide selection of chips, snacks, and candy. There was nothing quiet about those two boys, and I had to smile. There was probably never a dull moment when they were around.

We didn't have a pet store in Heyward Beach. I usually ordered supplies from an online warehouse or shopped in Charleston. Today, I studied the dog leashes available at the dollar store. There was a fairly good, and colorful, selection of nylon leashes and harnesses. Black and blue were the most popular colors available.

My gaze landed on a neon pink harness. I grabbed it and turned my attention to see if there was a matching leash. No luck.

"Boys!" The twins' mom yelled loud enough that everyone in the store grew quiet.

From my vantage point, I was able to witness the scene. The woman bent down to their eye level and spoke to the kids. They nodded and walked away from the junk food. The mom apologized to the clerk at the cash register, then the three of them exited the store.

Kudos to her for instilling discipline. The mother didn't act entitled despite her wealthy and powerful parents.

Back to the leashes. I had confirmed the leash used to strangle Norris could've been bought here. I paid for the harness and planned to take it to the sheriff's office. If it matched the leash at the murder scene, Wade could decide what to do next.

I stepped onto the sidewalk and bumped into the not-so-grief-stricken widow. "Hi, Ivey. I saw your family inside a few minutes ago."

One side of her mouth quirked up. "The twins are incorrigible."

"I think it's probably just their age. They must be a lot of fun."

"The boys have their good moments. I need to buy snacks. We're having game night at the house later. I had meant to stay in the car and return messages, but as you can see, it didn't work out."

"Have fun tonight." Once I was in my Highlander, I set my purchase in the passenger seat. The thin, almost clear plastic bag didn't conceal the harness. Had Ivey noticed? Would she be suspicious? After all, I did walk dogs for a living. In fact, I needed to get to Wade's house and take care of Duke.

The next two hours were spent walking dogs, and I ended my day caring for Captain and Pumpkin. Phyllis was in charge of taking meals to the church widows and usually hired me to care for the shepherds on those nights. I hadn't given up hope she and Pastor Mays would hire me to train their canine friends. Until then, I'd work with the animals whenever possible.

I pulled into my driveway and gathered my belongings. Phone, purse, water bottle, and that was all. The dollar store bag with the harness had disappeared. A quick search under the seat and in the back confirmed my suspicion. I sent a text to Wade, asking him to come by.

He replied he'd stop by within the next hour.

Anger, frustration, and a bit of fear settled in. I couldn't sit in my vehicle until the sheriff appeared, so I headed inside and took care of Sunny.

Chapter Thirty-eight

WADE AND I STOOD IN MY DRIVEWAY after I told him my story. He opened the passenger door. "It can't just have disappeared."

"I promise you, it did." Thunder rumbled in the distance. "The bag with the pink harness was in the passenger seat."

He stuck one hand under the seat and came up empty. After searching the glove compartment, console, and the rest of the interior, he faced me. "Where did you go between the store and here?"

"I started at your place to walk Duke." I gave him a blow-by-blow account of my schedule.

"Do you always lock your doors when you're at a client's house?"

The fight left me. "It's been so stinking hot, and I left the windows down."

He crossed his arms. "That explains the how."

At least he appeared to believe me now. "Wade, it's got to be Ivey Gilbert. She's the only one who knew I had the harness. I'm more convinced it matches the leash used to strangle Norris. The only reason I bought it was for you to see if they matched." I could see my reflection in his mirrored sunglasses, but I had no clue what he thought.

"It won't prove she killed her husband."

"I thought if the harness and leash matched, you could ask the store manager if they could tell when the leash was sold. If they said yes, and if they found the day and time, and if they have security footage, you could see who bought the leash."

"Those are five mighty big ifs, but I'll swing by or send one of my deputies to the store. It's possible we'll get lucky. Stranger things have happened."

"Wade, thanks for not laughing in my face."

"You're welcome. If Ivey bought the leash and strangled Norris, you could be seen as a threat. Some of my deputies will go to each of the homes you were at this afternoon and ask if neighbors saw anything suspicious."

"That's a great idea."

He laughed. "You sound surprised. Don't forget, I was trained to investigate crimes."

"I know you're a great sheriff. Thanks again."

"You bet." Wade walked away.

Marc appeared in his red truck and parked behind Wade's vehicle on the street. The two men talked, and I sat on the steps until Marc strolled up to me. "Sounds like you've had a little excitement." He loosened his tie.

"More than you know. I guess Wade caught you up on the most recent activities."

"The missing harness? Yes."

I reached for his hand and held it tight. "There's something inside I need to show you. I meant for it to be a surprise, then I got nervous."

He smiled. "Good or bad surprise?"

"I hope you think it's good."

"You shouldn't be nervous of my reaction. Lay it on me."

"You know how much I want the house to feel like our home. I want you to be comfortable and not feel like you're invading my space. So, I hired Griffin for a project. Then it occurred to me you might like to offer some input."

"Okay, now you're starting to make me nervous. Why don't you simply tell me what you did?"

I kept a grip on his hand and led him inside. The room being converted to his office was to our right, with the window facing the front yard. "Tada."

He released my hand and frowned. He filled the doorframe with his feet spread shoulder-width apart and arms crossed. "I'm not sure what you want me to envision. Is it going to be our future dining room? Another living room? Give me a hint."

"We're converting it into your home office." I found the plan Griffin had drawn up for me laying on a sawhorse and passed it to Marc. "It'll have bookshelves on this wall, a comfy chair, plenty of lights, and your desk can go in the center of the space. This is what I imagined you'd like, but Griffin will meet you here early tomorrow morning and make any revisions you'd prefer."

Marc studied the drawing then walked through the room. "I've never spent any time in here. Are you sure you don't want it for entertaining?"

"Nope. This is your space now." A memory of Norris dead behind his desk sent a shiver up my spine. I shook it off. "If you'd rather have a pool table or something else, that's fine. I like my little office in back of the house and thought you'd enjoy this space."

"I like the idea of working from home in the evenings. The office can be gloomy without anyone around."

His words pinched my heart. Marc had changed from a grumpy boat-building hermit to a social human being after nursing wounds from his childhood. I hated the thought of him feeling lonely. "You didn't remodel your law office when you rented the space. We can paint the walls at work and make it nicer. My first question is, would you like a home office?"

He bent down and ran his fingers over the floor. "I don't need a man cave, a movie theater room, or a pool table. I'd rather be outside when I have free time. Although a home office would give us more time together, and I like the thought of that. Maybe we can add a little TV so I can watch sports when I get tired of watching your mystery shows."

I chuckled. "I've always enjoyed trying to solve the crime whether it's a fictional mystery or true crime."

"Yeah, I know. I don't know about color preferences." He walked around the room again. "I'm more into blues. Light brown walls also appeal to me. I don't want you to go to a lot of trouble and expense though. If you just give me a little space in the garage area for kayaks and bikes, I'll be good."

"Sure, but aren't you keeping the boat shed by the river? I thought that was the only condition we'd given Lacey Jane and David when we gifted them your house." With my recent inheritance, we'd shared property with both of my siblings. The areas we'd saved for ourselves was the boat shed, the dock on the river, and some area on the Kennady farm for my dog business and future animal rescue shelter.

"Yeah, but we'll need a couple of kayaks for the marsh or to take out in the ocean. It'll also be nice to ride our bikes on nice days."

"Sounds fun. I've been meaning to get the garage space better organized. It sounds like the time is now." My house was raised, and the garage was under the house.

"Thanks." He placed the office plans on a ladder, then took me in his arms.

"You don't need to thank me. Maybe we should look for another house so you'll feel at home."

He kissed my forehead. "You're overthinking my moving in here. Home is more than a structure. Home is wherever you'll be. I love you, Andi Grace."

"I love you, too." I tiptoed up and kissed him. His words humbled and blessed me.

Chapter Thirty-nine

THE ROAR OF WAVES CRASHING ON THE BEACH confirmed there was a tropical storm in the Atlantic. I stood on the back porch waiting for Sunny to finish sniffing around.

Marc joined me. "I just received a storm warning alert on my phone. One of the models projects Heyward Beach will take a direct hit. Do you have a hurricane plan?"

"In the past, we packed up and headed inland. The island is prone to flooding, especially if a storm hits at high tide. King tides flood the island too. I feel like this house will survive a hurricane better than my old one, but I don't want to get stuck here. The bed-and-breakfast should be safe from flooding, but there are a lot of old trees and some of the sheds don't seem stable. The residual tornadoes could be dangerous there."

"Still, it'll be safer there than here."

"I agree."

Sunny lumbered up the steps and we took her inside.

Marc said, "I need to get home and prepare for the meeting with Griffin and another early morning meeting. There's plenty of time to get ready for Hurricane Gabe."

"You're right, and with a little luck, Gabe will fizzle out." I walked with Marc to the front door. "On a happier note, we need to decide on flowers for the wedding. Do you want to help make those decisions?"

He shrugged. "I'm not much of a flower person. Can you handle it? I'll touch base with Erin on food."

"Sounds good. Divide and conquer." I kissed him. "Hey, do you realize we've spent the evening together and never once discussed Norris's murder?"

"Su-weet. It's probably why I don't feel stressed. Do you feel safe by yourself?"

"Yeah, I don't think I made anyone mad enough to come after me tonight. Plus, Sunny will protect me."

"Okay. Lock up and set the security system. I'll talk to you tomorrow."

After Marc left, I played a Lincoln Zane album and checked my tote of hurricane supplies. The mosquito repellant had expired, and so had the supposedly non-perishable food. I started a list of supplies to add to my tote. If the National Hurricane Center and local weather forecasters firmed up their predictions of us getting hit hard, the stores would be packed. I added batteries, moist towelettes, food, water, and fresh first aid supplies to my list.

I scooted the tote under the table, grabbed my journals, and set the house alarm. Sunny followed me to my room and fell asleep while I prepared for bed. I stepped around her slumbering form and crawled into bed, propping up my pillows against the headboard.

Who had stolen the pink dog harness I'd bought at the dollar store?

Ivey probably saw my purchase when we were talking outside of the store. Nobody else besides the clerk knew I'd purchased the harness. Ivey's daughter and grandsons had been with her, and it was unlikely she'd bring them on a mission to steal the harness. I never rushed dog-walking appointments, so Ivey would've had time to take her family home and make up an excuse to leave again.

Heyward Beach was a small town, and Ivey probably knew some of my clients. It was doubtful she'd made the snatch at the sheriff's house.

Phyllis Mays and Ivey were good friends. Ivey probably knew Tuesdays were one of the nights our church took dinner to shut-ins. Did Ivey predict I'd stop by to take care of Captain and Pumpkin? Phyllis often hired me to care for the dogs when she was involved in church activities.

It wouldn't have been impossible for Ivey to park on the street and wait for my arrival. There were no HOA rules in Phyllis's neighborhood, and people often parallel parked in front of houses. Nothing unusual in that. If Ivey had driven a vehicle belonging to one of her kids, it'd be even less likely I'd notice her.

Had she been waiting for me in hopes I'd show up at Phyllis's place? When I entered the house to take care of Pumpkin and Captain, had Ivey hurried over and taken the package from my SUV? I'd left the Highlander in the shade with the windows down, and it would've been easy to retrieve the bag from the dollar store.

Why would she have stolen the harness? To prevent me from linking it to the leash? Again, why? Had she bought the flashy pink leash, intending to strangle Norris? It would've been less obvious if she'd bought a black leash. Not very smart, and Ivey was clever. It didn't make sense to buy something a clerk would remember.

If Ivey bought the neon pink leash, had she planned to use it as a murder weapon? Or could there have been a big argument and she strangled Norris in the heat of the moment?

How shrewd was Ivey? Did she call me pretending she needed me to check on Lady? Was I part of her intricate alibi?

Ivey told the authorities and me she was in Savannah to pick up food from Molly's Deli for the family vacation. I'd unpacked her cooler of food from the deli, but I'd forgotten to call the place to see if anyone remembered Ivey being there. The widow didn't seem to be grieving her husband's death, and it appeared she didn't want her family talking to anyone. Was it because there'd been no family vacation planned?

I couldn't fathom what she'd done on Friday morning. There was also the dognapping. Had Lady escaped the house when the murder occurred? Had the killer stolen Lady? It couldn't be a coincidence the murder and dognapping happened the same morning.

Norris had gone for a golf lesson with a man who'd been angry with him. After the lesson, Norris had returned home. Maybe it'd been to shower before driving to Savannah, or maybe it'd been to pick up Lady.

Oh, what had Norris been wearing when he was strangled? He came home, was strangled, and died. I squeezed my eyes shut and remembered the murder scene. Norris had worn a white polo and black shorts, but I didn't know if they were golf clothes or vacation attire. It probably didn't matter.

If Ivey was innocent of killing her husband, there was still something bizarre going on. Ivey and Norris had been up to no good. If I could discover the truth behind their secret, I might be able to prove if she was innocent or guilty.

Chapter Forty

IT WAS NINE THIRTY WEDNESDAY MORNING and I still hadn't homed in on the person who murdered Norris Gilbert. Marc had met Griffin at my house before I left for my dog-walking appointments. We'd barely had time to speak, and now that I had a break, I decided to pick up coffee at Daily Java and take a cup to him.

"Good morning," Erin greeted me when I entered the building.

"Morning." There weren't many people inside eating. A group of women sat in one corner, with their Bibles open and a plate of pastries in the middle of the table. Each person had a drink beside them as well. In the far corner was a man eating a breakfast sandwich and looking at his electronic tablet. A turquoise insulated mug sat on the table. It had to be Rhett Alton.

"What can I get you today?" She smiled but her eyes lacked sparkle.

"Erin, do you feel okay?" Poor thing had worked extra hours during the past weekend, and she was a one-woman show. "You must be exhausted."

"You sound like my family. The Labor Day activities helped my business, and I'm going to close on Mondays for the rest of September. I'll be fine, but thanks for asking."

"Okay, I hope you can hire more help soon." I read her chalkboard listing the daily specials. "I'd like one smores and one pumpkin spice latte. Iced, please."

"Two blended lattes, coming right up." We exchanged money. "I'm going over to speak to Rhett Alton. Take your time."

"Is that code for stall?" She laughed.

"Looks like you've got me figured out. Thanks." I moseyed over to the table and faced Rhett. "Hi there. Do you have a minute to chat?"

"Have a seat." He folded the wax paper around the remainder of his sandwich as if he was afraid my germs would reach it.

I sat before he changed his mind. "I'll get straight to the point. I know you wanted to sue Norris for insurance fraud, but how did that work? If patients had to pay cash for their appointments, how was it possible for the clinic to commit insurance fraud?"

"It's a little thing known as the anti-kickback statute." The tone of his voice insinuated I must be an idiot.

"Can you enlighten me how that works?" I didn't take notes because of Rhett's skittishness in the past.

"After Aunt Stephanie went to work for the clinic, she realized it was more of a pill mill than a place to help patients get life-changing treatment. She did her best to spend time creating care plans, but the clinic's owners booked her for multiple patients at a time. They only wanted her to hand out narcotic prescriptions, but I digress." He reached for his cup and turned it in his hands. "The clinic owners also owned laboratories and a couple of pharmacies. The owners didn't want Aunt Stephanie to order urine tests."

"Urine tests?"

"Yeah, to see if the patients were taking the pain medicines she prescribed. She tried to fight back, but it was useless. She cared about the patients and she was under contract, so she stayed. Before her death, a patient brought his insurance bill and questioned her about some of the expenses. There were reports of urine tests and steroid injections. The patient knew neither should have been billed to him. Aunt Stephanie investigated and that's when she discovered the same people owned the labs."

"And that's illegal because—"

"It's an improper relationship and leads to an increase in health-care expenses. Aunt Stephanie also found out that the doctors who played nice got kickbacks from the laboratories."

"Gotcha. Insurance fraud. Rhett, do you believe you're in danger?"

"Ah, it sounds like you heard the rumors of the clinic being owned by the mob. Aunt Stephanie didn't believe it, and neither do I." His hands stilled. "However, I wouldn't put anything past Norris Gilbert. The pressure he exerted on my aunt was tremendous, and I blame him for her suicide."

"Did you ever wonder if she was murdered?"

He looked at the table. "No. I'm out of here." Rhett snatched his sandwich and drink and huffed off.

The man's words didn't match his angry movements, making me wonder if he believed she really was murdered. If so, why did he deny it?

Erin sat across from me and set the drinks on the table. "Andi Grace, on Friday morning Rhett was here and bought two smoothies. It was around nine or ten o'clock."

"Okay." I gave her time to get to the point.

"When I watched him walk out of here this morning, it reminded me of Friday. Every other time he's ordered coffee here, he's had me put it in the turquoise travel mug. It didn't matter if he ordered a cold or hot drink. It was always his personal cup. Friday, he took the drinks in two paper cups. It could be nothing, like he ordered them for friends, but I thought it was worth mentioning."

I gripped her hand. "That's a brilliant observation. If you need to tell Wade, I understand. But I wouldn't tell anyone else."

"You're scaring me."

"Sorry, that wasn't my intention. Just be careful until they catch the killer."

I headed to Marc's office with the two lattes and texted him when I reached the parking lot. Marc's office manager was loyal to him to a fault. Whenever I showed up, she treated me like an unwelcome interruption.

Marc walked out to where I sat thinking in my SUV, and he hopped into the passenger seat. "Hey, this is a nice surprise."

I leaned over and kissed him. "I brought you a cold latte. Would you prefer pumpkin spice or smores?"

"The pumpkin sounds good, and boy am I glad it's cold."

"Blended, actually." I winked and passed him the requested drink. "How did you do with Griffin?"

"Good. My requests won't take much more money, and the time line will be the same."

"Really? I'm glad it'll be ready before our wedding. How's your morning going?"

"It's been busy, but that's not unusual for a week starting with a holiday. What about you?"

"Calling Molly's Deli is next on my to-do list. Rhett was at Daily Java and explained why he'd accused Low Country Pain Clinic of breaking the law. The same owners also have laboratories. The labs billed false claims for urine tests and somebody billed for steroid shots that weren't given. Rhett believes his aunt came here to help people suffering with pain." I finished updating him on my conversation with Rhett.

"Incredible. I would've bet money Rhett believed his aunt was murdered. My gut instinct must be off."

"Hold on. That's what he told me. After he exited in a huff, Erin shared he'd been in her place Friday morning. He ordered two smoothies. The interesting thing is he let her use paper cups instead of insisting on his travel mug for at least one drink."

Marc's watch beeped, and he glanced at it. "I've got a client waiting on me, but first remind me why the paper cups are bad. I mean, we're drinking out of paper cups right now."

"For such a strict environmentalist, it seems like he would've at least had his drink put in his personal mug. It's not proof, but what if Rhett was meeting with Norris and put the drugs in his cup beforehand?"

"You might be on to something. What's your next move?"

"Call the deli, and then maybe contact Ivey one more time. Later, I need to pick up Duke and take him to Stay and Play. Wade says this case is causing him to neglect his dog."

"Okay. Please don't do anything dangerous." He reached for the door handle.

"I'll keep you posted, even if you can't reply to my texts."

"Sounds good." He gave me a brief kiss then returned to his office, paper coffee cup in hand.

I dialed the number for Molly's Deli and asked to speak to the owner.

"This is Molly."

"Hi, I'm Andi Grace Scott, and I live in Heyward Beach, South Carolina."

"How can I help you?" Her voice had a lilting Southern accent and no hint of an Irish dialect.

"My friend Ivey Gilbert was at your place Friday morning, and I was wondering if she left her blue scarf with the palmetto tree. Do you remember seeing Ivey on Friday?"

"I can't forget her. She was waiting when I arrived to open the deli. She's been a good customer over the years, and she's a good tipper. Anyway, she said she'd placed an order for the weekend, and I couldn't find it anywhere. I offered her a cup of coffee while she waited. It took me a bit to get her food together, and some people would've pitched a hissy fit. Not Mrs. Gilbert. She couldn't have been nicer."

If Molly had reported that Ivey blew her stack, it would've been more believable. She wasn't the most tolerant person around. I needed to put some thought into Ivey's reaction.

"You know, I questioned my employees later and nobody remembers taking an order from Mrs. Gilbert." Molly sighed. "As for the blue scarf, she must've lost it somewhere else. I don't remember her wearing a scarf while she was here."

"Okay. Don't worry about it." I felt guilty for misleading the woman. "Say, what time do you open?"

"Seven o'clock. Sharp."

"Right. Thanks for your time, and I'm sorry to have bothered you."

"You were no bother. Have a nice day."

"You too." I sipped my blended drink and made notes about our conversation.

Ivey had gotten to the deli way earlier than I had imagined. Her order wasn't ready, and she had remained calm. Ivey had high standards, and she expected them to be met. Maybe the thought of vacation with her family had put her in a good mood, if there really was a family vacation planned. The home security system being completely shut down still disturbed me. What wealthy person intentionally shut off the house alarm when they left town?

Why did Ivey leave so early Friday morning? Had she really placed the food order, or was it a last-minute thought to prove she was in Savannah? Could Ivey have driven to Savannah, picked up the food, then come back home to strangle Norris?

I slurped my drink. Sitting here and thinking about the murder wouldn't catch the killer.

I looked up the distance from here to Molly's Deli and calculated the time. Well, what do you know? The time line was doable.

I pulled out of Marc's parking lot and headed to Ivey Gilbert's home.

Chapter Forty-one

THE GUARD WAVED ME THROUGH THE ACCESS to the gated community, and I passed Ivey's middle daughter and granddaughter on the street driving a Suburban. They appeared to be in deep conversation and didn't return my wave.

The driveway at the Gilberts' house was empty except for Ivey's Lexus. I parked behind it, then climbed the stairs to the front door.

The ferocious crash of waves on the sand warned me to check the latest hurricane predictions. Even if the hurricane didn't hit us, we were in for some rough weather.

Lady barked before I could ring the bell.

The door swung open. "What'd you forget?" Ivey didn't look up from the screen of her tablet.

"Um, hey, it's me." I caught a glance of what she'd been looking at but pretended not to notice. It appeared to be a seating chart for an airplane.

Lady ran outside, licked my hand, then trotted inside.

Ivey met my gaze then turned off her tablet, preventing me from getting a closer look at her screen. "Andi Grace, I'd invite you in but I'm terribly busy."

"That's okay. Has your family left?"

"Yes, they all have busy lives. As do I." She wore a navy-and-white-checked shirtdress and black sandals.

"This was supposed to be your family vacation. Why would they leave you alone when you're grieving?"

"I'm going to take a little trip to mourn on my own. There are too many memories here. It makes sense to me that I can deal with Norris's death better without so many memories of him all around." She rolled her head. "What do you need?"

"Ivey, it's come to my attention that you were in Savannah before seven o'clock Friday morning."

Her eyes widened. "Are you spying on me, Andi Grace? Should I report you to the sheriff for stalking me?"

I had no intention of revealing my source. "No. Have you told the sheriff you're leaving town?"

"That's none of your business, nor is it Sheriff Stone's."

"You've got to realize you're a murder suspect."

Her shoulders slumped. "Come inside."

I followed her to the seating area. She took the couch, and I sat in a bamboo armchair with beige-linen-covered cushions. "What's going on, Ivey?"

Lady walked to me, and I rubbed her head.

"How much do you know?"

"To begin with, I don't believe you and Norris were planning to meet your family in Tybee Island for a vacation."

"That seems like an odd conclusion. You just admitted to knowing I was in Savannah early Friday morning." She leaned back and crossed one leg over the other. The sandal dangled on her foot.

"True." I reached for my phone and texted my location to Marc then found the map app and flashed it for her to see. "I verified the distance and time it'd take for you to drive to Molly's Deli. If you double it, there was ample time for you to make a round trip and strangle your husband without anyone suspecting you."

"That's ridiculous."

"I don't think so. What about your plane tickets to Bali? And why didn't you arm your security system? What was really going on?" I pretended to turn off my phone. Instead, I tapped the video mode of my camera app. It'd make a nice recording of our conversation.

She lifted her chin and pinched the bridge of her nose. "Norris had made a couple bad business decisions. He believed someone had begun to follow him, and we decided to leave town for a while."

"Did you report it to the cops?"

Lady settled at my feet instead of going to Ivey.

"They wouldn't believe us."

"Of course they would. Do you think the mob was following Norris?"

"Pish posh." She made a dismissive motion with her hand. "Whoever started the rumor that the mob was in Heyward Beach should get a good whipping."

"If Norris didn't have ties to the mob, who do you believe was following him?"

"You know good and well that I've said all along it must've been a disgruntled client."

Cheyenne Marther was the only person I knew who'd hired Norris to be her attorney. "How about Rhett Alton? His aunt was Stephanie Rich."

"He and Norris had a couple of altercations, but I assumed they had to do with the environment."

"Mr. Alton accused the clinic of committing crimes."

"My only responsibility was to sell the building. I know nothing about the pain clinic's billing methods." She held out her hand and inspected her red manicured nails. "Are you finished?"

"Let's make sure I've got the facts straight. First off, you and Norris were heading to Bali either forever or until he felt safe."

Her complexion paled.

"Wait, did you plan to never return?" It would explain why family pictures had been removed.

Ivey frowned. "We considered the possibility of living in Bali permanently."

I remembered the list of numbers Wade, Marc, and I had found, but I couldn't say anything. "If you commit a crime and move to Bali, you can't be extradited. Is that why you chose to go to Indonesia?"

Silence.

"You claim you don't believe there are any mobsters in Heyward Beach. Norris thought he had a stalker. In your opinion, the killer is one of Norris's clients."

"That sums it up." Her gaze left mine and traveled to the schnoodle snoozing by my feet. "Do you have room to board Lady at Stay and Play?"

"Yes. Will you return for her?"

Ivey walked to the long eating table and opened her purse. She removed a wad of money. "This should cover her visit. If you need more, text me."

I joined her and accepted the money without counting it. "Do you plan to return to South Carolina? If not, does anyone in your family want Lady, or should I find her a new home?"

"She preferred Norris to me. It's possible she needs a fresh environment to recover from his death."

If she wouldn't give me a straight answer, I needed to be clear. "If I don't hear from you when I run out of money, I will search for a family to adopt Lady."

"Your terms are acceptable to me. Give me a moment to gather her supplies."

Standing alone at the table, I texted Wade that Ivey planned to leave town.

"Here is her favorite food. She likes these snacks." Ivey lifted a box of treats. "You're the professional, so I don't need to explain all the other items in here."

"It always helps to know what a dog is used to. There's less chance of an upset tummy."

Ivey put the lid on the plastic tote and scooted it across the table to me. "You take that, and I'll bring the dog."

I followed Ivey and Lady down to my Highlander and got the dog settled in a crate in the back of my SUV. After a recent motion sickness episode with a dog I was transporting, I had taken to putting pets in the crate. No more dog vomit in my lap. The very remembrance made me want to gag.

The sheriff drove up and parked across the street from us.

Ivey glared at me. "It didn't take you long to report me, although I'm not sure how you accomplished it."

Wade walked to us. "Good morning, ladies. Mrs. Gilbert, do you mind if I have a word?"

"Fine." Her scowl deepened.

"Ivey, do you still want me to take Lady?"

"Yes." The word sizzled and hissed.

"Okay."

Wade and Ivey stood in the shade of her garage, and I drove to Wade's house. It was time to pick up Duke and take both dogs to Stay and Play.

Chapter Forty-two

LINCOLN ZANE STOOD BY HIS BLUE CHEVY PICKUP, talking on a cell phone, when I drove up to the dog barn.

I parked in the shade, and Belle greeted me when I hopped out. "Hi, Miss Andi Grace."

"Hi there. Please, just call me Andi Grace."

"Yes, ma'am. Dad brought me here to discuss the job opening." Her thick dark hair had been pulled back in a messy bun, and her blue eyes shone.

I opened the back of my SUV and opened Duke's crate first. "This is the sheriff's dog. Duke is part collie, friendly, and high energy. He's going to spend the afternoon with us, and Sheriff Stone will pick him up this evening."

She nodded. "The sheriff is probably too busy to play with his dog while trying to solve the murder. Dad said you're pretty good at catching killers."

"I've helped out a time or two."

"Cool."

Duke barked and ran to the barn, where Dylan greeted him.

I reached for Lady and cuddled the little black-and-white bundle of fur to my chest. "This little one is a schnoodle. Her name is Lady, and she actually belonged to the latest murder victim."

"Aw, she's so adorable. Can I hold her?"

"Absolutely." I passed the dog to Belle then reached for her container of supplies.

Lincoln remained on the phone and smiled as we passed by him.

Inside the barn, I introduced Belle to Dylan.

After a few moments of awkward conversation, I faced Dylan. "Belle could be your replacement, and I need you to train her today."

"Great."

I turned to Belle. "This will give you a chance to see if this job is a good fit. Have you figured out transportation?"

"Yes. We bought a used Jeep Cherokee yesterday. If you give me the job, I can start anytime."

"Sounds good. I'll let Dylan start explaining what the job entails. Feel free to be honest if you decide it's not for you. There's no pressure." I walked to my office. If Belle worked out, it'd be perfect. Dylan could continue living in his studio apartment in the barn, and Belle could commute from the beach house where she lived with her dad.

I pulled the wad of money Ivey had given me from the pocket in my shorts. Whoa, all hundred-dollar bills. I counted them, then counted again. Seventeen hundred dollars.

"Knock, knock." Lincoln tapped on my door.

"Come in."

"Belle didn't come back out, so I decided to investigate."

"Hey, that's my second job." I laughed. "Dylan is going to train her. Is it okay if she spends the day here? She can leave with me and go to some of my dog-walking appointments. I'll have her home after six."

"I don't want to take advantage."

"You're not. I offered. It'll give me the opportunity to get to know Belle better and see what she thinks about taking the job."

Lincoln ran his fingers over the rim of his ballcap. "Thanks, Andi Grace. I'll speak to her on my way out."

"See you tonight." When he left, I sat down and filled out a deposit slip. It might not be a lot of money to Ivey, but it was huge to my business.

Cheyenne had offered to be my bookkeeper. She claimed to have experience, but it must've been before her addiction problems. It didn't seem smart to trust an addict with money.

Cheyenne wasn't much younger than me. From a distance, the woman's small frame led you to believe she was a teenager. Up close, it was easier to see how the drugs had taken a toll on her appearance.

I smoothed the money. Why did Ivey have so much cash on her? Had it been part of her attempt to disappear with Gilbert? No trail of credit card receipts?

When I'd arrived at her place earlier, she'd admitted she needed to leave town to grieve her loss. Maybe her plan had been to completely disappear. There wouldn't be a paper trail if she only used cash. Or could the money be to buy herself a new identity? Nobody would find her if she didn't use credit cards, her passport, or any other identification.

If Ivey wasn't guilty of murdering Norris, why would she plan to leave town and probably the country?

Chapter Forty-three

AFTERNOON SHOWERS always made walking dogs more challenging. Good. It would give Belle a better understanding of what this job required. The hard rainfall demanded the highest speed of my wipers. The trip down River Road wracked my nerves, and I would admit it was in part due to my experience with Freddie Fisher trying to run me off the road.

Belle rode shotgun and hummed an unfamiliar tune. Chubb rode in a crate in the back. We'd picked him up right after we left Stay and Play. He didn't need to be contained because of motion sickness, but it was the safest option given the driving conditions.

First stop was to check on Yoyo. The black Lab had been training with me for longer than necessary. His owners, Ethan and Violet Seitz, needed the lessons as much as the Lab.

"There's a cheap poncho in the console that you can wear. You'll want a sturdier one if you take the job. Most of your time will be at the farm, but there will be days I need to schedule you for dog-walking appointments."

"Yes, ma'am." Belle removed the frosted white plastic rain garment. "Is this better than a rain jacket?"

"In my experience, a poncho keeps your clothes drier, and it's easier to move around in it. Umbrellas keep the water off you until the wind blows. Then you may as well call it quits."

"Okay. Poncho it is. I have rain boots."

"They will be perfect if you need to step into the grass to pick up dog droppings. The only time I don't mind wet feet is when I'm in the ocean or a pool."

"I hear ya."

We took care of Yoyo and drove to Waccamaw Retirement Community. I discovered Belle was not only good with the pets, but she did an amazing job with the older adults.

The rain had lessened by the time we finished our appointments. I drove to the island. "Belle, you've impressed me today. The job is yours, if you still want it. Dylan can continue training you the next few days, and then you can fly solo. What do you think?"

"Yes!" She squealed in the passenger seat. "Thank you so much. You won't regret hiring me. I've got to text my dad." She hummed while texting.

I motored over the causeway and made my way to Lincoln's place. From the look of the marsh, it was high tide. Lincoln was standing in the garage when we arrived at his beach house.

Belle unbuckled her seat belt. "Thanks again for believing in me. I promise not to disappoint you."

"I have faith you'll do a terrific job. See you later."

Lincoln hugged his daughter when she got out of my vehicle. She ran inside, and he slid into the passenger seat. "You made her day. I owe you one."

"She's amazing, and I'm lucky she wants to work for me. What did you do today?"

"I mostly researched how to survive a hurricane. Tonight, I'll stock up on supplies."

"Brace yourself for a mob, because if the latest weather model shows it hitting us, you're going to deal with crowds."

"Guess that's to be expected."

Chubb whined in back.

"I should get him home. He and Sunny need time to run around while it's only sprinkling." I smiled at Marc's best friend. "You're welcome to stay at the bed-and-breakfast or with Marc. Don't put yourself in danger, thinking you should ride out the hurricane."

"You're right. Just like you shouldn't put your life in danger trying to solve a murder when we have a good sheriff's department."

"Ouch, that hurt." I laughed.

"See ya around." He stepped out of my Highlander and jogged the short distance to his garage.

"One more stop, Chubb." I drove to the closet branch of the bank and made a deposit before heading home.

Marc's truck was backed into my driveway, and the hurricane shutters had been lowered.

I hopped out of my vehicle and released Chubb. "Go find Marc, boy."

The golden retriever raced to the gate, splashing in puddles along the way. He barked until Marc opened the gate. Sunny was at his side, and Marc knelt to pet his dog. "Hey, I wasn't sure if you heard the forecast. They predict the storm will be a Category Three by midnight." He motioned for me to follow him.

Chubb ran circles around Marc, then he and Sunny raced around the wet yard.

I secured the gate behind us and followed my fiancé up the steps to the back patio. "Cat Three, huh?"

"Afraid so." He wore athletic shorts and a faded T-shirt with the drawing of a boat and words warning the reader not to rock his boat. Marc fisted his hands on his hips. "At first, I thought we could move the patio furniture into the kitchen, but it's wet. I should've come over sooner. I believe the best thing to do is carry it to the garage. Care to lend a hand?"

In the past, Nate had helped me with hurricane preparations. Was it fair to expect Marc to step in before we were married? "I'll figure something out. Don't you need to prepare your office and the boat shed? If we're looking at a Cat Three, the river might flood your shed."

"Hey now, you keep telling me to think of this place as my home too, and I'm here to help get it ready so there's minimum storm damage." One side of his mouth lifted.

"Touché." I threw my arms around his neck and kissed him. "You are so good to me."

He kissed me again, then pulled back. "As much as I'd like to continue this romantic moment, my gut tells me we need to get cracking. I've lived through hurricanes before, but this is the first time on an island."

"And it'll be my first time in this house, so we'll experience our first hurricane together here. I've got tarps in the garage. Let's bring them up and cram all this into the kitchen. It'll conserve our energy if we don't have to carry everything around the house and down to the garage."

"I like the way you think. So we'll gather the tarps, and maybe rags or old towels to dry the furniture as we go."

It sprinkled on and off for the next hour, but we moved the furniture, flower pots, dog bowls, and basically anything the wind could turn into a dangerous projectile. When we finished, we collapsed on the couch.

Marc patted his flat stomach. "I'm starving."

"Me, too."

"Let's call Tony's and order a pizza. Unless you prefer something healthier."

I laughed. "Pizza is always a good option. After supper, should we work on your office?"

"The furniture doesn't worry me, and Griffin has a guy coming to board up my windows. I don't have the plywood, and he offered, so I took him up on it. My files and computers are the real issue." Marc swiped his phone and called the pizza place.

The closed shutters made the interior of my house darker, so I walked around and turned on every light. I sat on the couch and leaned my head on

Marc's shoulder. "Thanks for all your hard work."

"You're welcome."

Sunny snoozed, but Chubb walked restlessly around the dim interior of the house.

"If you decided to leave the country, how would you hide your client files?"

"We're not discussing me anymore, are we?" He squeezed my hand. "I guess you're thinking about Norris."

"Yeah. The ransom demand for Lady wasn't for money. The dognapper wanted files from the clinic and the law practice."

"Right. And Cheyenne said she wanted the files to blackmail Norris's clients." Marc rubbed his chin. "My hunch is Norris recommended the clinic to all of his clients who'd been in accidents."

"And the clinic would refer Norris to patients who wanted to file a lawsuit."

"Exactly." I turned my body so my shoulder was on the couch cushion, and I faced Marc.

He adjusted his position so we were face-to-face and still holding hands. "You are so smart, Andi Grace. It's amazing how you can put the pieces of a puzzle together and solve a murder."

My face grew warm. He was the smart one, and I didn't feel worthy of his compliment. I didn't want to be the type of person, though, who argued in order to get more positive feedback. "Thanks."

Thunder rumbled, and both dogs growled. Sunny leapt to her feet and looked at the back door.

Marc said, "When will you leave here?"

"I plan to spend at least one more night. If Hurricane Gabe slows down, I'll stay longer."

"But not so long as to put yourself in danger." His eyebrows rose. "Right?"

"For sure. I'll get up early and check the forecast. If Gabe gains strength and heads toward us, I'll pack a bag before leaving for my morning appointments. I wish he'd fizzle out in the Atlantic."

"Me, too."

Chubb barked and raced to the front door right before the doorbell rang.

Marc laughed. "That must be our pizza."

"I hope you're right." I fixed drinks for us while he dealt with the delivery person. We bounced murder theories around while we chowed down.

Who besides Cheyenne went to the pain clinic and used Norris Gilbert as their attorney? If we could figure out the answer, we might be closer to catching the killer.

Chapter Forty-four

MARC'S OFFICE WINDOWS HAD BEEN BOARDED, and there was a sense of gloom inside the building. Most evenings there'd be a bit of moonlight or lights from local businesses seeping in. Just like my home, the place was dark. Turning on all the lights helped, but there was a chill in the room.

We wasted no time preparing for the storm. Marc wrapped cords and labeled them. Some electronics fit in plastic containers. Others we wrapped in large garbage bags to keep dry. Chubb sniffed around the rooms and found something to munch on in the conference room.

Marc glanced around the large conference room, which was furnished with a long table and chairs. "There's nothing in here to move."

"Good. It's not raining as hard right now. Should we move the items you've got ready to the truck?"

"May as well." He grabbed the heaviest objects, and together we loaded the backseat of his truck with computers and other electronics. He locked his vehicle and returned to the office.

Chubb paced near the door.

"Marc, if you hand me his leash, I'll walk him around the building."

"Are you sure you don't mind? It's starting to rain harder."

"It's what I do, plus, you need to decide what to do to protect your paper files. I can't help with that."

"True." He attached the leash to Chubb's collar, and I led him to the azaleas along the side of the parking lot.

A little car drove by at a slow rate of speed. The vehicle was dark, low to the ground, and appeared to be a Mini Cooper.

Chubb tugged on the leash, and I followed him to the next bush while keeping an eye on the vehicle. It'd be ridiculous to think Rhett Alton was driving on the island, at night, and in the rain. He lived on the mainland. "Hey, Chubb. Let's go this way."

The golden retriever barked, and we splashed our way across the parking lot and down the sidewalk. I wore a poncho and rain boots, and water swirled above my ankles. A gust of wind blew my cover toward the sky, and I slapped it down. Puddles got deeper, and I stopped sloshing through the water. I lost sight of the car, but I didn't want the water to knock me down.

"Andi Grace, where are you?" Marc's voice rang out.

"We're coming." We retraced our steps at a much slower pace. "Sorry about that. Do you have a towel for Chubb?"

"Yeah. Come back inside." He hurried down the hall and soon returned with beach towels. "I'll dry Chubb, and you can use this one." He passed me a bright blue towel.

"Thanks." I removed my rain gear and began blotting my damp hair. "We saw a Mini Cooper drive by. Do you think it could've been Rhett?"

"Why would he be driving around here tonight?"

"You know Ethan saw Rhett cruising in their neighborhood Friday morning. Oh, I'll text him and ask him to look out the window." I pulled the phone out of my pocket with pruney fingers and fired off a text message. "People usually remove the gates from their private communities when storms brew in the ocean."

"Yeah, a flood will destroy the mechanisms of the security system. Even if people are free to drive to that end of the beach, Ethan won't be able to see much if his windows are already covered."

My phone vibrated. It was Ethan. *I'll stand on the front porch and watch.*

"Look, he might be suspicious of Rhett too."

Marc's eyes narrowed, but he ran the towel over Chubb's body.

I dried off to the best of my ability, but the damp clothes clung to my skin. "What's next?"

He motioned for me to follow him. We walked down the main hall, and he opened accordion closet doors. The space was lined with white wire shelves. "In case I have flooding, let's move everything from the bottom shelves to the top."

I eyed the space. "Should we use all the shelves taller than four feet?"

"That works for me. I'll empty the desks in case they float around or tip over."

We got busy. I moved packages of copy paper, boxes of office supplies, as well as tissue boxes and paper towels to high shelves.

Thirty minutes later my phone vibrated. Another message appeared from Ethan. *Sorry. No sign of the Mini Cooper.*

I texted a reply to him. *Thanks for trying. Stay safe.*

Either the driver wasn't Rhett Alton or he went somewhere other than the gated community.

We returned to working on our projects. After I crammed as much as possible into the closet, I headed to Marc's office.

He was pulling files out of his cabinet. Some he dropped onto the desk, and others he fit into a fireproof box.

"You've got a lot of paper files to deal with. How can I help?"

"This is all confidential." He stuffed another folder into the box. "I'll drive you home."

"No way. It's not far, and Sunny's waiting for me. It's safe enough to drive myself."

He opened his mouth.

"Really. I can even text you when I'm inside with the security system armed." I kissed his cheek. "Keep working so you can make it home before it gets late."

He dropped the papers onto the desk. "I may agree to you driving yourself home, but that kiss wasn't much to brag about." His eyes twinkled.

"Challenge accepted." I wrapped my arms around his neck. He leaned down, and our lips met. Nothing else mattered for the moment but this kiss.

Chapter Forty-five

I DIDN'T SEE ANY VEHICLES until I got ready to turn off Charleston Street onto Dolphin Drive. A car drove toward me and swerved.

Fear washed over me. My heart sank. Was Freddie making another attempt on my life? I slammed on the brakes and hydroplaned into the other lane.

The little car spun in a circle.

My Highlander hit the curb. The other car smashed into a mailbox, then the horn blared.

Reality slapped me. It was a car. Not Freddie's big truck.

I shifted into Park, pulled my poncho hood over my head, and waded outside to check on the driver. Shaky legs made it a struggle to walk to the other vehicle. I leaned against the side of my SUV and dialed Wade's contact information.

"This better be good."

"Wade, I've been in an accident. I'm okay but not sure about the other driver." I swiped the rain off my face and informed Wade where to find us.

"An ambulance is on the way, and I'm coming too. Is Marc there?"

"No, can you call him? I'll check on the other driver."

"Sure."

I didn't know if he'd hung up or put me on hold, so I shoved the phone into the pocket of my shorts and slogged through the rain covering the street. The vehicle was a Mini Cooper. No doubt the one I'd spotted earlier. I tapped on the window. It lowered, and I stared into the face of Rhett Alton. "Are you hurt?"

"My wrist hurts, but that doesn't make sense. Basically, I'm okay." He looked at his arm then back toward me. "What about you?"

The sky filled with light, then thunder boomed over the ocean.

I squealed and jumped. My heart raced. "Yeah, I think I'm fine."

Sirens filled the air, and red lights approached from the west.

Rhett said, "You were all over the road."

"Hey, I hydroplaned. You hit the mailbox, and I figured the same thing happened to you. Why are you on the island?"

"I needed to check on something."

"While it's raining?"

Thunder rumbled again.

"It was the perfect time to check for erosion around the building at the pier."

Erosion. Environmentalist. His story seemed plausible.

Marc parked behind my SUV. He ran over to me and clasped my shoulders. "Did y'all crash into each other? You scared the tar out of me. Next time I offer to follow you home, just agree. Are you okay?"

It was rare for Marc to be discombobulated, and it unnerved me more than a little. "I'm so glad you're here, and I'm fine. But you should be wearing rain gear."

He held me tight. "When you hear that the woman you plan to spend the rest of your life with has been in an accident, you don't stop and dress for the weather. I dropped everything and came straight here. Good thing you were nearby."

I clung tighter to him, resting my head on his chest. His heart raced. Rain splashed down on us.

The ambulance arrived, followed by Sheriff Stone. Wade wore his official lime green high-visibility raincoat. Plastic covered his official hat. He made eye contact with me through the rain and strobe lights, but he approached Rhett.

A deputy's Charger arrived and parked at a slant to block traffic, not that I imagined many vehicles would be out and about. David Wayne walked straight to us. "Andi Grace, are you okay?"

"Yeah, except for having my life flash before my eyes, I'm fine. The sight of Rhett Alton's car surprised me, and then I was sliding across the road smooth as can be until I crashed into the curb."

A streak of lightning crossed the sky followed by the boom of thunder and an echo off the water. I squealed. "We all know better than to stand outside during a storm."

"Hold on one second." David walked around my Highlander and inspected the tires against the curb.

Wade joined David, and they had a brief discussion before approaching me. Wade said, "This is two separate accidents. Nobody got hurt, and there's no need for us to stand out in the storm. Go on home, and one of us will touch base with you tomorrow, Andi Grace."

"Sounds good." I waved to the sheriff when he walked away, but David got a hug. "Thanks for coming to check on me."

He patted my back. "Of course. Is Marc going to follow you home?"

"You better believe it." I smiled at my brother-in-law. "Hey, Rhett told me he came over to the island to check on the rain and erosion around the pier restaurant."

"You don't believe him?"

I shrugged. "Maybe. It's just that Ethan Seitz saw him drive by the Gilberts' house on Friday morning."

David nodded. "The day of the murder. I'll mention it to Wade."

We all departed the scene in our own vehicles, and Marc followed me the short distance to my house. He proceeded to walk me inside and check for bogeymen. Sunny followed him through the rooms, and they rejoined me in the kitchen.

Marc reached for a paper towel and swiped at the rainwater running down his neck. "All clear. I better go get Chubb and head home. Call me if you need anything."

"Will you contact me when you get home? I'd hate for you to have an accident and not be able to call for help. This weather is dreadful."

"I'll be sure to call you." He tweaked my nose.

After he left, I took a hot shower, put on warm pajamas, and fixed a cup of hot herbal tea. If the rain let up long enough tomorrow, I'd look around the pier's diner for signs of the beach washing away. I might not work in construction or engineering, but surely it'd be obvious to the untrained eye.

My eyes grew heavy as I read through my journal of murder notes. Right after Marc texted me that he'd made it home, I crashed.

Chapter Forty-six

THE SKY WAS OVERCAST THURSDAY MORNING. Black, gray, and white clouds jockeyed for position. The heavy scent of ozone warned me more rain was coming. There were various spaghetti noodle models on the news of where Hurricane Gabe might land. The other big question was how hard the storm would hit.

All of my morning clients had contacted me, saying they were leaving town with their pets. My policy of charging for last-minute cancellations didn't apply to hurricane warnings.

With no dogs to walk, I decided to head to the pier and look for the signs of erosion Rhett claimed to have inspected the night before. I grabbed my phone and windbreaker and strolled to my destination.

Waves crashed and the wind blew, but no rain pelted me yet. The pier parking lot was full. Fathers and teenage sons pulled surfboards from their vehicles. A van with bumper stickers covering the back window parked, and giggling girls spilled out. Working together they removed eight surfboards. The girls attached surfboard leashes to their ankles and hurried to the beach access, with me following in their wake.

The beach was packed. Oh, dear. Many surfers liked the challenge of waves before and after a hurricane, but it was much more dangerous than regular days. On a bright note, the activity would make it less obvious I was hanging around. Heyward Beach's pier had weathered many storms in the past, and I was confident it'd survive whatever came our way.

Upon reaching the sand dunes, I returned to the parking lot and walked around the building. Nothing looked suspicious to me, but I wasn't an environmentalist.

I called my brother-in-law.

David's voice sounded groggy and low when he answered.

"David, I'm so sorry. Were you sleeping?"

"Yeah. It was a late night, but I should get moving. What's up?" He yawned.

"Did you ask Wade about Rhett's reason for being on the island last night?"

"His excuse had something to do with beach erosion at the diner."

"At least he was consistent. Sorry to have bothered you. Be safe."

He chuckled. "You be safe too. Bye."

Cheyenne Marther walked out of the diner with her shoulders slumped and wearing a frown.

I almost spoke to her but decided it might be a good time to follow her. So I stepped behind a van and watched.

With her head down, Cheyenne snaked between the vehicles. Once she bent over and picked up a coin. She eyed a trash receptacle but jumped away when two teens with surfboards walked by. One of the boys spoke to her, then reached into his backpack and pulled out two power bars. After a brief conversation, the youths followed the path to the beach.

I must be a terrible person to suspect Cheyenne was going to do something bad when she was probably just hungry. With resolve in my step, I began to make my way to where she stood. Before I reached her, Rhett circled the parking lot in his turquoise car. One headlight was crooked, and the front fender was bent. All in all, the car didn't appear to have much damage from running into the mailbox.

He stopped by Cheyenne and spoke to her. Their conversation was brief, then he took off.

I joined her. "Do you know that guy?"

Her head jerked back. "Not really. We crossed paths at the sheriff's department."

"What did he say to you?"

"Um, nothing really." She pointed to the parking lot. "He asked if I knew of another place to park, and I suggested looking on the secondary streets."

"Did you walk to the island?"

"No, I caught a ride with Leroy."

Interesting. I pointed to the pier. "Is he fishing?"

"Yeah. He offered to teach me how to fish, but I need to find a job."

"I saw you walk out of the diner."

"Yeah, they plan to start closing earlier now that summer's over. So they're definitely not hiring." She wore capris with holes in the knees and a black bra under her faded yellow T-shirt.

"Where to next?" Without a car, I wasn't sure how she'd get to work on the island. In fact, I didn't even know if she had a license.

"I'm heading to the ice cream store. If they turn me down, I'll try every business on the island." Her fists clenched. "I better go."

"Would you like to come home with me and maybe borrow one of my outfits?"

Cheyenne looked down at her tattered clothes. "This is one of my best shirts."

"I'm not being critical, but if you wear a dark blouse that doesn't reveal what's underneath and maybe sturdy tennis shoes, a manager might take you more seriously. Does that make sense?" Did I sound condescending? "You shouldn't have to go all the way back to your apartment when you could wear something I own. Besides, my place is on the way."

She hung her head and avoided eye contact. "If you're sure you don't mind. I'll take good care of your stuff."

"I'm happy to help. Let's go." We discussed Hurricane Gabe as we walked.

A Lexus drove by, and Cheyenne stopped mid-stride and turned to watch the vehicle until it turned onto Ocean Drive. "Can you believe the nerve of that woman? Mrs. Gilbert probably knew everything her crooked husband was doing. He's dead, but she's driving her expensive car to her fancy big house on the beach. Some people have all the luck."

"Her husband just died. I wouldn't say she's lucky."

Cheyenne frowned.

I said, "Why do you believe Norris was crooked?"

"He gave my settlement money to my ex. It wasn't his decision to make. Whenever I had an appointment, the waiting room was always packed. Nobody was happy. People would go into their appointments empty-handed and walk out carrying a file. They always looked angry or despondent. I sure wish I knew what was in those files. Deep down I believe he was blackmailing them."

"Did Norris give you a file?"

"No, and I couldn't figure out why."

"Why did you ask for a copy of the files instead of demanding money in the ransom note?"

She turned and flip-flopped away from me and headed in the direction of my house. "It's none of your business, but what if there was an opportunity for me to blackmail the law firm or the family?"

I caught up with her in two long strides. "Blackmail is illegal."

"Ha, is it? Really? Or is it only illegal if you're poor and get caught?" She stopped at the intersection and looked both ways. It was clear, but she looked in each direction again, stepped forward and checked once more before actually crossing.

Poor thing. If I'd been hit by a car, I might act the same way. "Cheyenne, you seem bitter toward Norris. Why didn't you find another attorney?"

"If I changed to another lawyer, Norris would bill me for all of the hours he'd worked on my case. But if I remained with him, he'd only take a percentage of what the insurance paid. Here's the kicker. He never told me how much I got." Her jaw clenched. "Correction, I got nothing. Jordan got everything."

"Have you spoken to your ex-husband about the money? Maybe he'd give it to you, if you asked."

"Nah, we didn't part on the best of terms. I don't plan to humiliate myself asking for money."

We reached my house, and I unlocked the door. Sunny greeted us with a bark and licked my face. "Come in, Cheyenne. Would you like a Coke?"

Her eyes sparkled for a second, then her face fell. "Sure."

Oh, man. Had she believed I was offering her cocaine? I pulled a can from the refrigerator then opened a cabinet.

"I'll drink it straight from the can. That way I can take it with me and toss the can when it's empty."

"Okay. I'll be right back." I rubbed Sunny's head before running upstairs to grab a few nice T-shirts and a blouse for her to choose from. I also snagged tennis shoes and footies, and it hit me. A person of interest was in my house, and I was helping her. Except for Sunny, we were alone, and the windows were boarded up. I sat on the corner of the bed and texted Marc.

Cheyenne is in the house with me. I'm okay but wanted you to be aware.

"What are you doing?"

My heart leapt at the sight of Cheyenne leaning against the doorframe holding Sunny's dog leash.

Chapter Forty-seven

I STOOD BUT DIDN'T APPROACH CHEYENNE. "Why do you have Sunny's leash?"

"She started pacing, and it seems like she wants to go outside." Cheyenne smirked.

The darkness of the room from the hurricane shutters created a sinister air. The sight of Cheyenne holding a leash pumped anxiety through my veins. "Okay. Give me the leash and I'll take her out while you try these on."

"Oh, I like the red shirt." She entered my room and dropped the leash into my outstretched hand.

"Take your time deciding." I hustled out of my bedroom and raced down the stairs. "Sunny."

No bark. No nails scratching the floor. No sign of my German shepherd. I ran through each room. "Sunny." I called her name so much it sounded like a chant.

I raced to the back patio and looked over my small yard.

Sunny stood in the wet grass. Safe. It wasn't raining, so I left her outside and returned to face Cheyenne.

I got myself a Coke. I needed to be calm and get Cheyenne out of my house. *Un, deux, trois* . . . the leash. I'd stuffed it in the pocket of my shorts. Surely, Cheyenne hadn't been able to strangle Norris. He'd been so much bigger than her. Still. I removed the leash and stuffed it in the refrigerator. She wouldn't look there, right?

"I chose the red shirt, and the shoes are a little big, but I found your sock drawer and stuffed the toes of the shoes. They fit great now." She lifted a foot.

The woman had the stealth of a cat. How had she snuck up on me twice? "Let me walk you to the door. Good luck on finding a job."

She brushed past me. "Do you mind if I get another drink? I finished the first one." She whipped open the refrigerator door before I could reply. "Why is the leash in here?"

She must have watched me put it in there. I laughed, pretending to play along. "Oh, that's where it went."

Cheyenne pulled it out along with a canned drink and walked to the front hall. "Thanks for the clothes."

"You're welcome." This time I zipped past her and opened the front door.

When she caught up, she stretched the leash out with both hands. Her eyes traveled the distance of the nylon webbing from one hand with fingers gripping the handle to the other hand holding the metal snap clip and her Coke. She laughed and dropped the leash at my feet. Seconds ticked by before Cheyenne stepped outside. "Be careful of the storm, Andi Grace."

"You too." I stood on the front porch until she was a safe distance down the street. Then I locked the door, raced through my house, brought Sunny inside, and armed my security system. My heart raced. It was hard to breathe.

My phone vibrated in my pocket. It was a weather alert. I was disappointed Marc hadn't replied, but Cheyenne was gone, and I was safe.

Had she strangled Norris? Was she goading me today with Sunny's leash?

"Okay, girl. We need to load up the Highlander so we're ready to leave before flooding begins." I shot a glance at the front door before walking up the stairs. Cheyenne had unnerved me, and upon entering my bedroom I almost freaked. Drawers were open, clothes were strewn about, the duffle bag I'd packed in case Gabe hit us had been dumped out. I reached for my phone and took pictures of the damage.

Events of the morning flashed through my mind. Cheyenne speaking to Rhett. Cheyenne's anger toward the Gilberts. Norris made sense, but I wasn't positive about the antagonism directed at Ivey. Then there had been Cheyenne's fear of walking across the street. After she entered my home, her behavior shifted from being afraid to being scary.

I should've known better than to invite her here. Marc and Wade would be furious, but it was time to face the music. I sent the photos to both men before straightening the mess. My clothes were all going in the laundry after she'd touched them. Wait, that was extreme. No, it wasn't. Before I repacked my bag, the phone buzzed. Marc's face appeared on the screen. "Hi, sweetie."

He huffed. "Why in the world did you allow Cheyenne to enter the house?"

"It's a long story, but she's gone."

"Are you going to file a report with Wade?" Country music played in the background.

"He needs to know what kind of whackadoodle we're dealing with. Marc, I'm telling you, she seemed fine until we entered the house. Then it was like she transformed into a completely different person. She snuck up on me twice. The first time I came upstairs to find a shirt she could borrow.

When I looked up, she was standing near the door with Sunny's leash. I liked to have had a heart attack. It would've been easier to understand if she'd been drinking, but she was sober as far as I could tell."

"A leash?" The next words Marc uttered were indistinguishable. "What happened next?"

"Are you in the truck? You can call me back later."

"I'm in the truck, but I pulled over to check your message. If I hadn't been on the phone with a client, I would've seen your text earlier. Tell me everything."

Halfway through my story, the doorbell rang.

Sunny barked.

"Marc, someone's at the door."

"If it's Cheyenne, don't let her in again. I'll hold on while you check."

"If it's Cheyenne, I'm calling the cops, er, deputies." I jogged down the stairs and peeked out the window. Wade's new vehicle was parked on the street. "It's Wade. I'll call you back."

"I'm coming straight to you, but call if you need me sooner. It'll be about thirty minutes."

"Okay. Love you." I ended the call and opened the door to greet Sheriff Stone's frown. "Hi, Wade."

"Let's see the damage."

Sunny's tail wagged, and Wade leaned over and petted her.

I waved him in, and we faced each other in my large entry hall. "Wade, I'm sorry. After I took the pictures, I started straightening my room. With the storm coming, I'll probably need to leave the island. Cheyenne even unpacked my hurricane go bag."

He blew out a puff of air. "Do you mind if I see your room?"

"It's at the top of the stairs. I'll be right up." I led Sunny to the back door and let her out. "You should enjoy being outside before the rain returns."

White cumulus clouds filled the air. Had the rain before now been due to another weather system? Were these clouds a warning the hurricane was heading our way? Even if it hit south of us, Heyward Beach might experience massive rain, extreme flooding, and rip currents.

I went inside my shadowy house and joined Wade. "What do you think?"

"I can question Cheyenne. Is anything missing?"

"Let me think a minute." I walked into the bathroom. "Ugh, she may have used my hairbrush."

"Wait. Let me at least bag it up. If there are strands of Cheyenne's hair, we can use them as evidence." Wade snapped disposable gloves onto his hands and pulled an evidence bag from his pocket. He picked up the brush and deposited it into the bag. "What else?"

I eyed the toothbrush. It was too frightening to contemplate. We'd just bought toiletries for her, so she didn't need to use my items. It'd been pure meanness or an attempted show of power.

Wade nudged me with his elbow. "Any jewelry missing?"

"This engagement ring is the most valuable item I have." I lifted my hand, and the sparkling diamonds glittered. "I always wear it unless I'm in the ocean or river. Not only did Marc give it to me, but it was a family heirloom."

"What do you believe she was searching for?" Wade opened his little notepad and clicked his pen.

"If she was looking for jewelry to pawn, she must've been sorely disappointed. I always keep a few twenties with my socks for emergencies. It's possible she was searching for cash." I dug around, found the holey pair from middle school, and unfolded them. "Here's the money." I put the cash in my pocket, then tossed the socks into the stack of dirty clothes.

"Any more thoughts?"

"Maybe my journal. It should be either in my nightstand or my vehicle." I returned to the bedroom. "Cheyenne said she didn't steal Ivey's dog, but she did hatch the ransom scheme. She also mentioned something about Norris blackmailing clients."

"Keep going."

I opened one drawer in the bedside table. No journal. "My journal's gone."

"Is it important?"

"It has all of my murder notes." I shared what I'd learned earlier with the sheriff and walked to the other side of the bed. The contents of the drawer had been dumped out. I sat on the floor and sifted through the items while talking to Wade.

"Wade, you should've seen Cheyenne. It was like she was mocking me with the leash. Scratch that, she taunted me with it. I was worried she might strangle me, but would that mean she strangled Norris?"

"Seems likely." He shook his head. "Anything is possible with this case."

"I don't see how Cheyenne could accomplish such an attack. She's frail, and Norris must've been stronger than her. How in the world did she get the upper hand?"

"Let's don't assume she committed the murder. On the other hand, don't invite her back into your house or your vehicle. In fact, don't put yourself in a situation where you two are by yourselves. I'm not saying she's a killer, but judging by the way she acted today, there's something off."

I looked under the bed for my journal and came up empty. "Wade, would you go with me to look in the Highlander for my journal. Maybe she didn't steal it."

"I'd feel better if we did find your notes. It wasn't long ago when we looked for the dollar-store harness. Hopefully our luck will be better today."

"Did you get to watch security tapes from the dollar store?" I reached for my key fob.

"Not yet. The threat of Hurricane Gabe hitting us has been a huge distraction. In the next forty-eight hours, we'll need to decide whether to urge residents to leave the island. Worst-case scenario, we'll call for an evacuation of all residents living on the island and in flood zones on the mainland."

I went to the bowl on the hall table to grab my keys. It was empty. My pulse vibrated in my ears. "Oh, no."

"What?" Wade's voice carried a tone of disbelief.

"Cheyenne must've stolen my key ring. It has the fob to my Highlander, the keys to my house, and my office at the farm." I leaned against the wall.

"What about your clients' keys?"

"They better be in my office." I ran to the back of the house.

The doorbell rang.

Wade could answer it. At that moment I needed to check the box of supplies. Whenever I was home, the list of owners and their keys were kept in a fireproof lockbox. I dove under my desk and found the big tote of supplies. Holding my breath, I pulled it out and lifted the lid. There was the heavy black box. The key lay to the side, and I reached for it and opened the lockbox. Yes. My list of clients and their house keys were still there. I lay on the hard floor and my eyes flooded with tears of relief.

Marc knelt beside me. "What's wrong?"

My lips trembled. "I finally caught a break. The keys are here."

Wade cleared his throat. "Good, but if Cheyenne has your personal keys, we need to create a plan to protect you and get back all the things she stole from you."

Chapter Forty-eight

WITH MY SPARE KEYS, David drove the Highlander to the sheriff's office. His offer to drive my SUV sent a flood of relief through me, making me wonder if I might be scared to drive after my latest experience with hydroplaning.

Marc drove me in his truck, and we picked up Wade's dog. Duke and Sunny would ride out the storm with me at Stay and Play.

Kennady Bed and Breakfast had survived many hurricanes, tornadoes, and floods. We should be safe there from bad weather and from Cheyenne Marther.

Marc steered with one hand. "If Cheyenne somehow found the strength to strangle Norris, do you think she also murdered Dr. Rich?"

Sunny and Duke panted in the backseat and traded sides to hang their heads out the windows.

"No. I don't want to think about Dr. Rich's death unless it is changed from suicide to murder. For now, I don't believe Cheyenne is involved in Dr. Rich's death. Although she probably stole my journal of murder notes, and she definitely stole my keys, but neither of those things make her a killer."

"Don't be getting soft on me, Andi Grace. Cheyenne made suspicious gestures with the leash at your house. Next time you see her, you need to ask why she stole your keys and journal. On second thought, just stay away from Cheyenne."

"I hear ya. The keys make sense in a way. Steal my Highlander and drive to Greenville, where her kids are. But you're right. Why did she take my journal?"

"There's a notepad in my glove compartment where I record my gas and mileage. You can use it to take notes."

I squeezed his arm before finding the notebook and a pen. "You know me so well. Writing down my thoughts and clues helps me think better."

"Should we start with motives for Cheyenne?"

On a clean page I wrote Cheyenne's name and started to make a list of potential motives for her to murder Norris. "She was mad that he gave her insurance money to her husband, Jordan."

"What else?" Marc turned onto River Road, and the dogs switched sides of the truck to hang their heads out again.

"Hmm, if Norris referred her to LC Pain Clinic, she might blame him for her drug addiction."

"Okay, that makes for a stronger case against her. Who else?"

"Freddie Fisher, although the sheriff's department believes he has an alibi. I wonder if we could find out what lady booked him for a golf lesson that morning."

Marc groaned. "I suggest you scratch that plan, or at least put it on the back burner. If you deliberately question her after Wade used her testimony to clear a suspect, he'll be livid."

"You're right. We'll trust that Freddie is innocent."

"You ruled out Lincoln and Ike. Who's left?"

"Ivey Gilbert." Money and freedom were two strong motives.

"She may have stolen the harness you bought at the dollar store. It seems like she's got more to gain than anyone."

I turned to a clean page. "Exactly. There's the will, assuming Norris left the bulk of his wealth to her." I needed to dig deep, but how? "Do attorneys have to file wills in South Carolina?"

"Yep. The will must be filed in probate court within thirty days of the decedent's death."

"Good to know." I took a deep breath. "Then there's Rhett Alton. He and Norris argued. Rhett's aunt was the doctor at the pill mill. And there are the two mysterious drinks he bought Friday morning."

"Mysterious?"

"Kinda. Remember he had Erin put both drinks in paper cups? None of these things seem like much. When you add them together, they might not be strong enough to consider as circumstantial evidence."

"Does that mean you're taking him off your list?"

"No. He'll remain a person of interest, but only because he gives off a bad vibe."

Marc chuckled. "You won't get far with Wade if you emphasize your bad vibe."

"Yeah, you're right." We drove down the back road with the wind blowing through the cab of Marc's truck. We whizzed past trees, but not as fast as usual. "Why are you driving so slow? Did Lacey Jane tell you she thinks I'm a little jittery after my experience with Freddie?"

"Andi Grace, we're about to get married." Marc's face drooped. "I figured it out on my own."

"How? I've been trying to forget the incident."

The new sign for Kennady Bed and Breakfast pointed to the entrance ahead. Marc signaled his intention to turn, and soon we were traveling the newly paved drive to Juliet and Nate's B and B and Stay and Play. Nate had made a good deal with an asphalt company, and we'd split the cost. There'd been a huge increase in traffic on the lane in the past year, and making it easier to travel had become a must.

"Honey, you didn't answer my question. How'd you guess?"

Marc pointed to my hands. "You're clenching the console with one hand and the door with your other one. Your feet have wanted to hit the brake with every turn. You had the episode with Freddie then you hydroplaned last night, and it didn't help that Rhett ran off the road too. Either one of those events would make anyone skittish, and you lived through both in a week. So, yes, I'm driving slower to make you feel more comfortable." His jaw clenched.

Tears threatened. "I'm sorry, Marc. I didn't want to worry you with more of my problems, but it looks like my acting skills didn't work."

We left the shadows of the woods and entered the clearing leading to Kennady Bed and Breakfast. Marc stopped in the grass. The dogs panted, and Duke nosed Marc.

"Sunny, Duke, sit." I pointed at the dogs. Sunny obeyed immediately. Duke whined then settled down.

Marc faced me. "I should've expected they'd want to get out when the truck stopped, but we need to finish this conversation without an audience."

"You have my full attention." I angled my body to face him.

"Andi Grace, I love you. Please don't feel like you need to hide anything from me. I want you to share your goals, your dreams, your fears, your family, and your animals. Chubb is my dog because of your influence. Trust me to love you no matter what. We'll have arguments and disagreements, but I'll always love you. If you become too scared to ever drive again, I'll still love you."

Tears filled my eyes. How had I been so blessed for Marc to fall in love with me? "It seems like I've lost so many people in my life, and it's hard to allow myself to fully trust you won't disappear. Not that you'd do it on purpose, but you could have an accident like our parents. And to be honest, I don't know how I would recover from losing you."

He took my hand in his. "We can't live in fear. If you're always afraid something will rip us apart, you won't have any peace."

I met his gray-eyed gaze. Warmth filled me. "I honestly believed I was only trying to protect you, but listening to you, it occurs to me I've been shielding my heart. Please trust in me when I say that there's nothing I want more than to spend the rest of my life with you. Honestly, sometimes it seems like you're too good to be true, which makes me wonder how I got so lucky."

"You know me better than that. Sometimes I'm moody, I like my time alone in a kayak on the water, or sitting on the dock staring into space. I get absorbed in my cases and forget everything else. Don't start thinking I'm better than the flawed man I truly am."

Part of the beauty of Marc's personality was his humility. "Marc Williams, I love you, flaws and all."

"Good to know, and you're not going to keep any more secrets from me?"

I hated to be a burden.

His eyebrows rose. "I notice you're hesitating to answer."

His argument was logical, and if our marriage was going to succeed, I needed to be open and honest. "You're right. No more secrets. I promise."

"All right. I'm going to hold you to that."

A horn blared. We both jumped, and the dogs barked.

Marc laughed. "It's Lincoln. Wonder what he's doing here?"

The blue truck pulled up beside Marc and the passenger window lowered. "Hey, if you two plan to block the road, you should at least be smooching."

My face warmed.

Marc said, "You came all this way to say that?"

"Nah. Belle worked today and needs a change of clothes. Something about catching a muddy dog and giving him a bath and who knows what all happened?"

I leaned around Marc. "Lincoln, have you heard the news? The weather authorities may call for a mandatory evacuation of the island."

"Yeah. If it happens, we'll crash at Marc's place. He's my best friend and won't require advanced notice."

Marc smiled. "You're welcome anytime. If I'm not there, you know where the spare key is hidden."

"Thanks, man. I guess I best get these clothes to Belle."

Marc turned and met my gaze. "So how about some smooching?"

I laughed then lifted my lips to his. Not a bad way to make up from our misunderstanding.

Chapter Forty-nine

A FEW MINUTES LATER, we drove to the barn and let Sunny and Duke out. The dogs went straight to a big water bowl and lapped it dry.

Lincoln held Lady and crooned a song to the little schnoodle.

I refilled the water bowl then joined Marc and Lincoln. "Where's Belle, and why are you singing to Lady?"

"Belle's changing clothes, and she said Lady seemed sad. Dylan left earlier to help Griffin secure some supplies from blowing away in whatever kind of storm we have. The dog groomer, Melanie, is it? She's giving the new dog a second scrubbing."

"Yes, Melanie Bradshaw. I'll see if she needs a hand." I walked back to the dog grooming area. "Hey, I heard you got a new dog."

"Yeah, and he's a big one. No tags. Maybe Doc Hewitt can find a chip in this bad boy after the storm. I don't want to bother him just yet." Melanie shouldered her glasses up. "I'm using a special shampoo that won't dry his skin out too bad. If I had to guess, he swam across the river to get here. I also believe he's been abused." She detailed her hypothesis and convinced me.

"Like you said, the timing is terrible to alert anyone in case Hurricane Gabe hits us. For now, we'll take good care of him."

Melanie led the dog out of the tub and down the ramp. "I think he has a slight limp, and I'll keep an eye on him." She dried the mutt with a fluffy white towel.

"He's big. I'll clean the tub out for you while you continue drying him." I found the safe cleaning supplies and went to work. "You're right. There are twigs and grass in the sink stopper."

"Told you so. I even cut some briars out of his coat. He reminds me of a Siberian husky I used to groom, but there are some differences. This guy's face is more squared off compared to the rounder shape."

I paused cleaning to study the big dog. "Part Siberian and possibly part Lab. Oh, I recently heard about a new breed called Siberian Retriever Lab. That's my best guess."

"Cool." The next few moments passed in silence. "I'm going to put antibiotic salve on some of his wounds."

"Okay. I'm finished with this. I'll be out front if you need me." I dropped the dirty towels into the proper bin and returned the cleaning supplies to the appropriate shelf before joining Marc and Lincoln.

Sunny lay at Marc's feet, but Duke and another dog ran in circles around the play yard.

"Honey, you'll want to hear this." Marc crossed his arms.

"What's up?"

Lincoln still held Lady. "After all of the rain last night, I decided to check for leaks. I went onto the front porch, and a Mini Cooper drove by. It made me think of that guy Rhett Alton."

My heart missed a beat. "Was it Rhett?"

"Can't say for sure, but he came from the south end where the gated community is."

"Did you notice if he went to the pier's diner?"

"No, as in, no he didn't go to the pier. Leastways not after I saw the car. Mind you, I never saw the driver. Marc told me about your accident last night, and it seemed worth mentioning."

"Thanks. Would you tell Sheriff Stone?"

"Sure will. Just as soon as I tell Belle goodbye."

The singer's daughter returned wearing a clean white T-shirt and denim shorts. She took the dog from her dad. "Thanks again for coming out with the fresh clothes."

He kissed the top of her head. "That's what dads do. Call me before you head home."

Marc said, "Don't forget, you're welcome at my place if the hurricane comes our way."

"I appreciate the offer. We'll be happy to crash with you. Okay, y'all. I'm off to talk to the sheriff. Have a good afternoon."

"Bye, Daddy." Belle waved to her father before turning to me. "Did you hear I rescued a dog today? He was running in the woods, and I took him some dog treats. He was all excited until I tried to attach a collar and leash. The poor thing ran this way and that before I caught him. Until we can learn his identity, I'm calling him Chase."

"Perfect name. I was talking to Melanie, and we'll wait until after the storm danger passes before contacting Doc Hewitt." I rubbed Lady's ear between my fingers. "Did you tell your dad you might have an opportunity to adopt Lady?"

"Yes, ma'am. He didn't say no." Her smile stretched across her face.

"That sounds like a good sign."

Marc's eyes had grown wide. "It sounds like a good country song title. He didn't say no—and what? I'll be thinking about it."

I reached for his hand. "Belle, I'll be back in a few minutes. I need to unload my belongings from Marc's truck. I plan to ride out the storm with Juliet. Duke's in the play area with Sunny. Will you keep an eye on them?"

"Sure."

We carried my luggage to the big house, and Juliet opened the back door for us. "Welcome, welcome."

The smell of chocolate chip cookies greeted us, and my stomach growled. "It smells great in here."

"I'll fix sandwiches for you two, then you can have cookies."

"Yum." I dropped my duffle and hugged my best friend. "Thanks for squeezing me in."

"No problem. Most vacationers canceled their reservations because of the threat from Gabe."

Marc gave Juliet a quick hug. "Where should I take Andi Grace's luggage."

"The pink room. There's only one window, and I feel like it's the safest option in case a tornado pops up. Although if we have enough warning, we'll seek shelter down here."

"I'll help." I grabbed my duffle, and we went through the spacious rooms to the stairs leading to the second floor. When we reached my room and deposited the luggage, I faced Marc. "What did you think about Lincoln's story?"

"I believe him, so Rhett lied to Wade."

"What do you think he was doing in the gated community that has no gates in case of flooding? Was it a coincidence he ran into Cheyenne this morning at the pier parking lot?" I paced on the squeaky old wood floor in the guest room. "Both of them are newcomers, and both have been questioned by the sheriff's department regarding Norris's murder. Have they become friends?"

"If one of them committed the murder, could the other be extorting them?" Marc leaned against the doorframe and folded his arms. "Cheyenne mentioned she'd have no qualms about blackmailing someone."

"Great. I need clues to rule out suspects." I continued walking back and forth across the room. "Then there's Ivey. It makes the most sense she'd be guilty. She gave me her dog and told me to find her a new home if she doesn't return."

"Hmm." Marc crossed my path, sat in a pink wingback chair, and propped one ankle on the other thigh. His foot bounced. "You were suspicious from the beginning that Ivey and Norris had planned to leave the country in secret."

"True, but why? And why Bali?" I turned and retraced my steps. Between the murder and storm, I couldn't stop moving.

"Ivey told you the mob had nothing to do with the pain clinic, but what if she lied? What if the mob was involved, Norris made them mad, and they were running for their lives?"

"It's possible." I removed the band around my ponytail and rubbed my head. "I don't believe oceanic cruise ships leave from Savannah. Is there a link to Savannah that we're missing? Or is it a red herring?"

Marc stood and reached for my hand. "We'll think better after we eat. Come on."

We rejoined Juliet in the kitchen, and I sent a text to Ivey. *Help me prove you didn't kill Norris. Why were you really going to Bali?*

I poured glasses of water for us, and we sat down with Juliet to eat homemade chicken salad sandwiches. Just as I took the first bite my cell phone rang, and Ivey's name appeared on the screen.

Chapter Fifty

"SHH, THIS IS IVEY." I swiped my phone.

"Andi Grace, you've plumb worn me out with questions about my husband's murder."

I touched the speaker button but motioned for Juliet and Marc to remain quiet. "I'm down to three people on my list of suspects. Help me prove you're innocent."

"You have no power to arrest me, so why should I help?"

"Because I always share information with Sheriff Stone. If you convince me you're innocent, I'll tell the sheriff. I'll also focus on other persons of interest."

"Andi Grace, why can't you leave well enough alone? Focus on the dogs you walk and forget about trying to solve murders." Her angry tone made me glad we weren't talking face-to-face.

"The murder affects many people I know, so I can't forget about my personal investigation. Why were you and Norris going to Bali?"

Ivey groaned. "Norris stole money from the pain clinic, and the owners were about to come after him. Legally, I might add. It was only a matter of time before he was sued."

"It seems like he would've been arrested."

"That too, which is why we chose Bali. Indonesia wouldn't send him back to the States for his crimes."

Juliet hurried to her kitchen drawer with office supplies and returned with a pen and pad of paper. Marc took it from her and began writing.

"Okay, but how did he steal from the clinic? I thought he only introduced you to the people looking for office space."

"He referred people to them, and vice versa. There were kickbacks for the referrals. Somehow through all of the back-and-forth recommendations, Norris stole funds from the clinic. The owners got wind of missing money, and things turned ugly. For the first time since I've known Norris, he was visibly shaken."

"Do you think someone associated with the pain clinic murdered Norris?"

"Yes. I'm not talking about a few thousand dollars. He misappropriated hundreds of thousands. Norris hid the money in cryptocurrency. In addition to the bad money, he moved all of our investments to secret accounts overseas."

Marc held up a finger for me to wait, then he wrote a question on the next sheet of paper.

I read it. "Ivey, how did Norris think you wouldn't get caught?"

"He had a guy. Norris always had a guy. Anyway, this particular man was going to help us change our identities. I agreed to his plan because I didn't want to be left behind to pay for his misdeeds."

The pieces of the puzzle fell into place. "Norris dies, and you are left behind. You gave Lady to me. Are you planning to leave the country by yourself?"

"I refuse to admit to anything else, Andi Grace. However, if I'm going to lose the life I've come to love, it'll be on my terms."

"Okay. Thanks for this information."

"Goodbye." She ended the call.

"At last, I believe Ivey didn't kill Norris. Did you hear her say she didn't want to be left behind to deal with his crimes?"

Marc said, "Yes."

Juliet nodded.

"Leaving the country with Norris would save her from the humiliation and possibly jail."

"Prison." Marc wrote and underlined the word. "If not prison, she may have lost all of her possessions."

"Okay, prison was a possibility. It wouldn't make sense for Ivey to murder Norris in Heyward Beach. If she really wanted to kill her husband, she might have planned to do it in another country."

Juliet had been drumming her fingers on the table. "That's how I would do it. Wait until Norris had me safely out of the country. Get my new identity. Then on the way to our final destination, find a way to get rid of him."

Marc's eyes grew wide. "Juliet, remind me not to ever get on your bad side."

I laughed. Marc had no idea of how rough life had been for Juliet when she was growing up. "She'd never do that to you. Nate might be another story."

Juliet smiled. "Nate would never do the things Norris did. He's too kind, and maybe a little bit on the innocent side."

Marc pushed the notes aside and bit into his sandwich.

"If you two agree we should rule out Ivey, that leaves us with Cheyenne and Rhett. What do you think?"

Juliet pointed to my plate. "I believe you should eat your sandwich and think about the murder later."

My stomach growled in agreement.

Chapter Fifty-one

AFTER LUNCH, Marc and I called Wade from my office at Stay and Play. We updated the sheriff on the situation with Ivey.

Wade said, "I'll put out an all-points bulletin on Ivey. She's a flight risk, and I need to get her official statement. We also need to dig in and see how involved she was with her husband's crimes."

Marc said, "On a bright note, the latest weather prediction is Hurricane Gabe has been downgraded to a tropical storm, and it's heading for Florida."

"For the first time in days we're catching a break. We'll still have rain, but life will be much easier if we don't have to call for an evacuation. Andi Grace, you're a pain sometimes, but you're also amazing. Thanks for the info. I've gotta run."

"Bye, Wade."

Marc told him bye also, and we hung up.

Marc winked at me. "Too bad you didn't record our conversation. Wade doesn't compliment you very often."

"Yeah, I'll just have to remember this the next time I make him mad."

"I need to check on Chubb and make a few calls. I'll come back later to check on you, but do you need a vehicle?"

"I don't plan to go anywhere today unless I get a lead on Cheyenne or Rhett."

"Call me if you do."

"Absolutely." I walked with Marc to his truck and kissed him before he took off.

The gray sky and strong wind left me unsettled. The best solution for my mood was to play with the dogs. I returned to the barn. "Belle, where are you?"

She appeared from the grooming area. "I'm here. Melanie was giving me tips on bathing dogs."

"Oh, that might come in handy. We'll find a place for you to keep a change of clothes. More than likely this won't be the only time you'll need two outfits in one day."

"There's no need to make room for me. I can keep extras in my Cherokee. In fact, I don't know why it didn't occur to me earlier."

"New jobs can be stressful. There's always a learning curve."

"Thanks for understanding." She shot me a big smile.

"I see you put Sunny and Chase together in their own area." Fences around the dog areas could be adjusted. Sometimes we let more dogs play together, and other times we divided them into smaller groups.

"Yes, ma'am. Chase seems anxious, and Sunny is usually calm. It seemed like a good duo. Duke is playing with some of the others and seems happy. Lady is whining and seems skittish. She's so little though, and I wasn't sure how she'd do with the big dogs. Not that they would hurt her, but would she feel threatened by their size? I just wasn't sure what to do."

"I don't see Lady, so what did you decide?"

"I put her in a crate with a soft dog bed. She closed her eyes and fell asleep."

"All good decisions. I think you've got a long future here, at least until your singing career takes off."

Her dark ponytail swung forward, and she ran her hands through it. "I want to earn success on my own and not make it because I'm Lincoln Zane's daughter."

"I understand, but don't rebuff your dad. He might be able to introduce you to important people in the industry. Don't avoid walking through a door just because your dad opened it. Nobody will offer you a recording contract if you stink no matter who your dad is."

Belle's hands stilled. "Hey, you're right."

Twice in one day I'd received positive feedback. "Thanks. I'll play with Sunny and Chase."

"I'm going to finish with Melanie then check and see if we need more dog food. Dylan explained your system for analyzing and ordering supplies."

"Knock yourself out." I left her and opened the gate to join Sunny and Chase. "Hey there, how are y'all?" I sat on the ground and loved on Sunny. We played with her favorite rope toy, and I gave her a treat. At last, I turned my attention to the new dog.

Chase flinched when I reached for him. Time to change tactics. Instead of trying to pick him up, I sat beside him and spoke softly. "Hey, buddy. You've had quite a day. Were you scared swimming across the Waccamaw River? Did you hurt your paws?" With slow, cautious movements, I reached over and examined each foot. One of the girls had applied ointment. "We might clean again, reapply the medicated ointment, then wrap your paws. How does that sound? You'll have more fun if your feet don't hurt. Who treated you so badly that you'd swim in the river?" I rubbed his back and hummed. "Sunny and Chubb swim in the river, but they stay close to shore. You were very brave or else very terrified."

The big dog crawled into my lap.

"Hey, I won you over faster than expected. You must be love-starved." Chase was even bigger than Sunny, and he was more than a lapful. I was delighted he trusted me enough to take a leap of faith. Sunny deserved partial credit. Chase probably watched how I treated my German shepherd, then he decided to give me a chance.

My phone vibrated, but I hated to disturb Chase. I let the call go to voicemail. The dog had thick hair, but it wasn't very long. I continued to pet him, and my thoughts drifted to Rhett and Cheyenne. Who had the most to gain by killing Norris?

When I had found Norris, his body had been in the desk chair. The weapon was a hot pink dog leash. It was hard to picture Rhett buying it at the dollar store, but Cheyenne was poor. Ivey could've bought it and left it out in plain sight. Had the killer grabbed it in a fit of anger?

The issue of strength also needed to be considered. Was there any possible way Cheyenne was strong enough to strangle Norris?

An approaching vehicle rumbling up the drive brought my wandering thoughts to an end. "Chase, I've got to go now, but the girls will come back and work on your paws." The dog stood and looked at me with a forlorn expression. "You'll be safe here."

Marc entered the barn. "Andi Grace, David's trying to get ahold of you. Lacey Jane is having contractions, and they're on the way to see her doctor. Are you okay? Why didn't you answer the phone?"

"Sorry. I was with the new dog, but I'm fine. Give me a second." I hurried to my office and reached for my purse. Where was my portable phone charger? I lifted a stack of files. Nope.

Melanie appeared. "Is there anything we can do?"

"Would you treat Chase's feet again this afternoon and bandage them? Thanks." I opened the top drawer and spotted the charger. "Call if you need me. Lacey Jane is having contractions, and it's way too early."

"We'll be fine. Go check on your sister."

"Thanks." I hurried to Marc, and we jogged to his truck without uttering a word.

On the drive, I prayed for the safety of my sister and her baby.

When we approached town, I checked to see if I'd missed any other messages.

Wade had texted. Crime scene techs found paper cups from Daily Java in the outside garbage cans at the Gilberts' house.

What did his information mean? If they checked my garbage cans, they'd find Daily Java cups too.

I couldn't think about it now. I only wanted to see Lacey Jane and know she was safe.

Chapter Fifty-two

FALSE ALARM, and boy, had I been relieved. David and Ike took Lacey Jane home to rest. Ike had offered to stay with my sister because David was on duty. With Ivey on the lam and the killer loose, David had to return to work.

Marc and I sat in his truck in front of the doctor's office. "Crisis averted. Where would you like to go?"

"I need to think for a few minutes. Can we stay here?"

Marc met my gaze. "Sure. Do you want to bounce some of your ideas around?"

"Suppose the pink leash belonged to Ivey. One of the Gilberts could've laid it out for the trip. What if Cheyenne went to the house to ask Norris for more information on her settlement?"

"Or there may have been another issue she wanted to discuss in private." Raindrops appeared on the truck windshield in a slow dance.

I snapped my fingers. "Right. Whatever the reason, she must have gone to the house to speak to Norris. He wasn't afraid of her and sat at his desk. At some point she picks the leash up and strangles him. No, wait. I'm missing something. It seems like there's a vital clue just out of reach."

"Take your time." Marc rubbed my shoulder.

I replayed the scene in my mind the day we went to check on Lady. "The dog is part of the puzzle. She wasn't there when we got to the house. Cheyenne claimed to have found Lady running loose. She chalked it up to good luck."

Marc said, "The day we found Cheyenne near the apartments, she claimed to have found Lady. She kept acting like she was worried we'd steal the reward money from her."

"She fooled me. I'm not sure if she's an amazing actress or good at manipulating others."

"My money's on being a great manipulator." Marc tapped his fingers on the steering wheel.

"I think you're right. We'll assume Cheyenne went to the house, confronted Norris, then strangled him. It doesn't matter if the act was premeditated or executed in the heat of the moment. She sees Lady and thinks she can make a quick buck off the dog."

"Hold up. She wanted files, not money, in exchange for Lady."

His words took the wind out of my sails. "You're right. Cheyenne must have searched the office for her file—"

"Maybe it was an act of liberation for all of Norris's clients. She told you while waiting for her appointments, people often left the office carrying a file and looking distraught."

I turned my eyes to the windshield. The rain had transitioned from random sprinkles to a slow and steady rain. Trails of water slithered down the glass. "Had Norris failed other clients with their insurance lawsuits?"

Marc ran a hand over his face. "I'd always been under the impression divorce cases were Norris's bread and butter. I can't imagine he'd ask to meet with the spouses of his clients. It's unethical. It seems mighty brazen for Norris to call the soon-to-be ex-spouses to his office."

"Norris fit the definition of brazen. Unfortunately, he was smart in addition to being bold."

Marc drummed the steering wheel with his fingers. "What is Cheyenne's motive?"

"Norris suggested she go to the pain clinic. She went, but instead of getting better, she got hooked on painkillers. The addiction caused her to lose her family. Norris also gave the money she should have received from the insurance company to her husband. Next to the driver of the car who hit Cheyenne, Norris was probably the person who caused her the most harm."

"In theory, we've got a solid motive. Drug addiction, loss of family, and not collecting what the insurance company owed her."

I shivered. "Let's go get some coffee and check on Erin."

"Buckle up."

I fastened my seat belt. "Should we remove Rhett from our list?"

Marc started his truck and pulled out of the doctor's parking lot. "We know Rhett and Norris had a heated argument, and he was in the vicinity of the murder Friday morning."

"You're right. Rhett had accused Norris of taking part in the clinic's insurance fraud."

"I get that they may have argued over insurance fraud, but Stephanie Rich's death is a stronger motive." Marc turned onto the causeway.

"You're right. It doesn't matter if Dr. Rich died from suicide or murder. Rhett may have blamed Norris for her death."

Marc increased the speed of his wipers. "Erin may have closed for the day."

"Yeah, the threat of a hurricane has made life chaotic. Buying coffee and pastries probably isn't a priority for many people this week." We crossed over the marsh. Seagulls huddled on a deserted dock. "Next time we see Rhett, let's ask why he didn't use his travel cup for at least one of the smoothies he bought last week."

"Rhett lied about where he was last night when you two had your accidents. I'm not sure he'll give us the truth on the cups either." Marc slowed the truck and moved to the center of the empty road. Water from the street sprayed up as high as our windows. "There's been more rain on the island than on the other side of the marsh. I hope the roads aren't completely flooded."

I sat straighter and gripped the console and door. "Marc, I'm so sorry for suggesting we get coffee. This was a bad idea."

"I can't turn around just yet." He leaned forward and white-knuckled the steering wheel.

I closed my eyes and prayed for safety.

Marc neared the ice cream shop and slowed. "We made it this far. May as well check on Erin."

I opened my eyes and glanced at him. "Okay. I trust your judgment."

"Then onward we go." He eased off the brake and turned onto Main Street.

"Marc, look. The *Open* sign is lit up." A friendly red and blue sign shone through the dreary weather.

"Do you see what's in the parking lot?"

I squinted, and my heart dropped. "It looks like a blue Mini Cooper to me."

"That's what I thought too. Do you still want that cup of coffee?"

"Yes, but will you park on the street? I don't want to scare Rhett away before we talk to him. I also intend to text Wade. Not that I believe Rhett is toting a gun, but we've been in dangerous situations before. Alerting the sheriff seems to be the smartest thing to do."

"I couldn't agree more."

Chapter Fifty-three

NOT ONLY DID I TEXT WADE, but I included David.

Marc parallel parked and shut off the truck. "What do you think?"

"Let's go inside and place an order. We'll be causal. If we make eye contact with Rhett, we'll greet him. Otherwise, we'll leave him alone."

"Are you sure this is what you want to do?" He took my hand in his.

"We've come this far. Don't you think we should see it through?" My voice squeaked, but I pretended not to notice.

"I figured you'd say that. Let's go." He pulled the hood up on his athletic rain jacket.

The wind would make using an umbrella futile, so I slid on my rain poncho and darted out of the truck. I reached for Marc's hand. "Thank goodness for rain boots."

"Yeah." We jogged to the door and shook the rain off our cover-ups the best we could. Marc held open the door. "After you."

Erin stood behind the counter boxing up pastries. "Hi there. I didn't expect more customers with the bad weather. I'm boxing up pastries to deliver to the church. Even though we might not get a direct hit, there's bound to be flooding. People are already seeking shelter at the church."

"That's nice. What about your house?"

"You know, I'm not going to stress over it. Gabe has been downgraded to a tropical storm. I really stayed open because Griffin promised to stop by and board up the store windows. After that, I plan on closing." She glanced at her watch. "How are the streets?"

Marc said, "There's quite a bit of water on them, but they aren't flooded yet. Although, you may have trouble with your little Prius. We can give you a ride off the island."

"Thanks for the offer. I don't want to endanger your lives while I wait for Griffin." She looked out the window and frowned. "You two didn't come by to offer me a ride. What can I get you?"

"I'd like your largest white mocha latte."

"Okay. Marc, what about you?"

"How about green mint tea with a splash of lemon?"

"Coming right up. I'll bring your order out."

Marc placed a twenty on the counter and slid it to Erin. "Keep the change."

Her eyes sparkled. "Thanks so much."

I moved to the dining area.

Rhett sat in the corner and faced our direction, but his head was ducked. Across the table from him was a redhead wearing a white poncho. The two were deep in conversation.

I selected the first available table, making sure they couldn't accuse us of trying to listen to them. Marc sat beside me, and we each had a view of Rhett and Cheyenne.

Cheyenne did most of the talking and even shook her finger at Rhett multiple times. He shook his head but continued to look down.

Erin brought our drinks. "Enjoy."

We thanked her, and she walked away.

Marc removed the lid and blew on his drink. "They obviously know each other. What do you think they're discussing?"

"The murder? I don't guess they were in cahoots."

"We don't think they knew each other before each was questioned at the sheriff's office."

My shoulders slumped. "Oh, yeah." I sipped my latte, and the yummy warmth flowed through me.

Cheyenne jumped up so fast her chair crashed to the floor. "Don't you threaten me, Rhett."

I grabbed my phone and opened the text app. *Wade, we're at Daily Java. Cheyenne and Rhett are here.* I hit Send before I realized Cheyenne stood over me. A shiver slithered up my spine. I looked at her. "Hi, Cheyenne."

"Give me your phone, Andi Grace."

I didn't like the way she stood towering over me, but I refused to give in to her demands. We were in a public establishment. "No. You stole my journal and keys. There's no way I'll hand my phone over to you."

Marc rose from his chair. "Cheyenne, the sheriff's department is looking for you."

"Why?" She screeched. "If he's going to arrest me for Norris's murder, he'll have to arrest Rhett too."

At the sound of his name, Rhett joined us. "Why don't we take this conversation outside?"

"It's raining, Mr. College Professor." Cheyenne rolled her eyes.

Rhett called her an ugly name and stalked off.

I looked at Cheyenne. "Did you work with Rhett to kill Norris?"

"Not on purpose. It just turned out that way."

I gasped. "What do you mean?"

There was a muffled scream from the kitchen area, and it didn't seem likely that Erin had taken a spill in her sturdy cross trainers. There was no sign of Rhett. What had he done to Erin?

Chapter Fifty-four

MARC AND I DARTED TOWARD DAILY JAVA'S KITCHEN. Years earlier, I'd been in the back of the bakery often when Lacey Jane had worked for Erin. It had a concrete floor, lots of workspace, and top-of-the-line restaurant equipment.

I peeked in the kitchen. The sight of Rhett holding a chef's knife to Erin's throat stopped me in my tracks.

Marc halted beside me, and his hand touched my elbow.

Cheyenne approached and nudged us into the kitchen. "Move it."

We were trapped between her and Erin. Rhett remained behind Erin with the knife.

Rhett's gaze bounded from one to the next of us. He grinned. "Cheyenne, grab the keys from Erin's apron and lock the door. Andi Grace and Marc, give me your phones. Place them on the counter. Nice and easy."

"Be calm, man." Marc's smooth tone eased my nerves a bit. "We'll do whatever you ask. Just don't hurt Erin."

Rhett's nostrils flared. "You're not giving the orders today."

Cheyenne jerked the keys from Erin's apron pocket, then she brushed past us and hurried to lock the front door. Meanwhile, Marc and I placed our phones on the counter where I'd witnessed Erin mixing muffins in the past.

Marc said, "How do you see this playing out? If you didn't kill Norris, why are you helping Cheyenne escape?"

The redhead laughed. "Boy, does he have you fooled. He tried to kill Norris by spiking his smoothie."

"Shut up, Cheyenne." Rhett shook the knife at her. "You're the one who lost it when Norris laughed at your demand for your client files. You're the one who killed him."

"I'm not going down for the murder by myself. If you hadn't drugged Norris, it's doubtful I could've strangled him. So, you're just as guilty as I am."

So, both of them were involved in Norris's murder. That explained a lot.

A truck pulled into the parking lot and parked near the front door. It looked like Griffin's work truck.

"Oh, no. What are we going to do?" Cheyenne whined.

Rhett grunted. "Everyone shut up."

We obeyed his demand.

There was a pounding on the glass door.

Erin whimpered. "It's probably the maintenance man. He's here to board my windows."

Rhett cursed. "We don't need another hostage. Cheyenne, tell him Erin changed her mind, but don't open the door. No matter what he says, keep the door locked."

"Okay." She left us in the kitchen.

My ears tingled in anticipation of overhearing the conversation between Cheyenne and hopefully Griffin.

"Erin changed her mind," Cheyenne's voice boomed.

It was impossible to hear Griffin's reply from where I stood.

"No! Go home. She's not worried about the windows."

With one arm around Erin's body and the knife to her neck, Rhett edged toward the doorframe leading to the public area. He angled his head as if he too wanted to hear better.

While Rhett was distracted with the conversation, I looked around for a weapon. There were more knives, but could I reach one without drawing Rhett's attention? I met Marc's gaze, and he shook his head.

Erin's eyes were huge, and her complexion was white and gray like a seagull. She mouthed something to me. Her eyes darted from me to the desk along the wall. Then she mouthed the word again. *Desk.*

Rhett was absorbed in the ongoing conversation between Cheyenne and Griffin.

I pointed to the desk, and Erin nodded.

Yes, but what was I supposed to do about it?

Marc had witnessed our communication, and he stepped in front of me, blocking my body from Rhett's view. I studied the items on the desk. Bills, an empty mug, a framed photo of Erin and her family, and an oval plastic item about the size of a quarter. Oh, it was a panic button for a security system. A glance backward assured me Rhett was still engrossed in the conversation at the front door. I snatched the button and squeezed it before slipping the device into my pocket.

Cheyenne returned. "It was Griffin Reed, and yeah, he said he was here to board the windows. I didn't think he'd ever leave."

"Are you sure he's gone?"

"Yeah, I watched him drive away. He wanted to know where Erin was, then he offered to board up the windows anyway." Cheyenne looked from Rhett to Erin. "He seems like more than just a friend, but if Rhett slits your throat, you won't have romance on your mind."

Erin moaned. "Please, let me go."

Marc said, "She's innocent."

Rhett tightened his grip on Erin. "You two are the reason she's in danger."

There had to be a way for us to rescue Erin, but with that big knife at her throat, nothing seemed reasonable. "Rhett, if Cheyenne strangled Norris, it seems like she's the guiltiest party. The autopsy says death by strangulation." Nobody had revealed the autopsy report to me, but it had to be either strangulation or overdose of benzodiazepines.

"I can't take the chance. You two have royally screwed up my plans." His grip loosened on Erin. "Cheyenne, grab the biggest knife you can find."

Erin stomped on Rhett's foot. His knife fell and clinked on the concrete floor. Rhett howled.

Erin dropped to the hard floor and rolled away from her captor.

Marc tackled Rhett, and the man fell to the ground.

Cheyenne charged me with another knife. I lunged to the side, and she hit the wall. The knife clunked on the floor, and we both dove for it. We fought for control. Cheyenne grasped the knife handle.

Sirens wailed.

Erin crawled out of the kitchen.

I twisted Cheyenne's arm, and the weapon hit the floor with a clank. With her free hand, she raked her fingers down my face.

"Ow." I elbowed her in the jaw.

She groaned.

Erin reappeared at my side. "We need to search her for the door key. The cops are here."

Cheyenne clawed and kicked at both of us like a wild animal.

Together we subdued the redhead, and sat her on the floor.

Erin rooted in Cheyenne's pockets. "Here it is." She dashed away.

I tied Cheyenne's wrists together behind her back with an apron. I stood over the killer, unsure if the strings would hold her.

Marc pulled Rhett's arms behind him and shoved him toward the deputies.

David materialized beside me. "Andi Grace, let me help you."

"Thanks, David." I collapsed into the desk chair.

My brother-in-law handcuffed Cheyenne and led her away.

Wade entered the kitchen. "You don't look so good."

I touched my face and felt warm sticky dampness. Blood. "Cheyenne scratched me."

"One of the medics can treat your wounds, then I need to question you."

"Wade, don't let Rhett go. He's involved with the murder of Norris Gilbert."

He rubbed his whiskered chin. "Really? I was leaning toward Cheyenne."

"Don't let her go either."

"Oh, boy. This is going to be good."

Chapter Fifty-five

WADE PREVENTED ME FROM TALKING TO MARC OR ERIN. He wanted to question each one of us to get a full idea of what had really happened. David questioned Erin. Deputy Hanks took Marc, and Wade got me. We sat in the coffee shop, and I sipped my lukewarm latte. Wade placed a tape recorder on the table to record our conversation.

"Did you follow Rhett and Cheyenne here?"

"No. We were at the ob-gyn's office because my sister started having contractions. After we found out there wasn't going to be a baby today, Lacey Jane was put on bed rest. Ike decided to keep watch over her. Marc and I came here for a cup of coffee. To be perfectly honest, we saw Rhett's car in the parking lot. I texted you, and we decided it should be safe to go inside."

"Then what happened?"

"We ordered our drinks and sat at this table." I rubbed my hand over the surface. "Cheyenne and Rhett were in a serious conversation over there." I pointed out where they'd been sitting. "She acted like she planned to leave until she spotted us."

Wade looked up from his notes. "Did she bring up the murder?"

"Kinda, but it got pretty confusing for a bit. My understanding is Rhett tried to poison Norris to get back at him for his aunt's death. Either he didn't give Norris enough of the drug to kill him, or else it hadn't been long enough to work fully."

"Dr. Stephanie Alton Rich, the pain doctor, right?"

"That's the one. He blamed Norris for dragging his aunt into the pill mill and illegal business practices. He also doesn't believe his aunt committed suicide."

"She didn't die in our county, but I can reach out to the coroner of Blueburg County. She'll be able to go over the records of her death. Continue your story."

"On Friday morning, Cheyenne went to see Norris. She blamed him for her drug addiction, and he gave her settlement money from the accident to her husband. So, she went to ask for her files to see how much money she should've received. Norris laughed at her request to see proof of the settlement. Then she went ballistic."

"She was angry and killed him?"

"Right. Rhett bought two smoothies from Erin Friday morning. I don't know what excuse he used, but he went to see Norris at the house. He doped up Norris's drink, but evidently Rhett didn't calculate how much diazepam was needed. Instead of dying, Norris was nice and loopy."

"Let me guess. That made it easier for Cheyenne to strangle Norris. He wasn't strong enough after being drugged to fight back."

"Correct. When you make a list of charges against Cheyenne, be sure to include dognapping. She stole Lady that morning."

"She saw an opportunity and took advantage of it. She didn't just accidently find Lady and collect the reward money." He leaned forward. "Anything else?"

"I don't think so." I took another drink. "This has been the longest day. What's the latest on Tropical Storm Gabe?"

"He's fizzling out. We'll have rain but nothing else."

"I feel like going home and sleeping for a couple of days."

Wade stopped the recorder. "Thanks for your help on this case. Norris was a bad dude. The list of people wanting him dead made this a challenging case."

"It couldn't have helped that two people on the list tried to murder him on the same day."

"You got that right." One side of his mouth quirked up.

"Am I free to go?"

Wade looked past me. "Yes, and it looks like your fiancé is finished too. Take care of yourself, Andi Grace."

I stood. "If you hadn't questioned Ike Gage, I never would've gotten involved."

He laughed. "You're not seriously going to turn the tables and say it's my fault you butted into another one of my investigations."

"I think I just did. See you later." I left him at the table.

His laughter filled the restaurant.

Marc met me at the door. "Ready?"

"I'm ready to get back to planning our wedding." I stood on my tiptoes and kissed him.

"Su-weet. That's what I hoped to hear."

Chapter Fifty-six

A WEEK LATER, Juliet and I sat on my back patio finalizing plans for our double wedding. It would be small and outside at the farm. Sunny and Pinky, Juliet's little dog, rested in the shade of my backyard.

Traditional wedding cake remained the decision for Marc and me, while Juliet and Nate wanted to keep their cake selection a secret.

I turned to the next page in my wedding binder. "Did we agree on flowers? Are you okay if I have a wildflower bouquet with an emphasis on pink hibiscus? If you think it'll take away from your roses, I can change."

She flashed me a picture on her phone of soft pink roses. "I think it'll be perfect. We don't want to be matchy-matchy."

"Exactly. What else do we need to tackle?"

"Invitations have been mailed." Juliet raised one finger. "Pastor Mays has us on his schedule for the rehearsal and the wedding. Honeymoons are planned. The caterer is booked."

"Thanks for agreeing to hire Tony to do the rehearsal dinner. He would've been heartbroken if I didn't include him."

"No problem. I wouldn't hurt his feelings for the world."

"He promised it'll be fancy."

"Even if Tony serves his delicious pizza, I'll be fine. We're getting married to the best guys in the world." Juliet squealed.

I relaxed in my chair. "We've come a long way, my friend."

"You know that's right. I've loved your brother for years, and it's finally happening."

My friend had been more than patient waiting for Nate to realize he was in love with her. "Okay, how are the plans for the reception coming along?"

"The caterer agreed to our requests for Southern comfort foods." She patted her stomach. "I'm hungry just thinking about the mac and cheese, barbecue sliders, chicken and waffles, mini shrimp and grits—"

"Stop. We'll be starved by the time Marc and Nate pick us up for supper."

Sunny barked and ran to the gate. Pinky worked hard to catch up to my German shepherd.

"Hello, hello." Marc and Nate loved on both dogs, then joined us. "How is the wedding planning going?"

I closed my turquoise wedding binder. "The only thing that'd make it more perfect is if we could speed up time."

Marc leaned down and kissed my cheek. "I'm going to take the dogs inside. Wade and David pulled up behind us."

Juliet walked over and kissed Nate. "Hello, handsome."

"Hey, baby. I've got a feeling they're about to talk murder stuff. Let's blow this joint."

Juliet's face reddened. "Andi Grace, do you mind?"

"It's fine. We'll reschedule." I didn't want them to learn anything that would earn me a lecture on safety.

They left, and Wade and David appeared moments later.

"Hi, guys. Can I get y'all something to drink?"

Wade said, "We're fine."

David didn't argue, but his smile dimmed.

"Are you sure? I'm thirsty and was just about to get a Coke."

David said, "If you don't mind then, I'll be happy with anything you've got."

"Do you want to sit out here? There's a nice ocean breeze, and it's not humid today."

Marc joined us. "Which means it'll probably be a record-breaking scorcher the day we get married."

I laughed. "Be right back."

I went ahead and prepared four glasses of ice, added four cans of Coke, and napkins. In case they were hungry, I poured trail mix into a bowl and stuck a spoon in it. I carried everything outside on a turquoise lacquer tray we'd received for a wedding gift.

Marc spotted me and opened the door. "Nice tray. Is it new?"

"Yeah, it's an early wedding gift, but I don't recognize the name of who sent it. I'll show you later." I settled the drinks on the table and sat beside Marc.

Wade glanced up from a file he'd brought. "You know, I am thirsty. Thanks, Andi Grace."

It didn't take long for each of us to pour our Cokes into the glasses. David scooped trail mix onto a napkin.

After taking a sip, I asked, "Is there a new development in the case?"

Wade said, "I decided to officially catch you up. Cheyenne and Rhett will each be tried for murder. You'll see Ivey around town. Her passport has been confiscated until the government can decide her role in the laws Norris broke."

"Did you learn about all the people leaving his office with files and looking upset?"

"Norris often hired private investigators for his divorce cases. So he got the bright idea of having them follow the spouses of his accident claim clients too. When staking out spouses, they often discovered affairs, drug abuse, or lawbreaking, and that's exactly what they found with some of the clients' spouses. Norris decided it was only fair for him to cash in on their misdeeds, so he blackmailed the people who were due to get large insurance settlements."

"That's despicable, but Norris did a lot of appalling things." I leaned back in my chair.

Marc crossed his arms. "What did you decide about Dr. Rich, Rhett's aunt? Was it suicide or murder?"

"Her case was reopened, and the coroner still believes it was suicide. The sheriff over in Blueburg County assured me there was no foul play."

"That pill mill sure ruined a lot of lives." Marc frowned.

David nodded. "It sure did. Patients, employees, and relatives."

Wade said, "You'll be glad to know that Freddie Fisher enrolled in anger management classes. The instructor will report to me if he misses a class. I believe he's learned his lesson."

I shivered, remembering how he'd terrified me on River Road. "I hope you're right."

"The sheriff read him the riot act." David smiled. "He asked Freddie how he'd feel if a creep pulled the same stunt on his wife, sister, mother, or daughter. Freddie left the office with his tail tucked between his legs."

I turned to Wade. "Aw, it's nice to know you care."

"Hrmph." Wade drained his glass and stood. "David, let's roll."

"One more quick question. Was there any connection between the murder and the oyster knife?"

"There was no link that we could determine." He motioned for David to follow him. "Thanks for arresting the killer, Wade."

"It's my job, Andi Grace." His gaze darted to my fiancé. "Marc, try to keep her out of trouble."

David hugged me then ran down the steps and caught up with his boss.

Marc laughed. "You sure know how to clear a crowd."

I wrapped my arms around his neck. "I needed some time alone with my man."

He held me close. "Su-weet."

We kissed, and once again I couldn't wait to marry this wonderful man.

The ceremony was only a few weeks away, and there couldn't possibly be another murder between now and then.

About the Author

Former Kentuckian Jackie Layton loves her new life in the Low Country. She enjoys time on the beach, despite one vacation that ended with cracked ribs from riding her boogie board with the kids and another trip that ended with a fish hook in her foot and a trip to the emergency room. There's nothing like time at the beach, although she tends to be a bit more cautious these days. Jackie is the author of five Low Country Dog Walker Mysteries, including *Bite the Dust*, *Dog-Gone Dead*, *Bag of Bones*, *Caught and Collared* and *A Killer Unleashed*.

CPSIA information can be obtained
at www.ICGtesting.com
Printed in the USA
LVHW102026220223
740161LV00004B/394